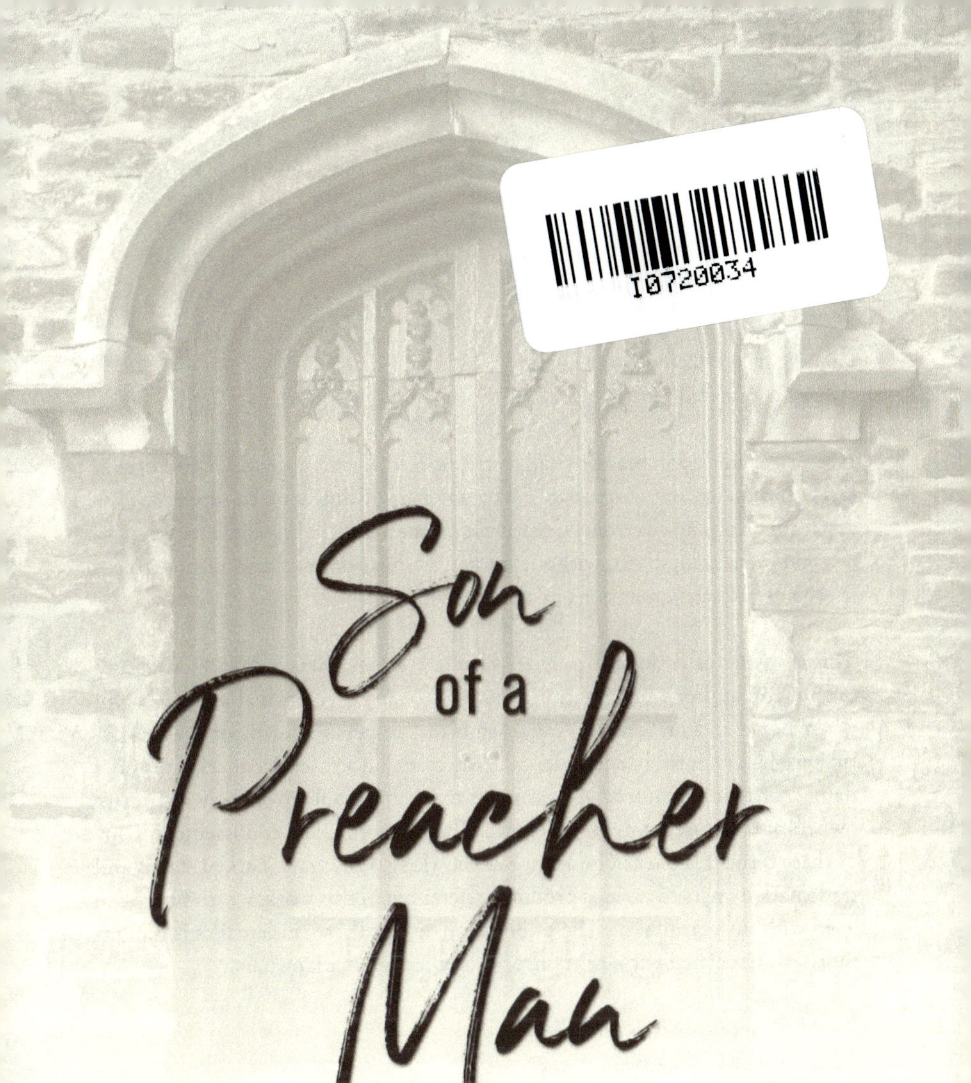

# Son of a Preacher Man

A RED DOOR NOVEL

# DYAN LAYNE

Cover/interior Photography: Michelle Lancaster, @lanefotograf
Cover/interior Model: Reeff Kuhn
Cover Designer: Lori Jackson, Lori Jackson Design
Formatting: Stacey Blake, Champagne Book Design

This book contains subject matter that may be sensitive or triggering to some and is intended for mature audiences.

# Playlist

Ghost | *Imperium*

Matt Mason | *Cringe (Stripped)*

Dusty Springfield | *Son of a Preacher Man*

Highly Suspect | *Little One*

Pearl Jam | *Black*

Nine Inch Nails | *Something I Can Never Have*

Mastodon | *Teardrinker*

Chase Atlantic | *Devilish*

I Prevail | *Bow Down*

Kings of Leon | *Crawl*

Incubus | *Monuments and Melodies*

Green Day | *Boulevard of Broken Dreams*

Korn | *Freak On a Leash*

Kidneythieves | *Before I'm Dead*

The Smiths | *How Soon Is Now?*

The Pretty Reckless | *Follow Me Down*

Bones | *ShameOnMe (МнеСтыдно)*

Marilyn Manson | *Personal Jesus*

Thrice | *My Soul*

Two Feet | *Grey*

Matt Mason | *Gravedigger*

MISSIO | *Demons*

Creed | *Bullets*

Jane's Addiction | *Sympathy for the Devil*

Zeal & Ardor | *Devil Is Fine*
Marilyn Manson | *Antichrist Superstar*
Disturbed | *Down with the Sickness*
Highly Suspect | *My Name Is Human*
Hozier | *Arsonist's Lullabye*
AWOLNATION | *Sail*
Jamie Bower | *Devil In Me*
Red Devil Vortex | *Ready*
Highly Suspect | *Send Me An Angel*
Of Virtue | *Sinner*
Dorothy | *Dark Nights*
Bohnes | *Holy Smokes*
Bad Omens | *The Death of Peace of Mind*
Def Leppard | *Pour Some Sugar On Me*
Bryce Fox | *Horns*
Bishop Briggs | *River*
Lowborn | *Demons and Angels*
Ghost | *He Is*
Halestorm | *The Steeple*
Ghost | *Ritual*
Disturbed | *Prayer*
The Plot In You | *Face Me*
Two Feet | *Tell Me The Truth*
Ghost | *Year Zero*
Black Veil Brides (feat. VV) | *Temple of Love*
In This Moment | *Half God Half Devil*
Red | *Darkest Part*
††† (Crosses) | *The Beginning Of The End*
Jamie Bower | *I Am*

Marilyn Manson | *Cry Little Sister*

Staind | *It's Been Awhile*

Ghost | *Ashes*

Red Devil Vortex | *The Devil's Place*

Ghost | *Devil Church*

The Bug (feat. Inga Copeland) | *Fall*

Black Label Society | *Scars*

Cobi | *Church Of The Lonely*

Chaoseum | *Unreal*

Alter Bridge | *Sin After Sin*

Jamie Bower (feat. King Sugar) | *Run On*

Kaleo | *Save Yourself*

David Kushner | *Daylight*

Matt Mason | *Gravedigger (Stripped)*

Ruelle | *Madness*

In This Moment | *Oh Lord*

Ghost | *Deus In Absentia*

Amber Run | *Amen*

Ghost | *See The Light*

Halestorm | *Amen*

Ghost | *Faith*

Ghost | *Respite On The Spitalfields*

Shinedown | *Daylight*

Sleep Token | *The Love You Want*

Bishop Briggs | *River (Acoustic)*

Hozier | *First Light*

# Author's Note

This book contains subject matter that may be sensitive or triggering to some readers and is intended for mature audiences. Seriously. I'm not just saying that. If you know Kodiak at all, and by now you should, then you won't be surprised that there's some heavy stuff on these pages. His story isn't pretty, but in the end, it's a story of healing, of hope, and most of all…love.

I usually don't list specific trigger warnings. It's not in the spirit of storytelling. But because this book contains elements you will undoubtedly find disconcerting, or at the very least make you uncomfortable, I will give you this much: PTSD, religious fanaticism, on-page accounts of minors undergoing LGBTQ conversion therapy and acts of dubious and/or non-consent.

Though parts of it may be distressing, I want you to enjoy this book. But I also don't want to hurt anyone. Please proceed with caution. I care about your mental health. If you have concerns regarding any specific triggers you may have, I urge you to contact me on social media or through my website.

I also usually tell you it isn't necessary to read the previous books in the series, as this is a standalone novel featuring a unique romance. Technically, this still holds true, but to avoid major spoilers and fully understand Kodiak's story, I _strongly_ encourage you to start at the beginning with **Serenity**. Trust me, you'll wish you had if you don't.

_Red Door_ is a series of interconnected standalone novels. All the main characters reappear, and some storylines connect throughout each book. For the best experience, the series should be read in order.

If you are following the series, **Son of a Preacher Man** overlaps with events in **The Other Brother** and **Drummer Boy**.

Two words. "Finish it."
If she hadn't pushed me to do it,
the Red Door would still only exist in my head.
These stories would never have been written,
and we wouldn't be here today.
This one's for you, Kim.
Love you!

*Tell me every terrible thing you ever did, and let me love you anyway.*
—Edgar Allan Poe

# Son of a Preacher Man

# Prologue

*Seth, ten years old.*

He sat buckled in the passenger seat of his father's old Chevy, Spice Girls playing on the radio. It reeked of cigarette smoke, whiskey, and cheap aftershave. Jarrid Black never smoked in the house. His congregation was blind to his fondness for the demon drink. Seth was more than well acquainted with it, though.

They were going to Miss Catherine's. He hated going there and he didn't like her very much. She was surly to everyone, except for his father. That didn't surprise him at all. Folks from church worshipped the preacher as if he were God himself. Sometimes Seth thought he really believed he was.

His father lit up a Marlboro. He cracked the window open, letting the cold, damp air of March rush in, and turned his face toward the glass.

"Seth." He glared sideways, taking a drag off his cancer stick. "Close it."

"But I can't breathe, and it stinks."

Turning his head toward him, he exhaled. "Must I tell you again?"

"No, sir." He cranked the window back up.

Seth knew better than to disobey him. He was in a halfway decent mood this morning, and if he wanted permission to ride his bike with Jonathan to the arcade this afternoon, it had to stay that way. He'd deal with the stench.

The Dairy Queen rolled by. Closed for the winter, it wouldn't open again until the end of April. *Dumb.* Did they really think no one wanted ice cream when it snowed?

Then the car took an all too familiar turn at the next corner. Lowering the window all the way down, his father flicked the cigarette out onto the street. It bounced a couple of times, the embers creating a cascade of sparks, before rolling into a puddle at the curb.

He left it down, despite the cold, waving his hand in the air around him. Then he spritzed on more of that nasty cologne. As if that smelled any better than his disgusting smoke.

It didn't.

At least the window was open so he could breathe.

They parked at the curb in front of the small two-story clapboard house. Catherine must have been waiting for them at the door. She opened it the moment they arrived.

Seth was sent to sit in the parlor, with the promise of a Coca-Cola that he knew would never come. Same as always. Glancing around the room he'd sat in a million times before, he twiddled his thumbs. A photo of Grace, when she was around his age, stood in a frame on the mantel. He liked her. She was nice. His father said she was his angel. When he was younger, she'd come to his house and stay with him while the preacher took care of church business. He was too old for a babysitter now.

After what felt like an eternity, Jarrid and Catherine stepped into the room. She carried a bundle, wrapped in a fluffy white blanket, in her arms. Grace stood by herself behind them. Hands balled into fists at her side. Head hanging low, her pale blonde hair covered her face.

"Son." His father stepped forward. "God has fulfilled his promise to you."

Miss Catherine placed the baby in his arms. "She's yours, Seth Thomas."

He gazed in awe at her beautiful, precious face.

"Now, you must make a promise to God and everyone here, that you will love, cherish, and protect the gift that has been bestowed upon you…" He bent over and kissed the baby's head. "…every day of your life."

"I promise."

She was given to him the day she was born.
*God's promised gift.*
He fell in love the second he held her in his arms.
And he'd loved her ever since.
Linnea. Was. His.

# One

t was that misty kind of rain. Not quite a drizzle, but enough to cling to the hairs on his skin. Glancing at his sister's house next door, Kodiak inhaled deep, then blowing it out, stepped off Dillon's front porch.

He didn't like leaving her there all alone. Never mind that's what she wanted. Linnea had given him and Chloe the boot, politely, yet firmly, insisting she was fine and sending them on their way.

*Bullshit.*

She wasn't fine.

She buried her husband yesterday.

And there was nothing he could do to take away her pain. He should know. Eighteen years later, his chest still ached at the thought of him.

But isn't that the inevitable consequence of loving someone?

While it wasn't within his power to free Linnea of all this

suffering, Kodiak could see her through it. Love her through it. Be whatever she needed him to be.

Maybe what she needed right then *was* some time by herself. To mourn Kyan on her own. To weep without an audience. He could understand that. He'd give Linnea some space and check in on her again later. No doubt, Dillon would be over there as soon as he showered the stench of whiskey from his pores anyway.

Though he didn't have a particular destination in mind, he didn't want to go back to the empty row house on Oak Street. He should probably check in on Bo too, being he was pretty fucked up when they parted ways at Dillon's last night. So, with the precipitous mist soaking through to his skin, Kodiak walked to the end of the block and softly knocked upon his door.

In better shape than he thought he'd find him, Bo opened it, and gathering Kodiak to his chest, they embraced. "Hey, man."

"Glad to see you didn't choke on your own vomit." Patting each other's back, they pulled apart.

"Heh." Bo hooked an arm around his neck, leading him toward the family room. "It was a close one, trust me. Been to Linn's yet?"

"Yeah, just left there."

"How's she doing? I wanna pop over and see her."

"Today's probably not a good day. She's…" With an exhale, Kodiak shrugged. "She wants to be alone right now."

Bo nodded, taking a seat on the sofa. "And Dill?"

"I'm glad I can report he didn't choke on his vomit, either."

The pretty blonde Bo took on tour to care for his two-year-old daughter, came into the room balancing Emery on her hip. "Oh, um…hi, Kodiak."

"Hello, Ava."

Placing the child in Bo's lap, she asked, "Want some coffee? I can make some."

"No, I'm not staying. Thanks, though."

"Coffee'd be great." Tugging on her arm, Bo pulled her in for a kiss. "Thanks, Avie."

His brow shot up watching Ava retreat into the kitchen. "You two?"

"Yeah." Bo couldn't contain his grin.

"Had a feeling that might happen." Teeth grazing over his lip, Kodiak nodded. "I'm happy for you, brother."

He meant it too. If anyone deserved that storybook happily ever after, it was Bo. And some good news was welcome in the midst of all this mind-numbing tragedy.

Studying him, his one-time lover tipped his head to the side. "You holding up okay?"

"I'm okay. It's just…"

"I know, man. I get it."

Bo was the only person on Earth who did.

Ava returned with the coffee and ruffling Emery's hair, Kodiak stood. "I need to get going."

"No, you don't." Bo held onto his wrist. "Stay."

"Yeah, I do," Kodiak countered, looking down at the floor. "I've got some work to catch up on at the house before I go back to Linnea's."

"Take a nap while you're at it, bro, 'cause you look like you could use one." And with a squeeze of his fingers, Bo let go.

"I'll be sure to do that. Be good for your daddy, little one," he said, patting the tot on the head. She gifted him with a cherubic smile. "Nice seeing you again, Ava."

Following him into the foyer, Bo stopped him at the door. "You know, I'm here for you. Always. Whatever you need."

Kodiak hugged him to his chest. "I know."

"You sure you're okay?"

He opened the door to the rain coming down in a steady drizzle. "Yeah, I'm fine."

At least that's what he kept telling himself. Maybe if he said it often enough, eventually he would be. Because nothing had been okay since he was sixteen. And truthfully, had it ever been?

He snickered. *Not even close.*

From the moment of conception, his existence was nothing

but a sordid, fucked up mess. Except for a name on his birth certificate, he didn't know who his mother was. *Brandy Sullivan.* Only fifteen when he was born, she'd never been in the picture. His father refused to even speak of her. Jarrid moved them out of their backwoods Missouri town to Crossfield before he was two.

The fucker fed all the church ladies this sob story of his pretty, young *wife* running off and leaving him. Tempted by Satan himself, she'd up and disappeared one day, saddling Jarrid with a newborn. *Lies. All lies.* He was never married. But the stupid bitches ate it up, fawning all over him and his father.

For years he'd tried to find her, but even with his skills, and the resources at his disposal, he never could. No records to be found of the girl anywhere. It was as if Brandy Sullivan never even existed. *Fake name. Had to be.* And so, he gave up looking for her a long time ago.

Kodiak opened the scrolled iron gate to Coventry Park. Cutting through it, he slowly walked the paved path that wound along the old oak trees, not caring that his shirt stuck to his flesh like a second skin. By the time he reached First Avenue, he was soaked to the bone, the steady drizzle had turned into a downpour.

Beanie's was up ahead at the corner. He figured he should run in and grab a hot cup of tea for the rest of his walk home. Eight blocks. Less than a mile. Kodiak could run that in a matter of minutes.

He pushed the door open, the jingle of brass bells announcing his arrival. The scent of fresh-baked snickerdoodles blending with the aromatic grounds warming his insides, he went up to the counter. Katie's brother, Kevin, looking bored as fuck, reached over for a paper cup, Sharpie at the ready to take his order. "Hey there, Kodiak. Matcha tea?"

Jesus, was he that predictable?

"Not today, Kev." He smirked, indecisively pursing his lips to the side. "I'll take an americano. Where's your sister?"

"Katie took the day off." Marking the cup, Kevin side-stepped

over to the coffee machine. "After the funeral yesterday, Brendan's…
well, you know."

He knew.

"Yeah," he sighed, nodding.

A heavy blanket of grief was weighing on them all.

"You got that, Kev?" The ice queen herself poked her head out
from the back. "Oh, Kodiak, it's you."

He wasn't in the frame of mind to deal with her. Not today.
Verbal sparring would require an energy he didn't possess at the
moment. Holding a hand up, he shot her a look that told her so.

Blue eyes taking him in, Kelly moved a couple of steps closer.
"I'm so sorry about Kyan. You doing okay?"

He wished everyone would quit asking him that.

"Thanks, I'm okay."

Snapping the lid on, Kevin handed him the blue paper cup
and took his card.

"Sometimes okay is okay, you know?"

He raised his brow at her. *Huh?*

"That's what Kyan told me the day he…"

Kevin returned his card. Sliding it back into his wallet, Kodiak
turned to leave.

"You're not going out in that, are you? It's pouring."

*Ain't it, though?*

He glanced back over his shoulder. "Yeah, and?"

Sipping on his coffee, Kodiak headed for the door. He almost
made it too.

"Wait."

His fingers fell from the doorknob.

"Cookies." Peering up at him, she pressed a bag into his hand.
"You look like you could use a friend."

*Could use more than that, Ice Queen.*

"You want to be my friend now, Kelly?"

"Why not?"

He snickered. "I have a dick, you know."

"I'm aware."

"Yeah." Kodiak smirked. "Be seeing you."

He lowered the lid on his Mac.

Rubbing his weary eyes, Kodiak kicked his feet up onto the coffee table. *Sorry, Anna.* Without a doubt, the hotshot attorney downtown was cheating on his wife. And his girlfriend. All of them. Judging by the surveillance footage and his text message history, the slimy bastard had a different one for every day of the week.

Of course, Anna likely knew of her husband's infidelity long before she hired him. Wives always know. It was when they needed irrefutable evidence for divorce proceedings, they retained his services.

"Hope she takes you to the cleaners, you stupid fuck."

Adultery jobs were a piece of cake. Not at all challenging. Cheating husbands aren't very smart. While they made for a steady stream of lucrative income, with his military background in intelligence, Kodiak preferred the more complex cases. Criminal stuff. Fraud. Embezzlement. Corporate espionage.

Ever since he helped Brendan get out of that whole Salena mess, Phil Beecham's firm sent a ton of work his way. It didn't take long for word to get around. With his expertise, courtesy of the United States Army, Kodiak had plenty of clients and more than enough to keep him busy.

And he needed busy.

To keep his mind occupied and the bad shit out of his head.

Jarrid always said idleness is the handmaiden of temptation, but then anything that came out of his father's mouth was to suit his own purposes. Kodiak threw it back at him to suit his back in high school, getting Daddy's permission to try out for the football team with Jonathan during his freshman year.

Nope. He couldn't allow his thoughts to go there.

Giving his head a brisk shake, Kodiak picked up the blue paper bag he'd tossed onto the coffee table when he got home.

He peeked inside and the corner of his mouth slowly lifted. Snickerdoodles.

What was up with her? It wasn't like Kelly to be so…nice. The girl was downright cold, almost to the point of being rude. They didn't refer to her as the ice queen for nothing. She voiced her disdain for anyone with a dick, especially Dillon and Brendan, loud and clear. Much too loud if you asked him. Leo seemed to be the only exception, but then he was gay. Go figure.

Okay, so Kelly adamantly claimed to be a lesbian. Just who was she trying to convince? Kodiak wasn't sure he believed her. He'd known plenty of them, but he'd never known any to hate on the male gender the way she did. Course, he'd never known any that were into sucking cock either.

And Kelly was sure into his.

Once.

Going on two years ago now. New Year's Eve at the Red Door. The night he first met her.

He and Dillon were having a drink at the bar when she walked into the private VIP space holding onto Katie's arm. Honey-blonde hair. Smoldering blue eyes. Knockout black dress. *Fucking stunning.* Kelly looked like she could be the answer to his prayers.

At least until she opened that snarky mouth of hers.

Chuckling to himself, Kodiak leaned back against the bar, observing Dillon's futile attempts to make nice with her. Kelly wasn't having it. Not at first. But as the clock ticked closer to midnight, she positioned herself smack dab in between them.

Dillon's birthday is New Year's Day, and he has a rule. Everyone has to kiss him at twelve. So, when Kelly kissed the birthday boy at the stroke of midnight, Kodiak wasn't exactly surprised. It's when she tugged on his hair, planting her lips on his, that knocked him on his ass.

He tasted strawberries and champagne on her tongue.

He felt her fingers slide over the bulge in his pants.

And for the first time in his life, Kodiak felt something for a woman who wasn't his sister.

With Kelly still rubbing him, he tore his mouth from hers. "I thought you don't like dick?"

"I don't."

"Oh, yeah?" Taking her by the hand, Kodiak led her away from the VIP space in the direction of the alcoves. "Could've fooled me. You seem to like touching mine."

"Maybe I'm a little drunk." Kelly giggled. "And a lot horny."

Opening the velvet drape, he pulled her inside. Fingering the thin strap of the slinky black dress that barely covered her tits, it slipped from her shoulder. "I want you to take this off for me."

She looked up at him from beneath her lashes, a puddle of fabric at her feet. "Are we gonna fuck?"

"Nah. Maybe one day." Unzipping himself, Kodiak smirked. "When you can admit you want this dick and beg me to put it inside you."

"Never gonna happen."

"Wanna bet?"

"Yeah, and I'll win." Kelly grinned, her tongue sweeping over her bottom lip.

"What makes you think so?" Stroking himself, he took a step toward her. "You're salivating just looking at it. Go on. You can touch me. I'll allow it."

She didn't hesitate. Slender fingers wrapped around his hardened flesh and squeezed. Her teeth sinking into her full, pouty lip, Kelly fisted his cock.

"That's a good girl." Thrusting his fingers into her long hair, Kodiak tipped his head back. "Now, get down on your knees. Suck me."

And she swallowed him whole.

*Yes, what a good fucking girl you are.*

Kelly was frosty to him after that—like it never happened. It was almost as if she was angry with herself for liking it. For wanting him. He could see through her shit, though. Something had fucked her up. The girl was broken. But as much as Kodiak wanted to, he was in no position to pursue her. He had nothing to offer.

Not then.

Not now.

Maybe not ever.

Because he was more damaged than she was.

# Two

S ix in the morning and the September sun was rising over Chicago.

Taking his third lap around the mile-long trail in the neighborhood park, Kodiak's gaze fell to the bench beneath the old oak tree. The place where they'd parted, tasting each other's tears.

*"You'll always be my Seth."*

*"You'll always be my little one."*

Leaving her was the hardest thing he'd ever had to do. Few would understand it, but what was left of his heart shattered that day. And he'd been trying to glue the shards back together ever since.

Six months in Cali.

Another three in Anchorage.

The second hardest thing he'd done was to come back. But she'd asked him to. And Kodiak made a promise he intended to keep. He would die for his sister. Linnea was the only good thing he ever had.

Halfway into his fourth mile, the sweat began to break on his skin. He picked up the pace, going faster, pushing himself harder.

Running always helped to clear his head. Kept him sane. Well, as sane as any man who'd lived his life could be.

His running habit started in basic training. Red Phase. Fort Sill, Oklahoma. Covered in sweat, dust caked to his skin, the endorphins would kick in, washing the bad shit away. Nothing remained, except a sense of peace. Calm. So, rain or shine, Kodiak ran, chasing after that feeling every single day.

Five miles, an hour of lifting, and a shower later, he was at his sister's doorstep. He didn't bother knocking and went right in. Setting his backpack on the table, Kodiak glanced around the room. Sunlight filtered through closed curtains, the house quiet and still, Linnea asleep on her turquoise sofa.

He stood there, watching her for a moment as she slept. She looked so small and delicate, like a porcelain doll on a nest of spun cotton, holding onto her pillow, tucked up tight in a fluffy white blanket.

Eyes twitching beneath closed lids, she whimpered. "Kyan?"

"It's me, little one." Taking her hand in his, Kodiak sat beside her. He kissed her forehead. "I'm here."

"I was dreaming, I think." Arms came around him, clutching his chest to hers. "Sometimes they seem so real."

"I know." Pulling away, he swept the hair back from her face.

Tears seeping from the corners, light green eyes, the same color as his own, looked up at him. "I didn't feel anything when my grandmother died. Nothing at all."

God, he should have been there for her then, but Jarrid didn't get word to him about Catherine's passing until it was too late to get leave. When he came home a month later, Linnea was gone. And to this day, Kodiak still regretted it.

*"Do you have any regrets?"*

*Shut up, Babs.*

He had so many.

She licked her lips. "I don't know how to do this."

"No one does." Pulling her up to sit, Kodiak gathered Linnea in his arms and stroked her hair.

"How did you do it?" She laid her head on his shoulder. "How do you get over it?"

With thoughts of the one person he'd loved and lost, his chest tightened.

"You don't." Her sweet almond fragrance enveloping him, he kissed her hair. "And you're not supposed to. It hurts right now, but love never dies, it becomes a part of you."

A strangled sob broke free.

Kodiak just held her, his palm gently cradling Charlotte in her tummy. "You're carrying Kyan's love right here." Then he placed his hand over Linnea's heart. "And right here is where it will always stay, safe inside you forever."

Chloe and Dillon arrived. Kodiak stayed until he couldn't take watching her heart bleed another minute. It tore him up that he was powerless to fix it. So, he went home, and wrote up his report for the cheater's wife, before coming out here to dig in the dirt.

Plunging the trowel into the damp earth, he dug the weeds out of the backyard flower beds his sister cajoled him into putting in. After the rain yesterday, fall was in the air. He could smell it. If he attacked the nuisance plants now, before they went to seed to lie in wait beneath the winter snow, there'd be less of them to deal with come spring.

Truth be told, it gave him something productive to do. Idle hands and all that. Couldn't keep his mind from wandering, though.

It was out of his way, but Kodiak contemplated stopping in at Beanie's after he left Linnea. Actually, he almost did. *Almost.* But he didn't.

See, he *could* use a friend. Someone to talk to who wasn't drowning in sorrow. Someone to spend his time with. Someone who knew how he took his coffee and that snickerdoodles were his favorite. Someone who could make him feel something other than fucked up.

And Kelly could be that someone.

That's why he kept right on walking.

Because how could he drag anyone into his shit? At the first whiff of it, she'd run for the hills anyway. He'd never be able to explain it all to her. The church. His father. Linnea. Jonathan. She'd never understand what growing up in Crossfield was like. The horrors he'd endured. The unspeakable things he'd done.

*Best to leave it be.*

Kodiak had given up on having a wife and kids when he signed those papers three years ago. At thirty-four, he'd resigned himself to leading a solitary life, and he'd finally made peace with it. He had a small circle of friends who'd become family, his sister, and a niece on the way.

*They would be enough.*

No, Kelly couldn't be that someone.

Nobody could.

Feet crossed in front of her, Kelly leaned back against the coffee bar, watching her nephew wipe down the table by the window, trance-like, as he stared through the glass. He'd been at it a full five minutes now. "It's good, Kev."

"Huh?"

"The table." She chuckled, shaking her head. "What's so interesting out there?"

"Nothin'. Keeping an eye out for Katie is all." Spray bottle in one hand, rag in the other, he turned around. "She had an afternoon class today. Her friend might be with her."

"What friend?"

"Ava." The curse of being a blond, Kevin's cheeks turned red. "Now that she's back, I think I'll ask her out again."

*Ohhh.*

"Good luck with that." Kelly smirked, moving toward the storefront window. "Your sister's not coming in. It's just you and me, kid."

"That sucks."

"Gee, thanks." She socked him.

"C'mon now, that's my throwing arm." He rubbed it. "And I didn't mean it like that."

A flash of denim out the window caught her eye. Motorcycle boots. His hair woven into a single braid down his back. She smiled. "Here comes Kodiak."

He seemed to hesitate at the door, but he didn't stop, walking by without so much as a glance in her direction.

"And there he goes."

The smile falling from her face, Kelly turned to her nephew. "I wonder why he didn't come in."

"Why do you even care?"

"I don't." She shrugged, watching Kodiak blend in with the shoppers on the sidewalk until he was gone, and she couldn't see him anymore.

Was she disappointed? Maybe a little, but then Kelly hardly expected some cookies to bring him around. A spur of the moment gesture, she wasn't even sure why she did it. Except he'd looked so… alone.

And Kelly knew what that felt like.

She'd always been alone, even during that disastrous farce of a relationship with Stacy. Especially then. Since college, Kelly just couldn't quite connect with anyone. Not on an intimate level, nor as a friend. Leo was probably the only exception, simply because he was Leo. And for one night, when she let her guard down with the help of a little alcohol—okay, maybe a lot—Kodiak.

The only man she'd ever willingly given herself over to. Kelly wanted him that night. Did she still?

*A real woman would.*

Six-plus feet of sculpted muscle, Kodiak was beautiful to look at. His quiet, reserved demeanor only added to the appeal. With a deep voice as smooth as honeyed whiskey, he spoke in this deliberate, easy cadence, that drew her in, forcing her to listen closely to every word.

It was his eyes that spoke to her, though. Like Jesus on the cross, he'd suffered. She could see it in the pale-green prisms. They held secrets, but even so, they told her enough. She and Kodiak were the same. Broken. Maybe they could fix each other, because as odd as it might seem, Kelly still wanted him.

*Just once.*

Before she was dead, Kelly wanted to know what it felt like. All of it. A strong, hard body covering her soft one. Hungry, heated kisses that stole her breath. Skin slick with sweat. Hot flesh penetrating her.

*His.*

Kelly had to know what it was like to be with a man *she* wanted. On her terms. A man who wanted her too. Christ, she was going on thirty, and she'd never experienced that. Not really. Was it crazy to think that with Kodiak she just might like it?

*"Are we gonna fuck?"*

*"Maybe one day. When you can admit you want this dick and beg me to put it inside you."*

She thought she could say it now.

It was probably too late for that anyway. A long time had gone by since that drunken encounter on New Year's Eve. But they could be friends at least, couldn't they?

*Maybe.*

She wanted to try.

# Three

One day rolled into the next, each day no different than the one before. Every morning Kodiak woke up in the little row house on Oak Street where Linnea once lived, then after putting in his five miles, walked the five city blocks to Park Place. Two weeks since that horrible day, and still, every morning he arrived to find his sister asleep on her couch.

It worried him.

He didn't wake her. Walking softly to the kitchen, he took a seat at the island and opened his laptop. They had a routine now. Kodiak came by every morning, staying through lunch, when Chloe joined them in the afternoon. Then he'd leave, returning in the evening with Dillon.

They weren't babysitting her—Linnea would never stand for that. But she needed the love and support of her people. To know she wasn't alone. Dillon did too, more so than his sister did probably, though he'd never allow himself to admit it.

Going through his emails, he saw he'd received one from

Barbara, checking in on him, at two in the morning. Course, that was only midnight to her. She was his shrink during his stint in Cali. He snickered to himself. God, how he'd hated her then—as much as he loved her now. He had a session with her on Zoom every couple of weeks. Kodiak could see someone else here, he supposed, but he was comfortable with good ole Babs. She knew his convoluted story. Every bit of it. And the last thing he wanted to do was relive it, by having to tell it all over again.

*Once was enough.*

Babs didn't seem to agree, encouraging Kodiak to confide in the people closest to him, those he loved and trusted—especially Linnea. She knew some of it. Bo most of it. But then some things were too abominable to ever be spoken of again. He'd carry them silently to his grave.

He already lost a wife.

He couldn't risk losing his sister too.

"Good morning, big brother." Her arms coming around his neck, Linnea kissed the top of his head. "Breakfast? I think I'll make us a frittata today."

Kodiak smiled. "Sounds good."

That was her thing of late. Her coping mechanism. One day she started tearing up the kitchen and she hadn't stopped yet. His sister was like him in that regard—anything to keep busy. He was just glad she was eating.

"What do you feel like for dinner tonight?" Her head buried in the fridge, she set a carton of eggs on the island behind her. "I was thinking eggplant parm. They're in season, not to mention on sale, so I ordered some." She turned around then. "Unless you want something else?"

"No, eggplant sounds good."

"You always say that." She stood there, raking her fingers through her hair.

*Truth.*

"I'm a guy, Linnea. I'll eat anything." Pushing his Mac to the side, Kodiak leaned forward onto his elbows. "You slept out here on the sofa again. How come?"

"Don't know." She shrugged. "Easier to fall asleep there, I guess."

He lifted his brow.

"Upstairs, in my room, I just stare at his empty pillow…or the bathroom door, waiting for him to come out of it." Squeezing her eyes shut, Linnea chewed on her lip. "The sheets…"

She paused and he went over to her.

"…I can still smell him."

*Shit.*

Holding her head on his shoulder, Kodiak stroked her hair. "I'm sorry."

"I should change them, but I just can't bring myself to do it."

"Do you want me to help you?"

"Yeah." She nodded. "Not now, though. Okay?"

"Okay." He pulled himself back, swiping tears away from her eyes. "Whenever you're ready."

Turning from him, Linnea went right to work on breakfast. It wasn't long before the savory scent of mushrooms and tarragon filled the kitchen, and by the time Kodiak answered all the emails in his inbox, she put a plate in front of him.

"Banana bread too?"

"I whipped it up last night after Dillon went home." Sitting down beside him, she took up her fork. "The bananas were turning all brown and I couldn't sleep."

Yeah, he was worried.

"Don't look at me like that."

"Like what? Concerned?" Wrapping his fingers around her wrist, Kodiak forced her to look at him. "Because I am, Linnea. You're having a baby. You need—."

"I know what I need." She blinked and tears rolled down her face. "I need to go visit Kyan."

"I'll take you."

"No," she insisted, shaking her head. "I need to do this by myself."

"Okay." Nodding, Kodiak exhaled through pursed lips.

"I love you, Seth." Linnea took his hand in hers and squeezed it. "I'm going to be okay; I promise."

"I know." He squeezed back. "And I love you too."

This was the hard part. Knowing when to give her space. And when not to.

So, after a subdued breakfast with his sister, he found himself walking along the trail in Coventry Park, coming out on First Avenue. Kodiak didn't hesitate this time. He opened the door and went in.

Katie ran out from behind the counter, wrapping her arms tight around his waist. "How are you?" she asked, gazing up at him. "And Linn?"

"I'm all right." With a tilt of his head, his lips pressed together. "My sister will be too."

*At least I hope so.*

"Koko." Crooking his finger, Leo beckoned him over. "We've missed you around here, *bebé*."

His hair was a lovely shade of burgundy today. Swept up in a high ponytail, his glossy lipstick matched. Tight pleather pants. Big hoop earrings.

Offering his cheek up for a smooch, Kodiak grinned. Leo was a walking ray of sassy-ass sunshine. How could anyone not love the guy?

"That's better," he cooed, after smacking his burgundy lips on Kodiak's face. "Now, what can we make for you, *bebé*?"

Kelly came out from the back, carrying a tray of baked goods. Acknowledging Kodiak with a tip of her chin, she went about her task, arranging the pastries in the display case. He glanced at Leo. "Americano, please."

He did this little shimmy move with his head. "To go?"

"Yeah."

"Room for cream?" And he winked.

"Sure."

Moving to the end of the counter to wait for his coffee, Kodiak watched Kelly. A delectable sight, bent over as she was, with her shapely ass in skintight jeans. Scalloped edges of pretty pink lace peeking out of her shirt, plump breasts pushed up against the fabric.

He licked his lips.

Clearing her throat, a smirking Katie pressed a cup into his hands. "Your americano."

"Uh, yeah. Thanks."

She leaned into his ear, and kissing him on the cheek, she whispered, "Go for it."

Brows pulling together, Kodiak shot her a look.

Katie scrunched her shoulders, and with a giggle, she turned away.

He was still staring after her when Kelly popped her head up from the display case. "You good? Want something else?"

*Uh-huh. Sure do.*

His gaze traveled from those hypnotic blue eyes, down her front, and back up again. He grinned. "I'll take a cookie."

Kelly handed him a giant-sized snickerdoodle.

"Do you run?"

"Huh?" She looked at him funny. "That's random."

"I thought maybe we could go for a run together sometime… *friend*. That's all."

"Oh." The corners of her mouth twitching upward, Kelly nodded. "Well, thanks, but I don't run. Maybe if a bear was chasing me in the woods or something."

*Now there's a thought.*

"A walk then?" He took a bite of the cookie, looking at her as he chewed. "Think you can do that?"

"Yeah, I can do that."

Taking her by the hand, Kodiak pulled Kelly out from behind the counter.

"Now?"

"Right now."

She glanced over her shoulder. Biting her lip, Katie stifled a grin. With a wink, Leo blew her a kiss. Kelly hesitated only a moment before turning her head back around.

"Okay, sure. Why not?"

They walked together without talking for a while. Sipping on coffee, he led her away from the shops and Coventry Park, toward the lake. "It's so noisy back there."

Sometimes the city overwhelmed him, the constant barrage of sounds too much. Cars whizzing past. Cabs honking. The clanking of the el overhead. Kodiak kept his earbuds in most of the time, listening to music helped cancel it all out.

"Where are we going?"

Halting his steps, he slipped his arm about her shoulders. "Wherever we end up."

She tipped her head to the side. Glancing up at him, a trace of a smile came upon her face. Kelly didn't seem to do that very often. She leaned into his side, and giving her a squeeze, Kodiak urged her onward.

"Here," he said, stopping at a shady tree on the asphalt path that ran along the shore of Lake Michigan.

They sat together, legs stretched out in front of them, his arm casually resting on her shoulder. Late-morning breezes softly rippled across the water, catching in her hair, wisps floating about her face. He reached for one, silk between his fingers, then let it go.

"This is nice." Sipping on her coffee, Kelly gazed at the panorama in front of them. "I hardly ever come out here."

"I run here sometimes."

She looked at him then. "Yeah?"

"North Avenue Beach to Montrose Harbor."

"Hm." Seemingly unimpressed, or maybe she was just nervous, Kelly pulled at the blades of grass beside her. "So, is Kodiak your real name?"

"It's real enough, but no, it's the nickname they gave me up at Richardson." Amused by her blank stare, he smirked. "In Alaska."

"…*Kodiak like the city in Alaska.*"

"*Kodiak like the bear.*"

"Oh." Her cheeks turned this lovely shade of pink. "What's your real name then?"

"Seth."

"I like it."

"I prefer Kodiak."

When he left Crossfield and that miserable life behind, Seth Thomas Black ceased to exist. Only his sister used the name their father gave him. That's how he intended to keep it.

"It's a K name."

*And?*

"My family has a thing for them. We all have one. Me, Katie, Kevin, Kristie, Kim, and Kara." Kelly spoke quickly, the names tumbling from her mouth. She paused, only to take a breath, then added, "My sisters."

"I met them at Brendan's wedding."

"Yeah, I guess you did." Her cheeks flushing pinker, she rolled her eyes. "Forgot about that. Speaking of sisters, how's Linnea doing?"

"Depends on the moment." Staring off at the water, Kodiak shrugged.

"Kyan was a good guy. I always liked him." Kelly took his hand and squeezed it. "You two were close, weren't you?"

Returning his gaze to her, he admitted, "I hated him in the beginning."

"Why? Didn't think he was good enough for your sister?"

"Something like that." Kodiak turned his head away. He couldn't exactly tell her the whole truth, now, could he? "But Kyan was the best thing that ever could've happened to Linnea. So, yeah, we were close."

"You ever been married?"

Emotion gathering in his throat, Kodiak lifted the cup to his lips. "Once."

"Didn't work out?"

He looked at her then. "It couldn't."

"Sorry."

*Me too.* "Your turn."

"What?" Limpid pools of blue questioned him.

"Ever been married?"

"God, no." Kelly sniggered with a shake of her honey-blonde head.

Warm and golden, dappled sunlight painted the lustrous locks. Glints of amber and chestnut. A hint of red. Kodiak swallowed the last dregs of his coffee to stop himself from running his fingers through it.

"I lived with someone for three years, though."

"Didn't work out?" But he already knew the answer.

"Well, I'm here and she isn't." Kelly inhaled, her brows pulling together, then released it with a sigh. "Stacy and I opened Beanie's together. She bailed three months later."

"Sorry." He went ahead and reached for her hair, winding a strand around his finger.

"Don't be," she uttered without any emotion at all. Cold as ice. "I wasn't."

"No one since?"

She didn't answer. "We should probably get back."

"Aren't we friends now, Kelly?" Kodiak released the silken wisp, watching it unravel.

Chewing on her lip, she nodded. "Yeah."

He thought she was getting up to leave, but in a move that surprised him, Kelly straddled his lap. Her pretty blue eyes locked on his. "We're friends."

And she kissed him.

# Four

The plane touched down on the tarmac and his eyes blinked open.

He couldn't recall the scenery that rolled past as they drove the Pacific Coast Highway. All he saw was her face streaked with tears as he held her tight one last time before he tore his soul in two and walked away.

They carried his bags up the stairs to his room. A sitting area with a window that looked out at the ocean. A small kitchenette. Bo had just set his bags down on the bed when there was a knock at the door.

Barbara was a severe-looking woman in her fifties with graying red hair pulled back in a tight twist. She introduced herself as his therapist and took a seat by the window so Bo could say his goodbyes.

*Babs.*

"It's gonna be okay, man." Bo hugged him.

He nodded. "Look out for her, Bo. Let me know how she's doing."

"I will," he promised with a squeeze of his hand on his shoulder. "And thank you."

Bo gave his shoulder one final pat, nodded his head and then he was gone.

The therapist motioned for him to take the chair across from her. He dragged himself over and reluctantly slumped into it.

"So, Seth…"

"It's Kodiak," he corrected. "There's only one person who can call me that."

"*You'll always be my Seth.*"

"Oh, I see."

Did she? No, she couldn't.

The air in the room was so still it was hard for him to breathe.

"Kodiak then. The first thing I always ask a client is do you have any regrets?"

He had a fuckload of them.

"Two."

She waited for him to go on and when he didn't, said, "Would you like to share them with me?"

*Not really.*

He ran his hand through his hair and rubbed the back of his neck. "I regret that I wasn't able to save him." He could feel the burn hit his eyes even now. "Jonathan. My best friend."

"And the other?"

"That I waited. If I had gone to Linnea as soon as I found her again…we'd have never known. We probably would have had a little baby by now. We could've lived such a happy life together if only…"

If only he'd acted sooner. If only he hadn't waited. If only they had never uncovered how diabolical Jarrid Black truly was.

It had been ingrained into him for as long as he could remember that Linnea was his to protect and to love. He didn't care if the same blood as his ran through her veins. That was his vow, a promise he intended to keep. To always protect her and love her. It was the sole reason he was here.

He unpacked his things from his suitcase and placed the framed photo he always kept with him on the nightstand next to the bed. He angled it so it would be the last thing he saw before he closed his eyes and the first thing he saw when he opened them. He traced the frame lovingly with his fingers and wondered if she did the same when she tore away the tissue paper he'd wrapped hers in.

Pigtails, pom-poms, and red sneakers.

*"Up you go, little one."*

"I see that you love her very much. You always will, and that's okay. Can you learn to love her as your sister?"

He couldn't give Barbara the answer she wanted to hear.

Looking at the little girl on his shoulder in the photograph, her arms wrapped around his neck as she held onto those pom-poms, he whispered, "I'm going to try."

Three years later, it sat on Linnea's dresser. The photo. Displayed amongst images from her lake house wedding, Venery concerts, Charley's, and Thanksgiving dinners, Kodiak found himself glancing at it as he stripped the sheets that still smelled of Kyan from her bed.

He was better now, wasn't he?

Before he had to see his sister cry again, Kodiak took the linens to the laundry room and threw them in the wash. Water cascaded into the machine. He tossed in a pod of soap and closed the lid.

"Thanks, Seth."

Tucking a new sheet under the mattress, he glanced up at Linnea. She appeared almost waif-like, in old, faded pajama pants, a shirt stretched over her burgeoning belly, and disheveled hair escaping its tie. And so very tired. Without makeup, the translucent skin beneath her eyes had taken on a purplish hue.

"Don't mention it." One small thing she didn't have to deal with. "Dillon left?"

"Yeah." With a tilt of her head, Linnea pushed the hair back from her face. "He has a meeting downtown first thing in the morning."

Most evenings, Kodiak made it a point to leave his sister in her brother-in-law's hands shortly after dinner. Why tempt fate? The two of them needed each other. And honestly, that made it easier for him.

He tipped his chin at her. "You trying to scare me? Or are you aiming to join the cast of *Zombieland*?"

"That your way of telling me I'm a hopeless mess?"

"You're not hopeless." Straightening, he smirked. "Some fresh air, sunshine, and a hairbrush can work wonders."

"I went out today."

*Yeah, to the cemetery.*

Grabbing the brush off her night table, Kodiak pointed to the bed. "Sit."

Linnea sat on the edge of the mattress. He knelt behind her, and after removing the tie, began to gently brush the tangles from her long blonde hair. "When's the last time you used one of these?"

Shaking her head, she blindly swatted at him. "You used to do this for me when I was little."

"Well, Catherine threatened to chop off all your pretty hair." *The witch would've done it too.* "Couldn't let that happen, now, could I?"

Linnea was four, maybe five. Kodiak and his father had been over for supper. Standing there in a pink flannel nightgown, she timidly handed her grandmother the brush. Catherine mercilessly tugged and yanked. The tears streaming down her face were silent at first, but ultimately, she cried out. Instead of comforting her granddaughter, the cruel woman slapped her. Then she went for the scissors.

"She always pulled so hard."

Kodiak put himself between them, and shielding Linnea from her grandmother, took the scissors out of Catherine's hand. Then he sat Linnea on the sofa beside him, and much like he was doing now, gently worked the snarls from her baby-fine hair.

Jarrid just watched, that ever-present smirk on his face. When they got home, he gave him a good whooping with the switch for interfering, but it was worth it. Linnea kept her hair, and after that, every time they were there, she came to him to brush it.

"There." Smoothing the hair down her back with his hand, Kodiak kissed her crown. "All done."

"Can you do me a favor?" She moved over, sitting up against the headboard.

"Anything."

"Stay with me until I fall asleep?"

*Anything but that.*

Did Linnea realize what she was asking of him? Probably not. But then she didn't go through the years of conditioning that he had. She never thought of him the way he'd thought of her. Since he came back, Kodiak had been very careful to avoid any situation where he might think of her like that again.

*"Can you learn to love her as your sister?"*

Should be easy enough, right? *Wrong.* Was he supposed to un-love someone he'd loved his whole life? He struggled with it for such a long time. And while it *had* been easier when Kyan was here, he wasn't here anymore.

Looking into Linnea's sad green eyes, Kodiak softly answered, "I can do that."

She got under the covers.

He laid down beside her on top of them.

"I can't smell him anymore." Her sweet voice trembled. "I still feel him, though."

"Close your eyes now." Looping his arm around Linnea's middle, he gave her hand a gentle squeeze.

She nodded, her head rubbing against his chest, and whispered, "Goodnight."

Shadows of swaying tree branches danced on the bedroom walls. Kodiak stared at them, while he waited for Linnea to fall asleep.

*"We're friends."*

Beneath a tree, along the shore of Lake Michigan, the sweetest lips he'd ever tasted softly brushed his own. It was so unexpected, he was stunned for a second. Then instinctively, his arms wrapped around her, holding Kelly to him closer. Her fingertips, which were lightly grazing his cheeks, slid into his hair and he took over.

Deepening the kiss, her lips parted. Kodiak slipped his tongue inside, and holy fuck, was she delicious. Coffee and cookies. Mocha and hazelnut. Those feelings came flooding back. And it was New Year's all over again.

Breaths staggering, he nipped her bottom lip. "What are you playing at, Kelly?"

Her answer was to kiss him once more.

Fingers gripping her hair, Kodiak pressed his cock, stiff and achy in his pants, between the thighs that straddled him. She whimpered, an encouraging sound, and kissed him harder. So, he reached inside the pink scalloped lace, her plump breast in his hand. Tearing his lips from hers, he squeezed it. "Answer me."

"Nothing."

"No, it's something." He smirked, his thumb rubbing circles on her nipple. *But what?* "What are you after?"

"A friend."

"Heh." Kodiak sucked that nipple deep into his mouth, biting it before he let go. "A friend, huh?"

"Fuck," Kelly squealed. "Yes, a friend."

"Unzip."

"What?"

"You heard me." The word was simple enough to understand, wasn't it? "Unzip."

Her head swiveled from side to side, surveying the area around them.

"No one can see." Kodiak grinned. "Now give me that pussy."

Kelly pulled her zipper down.

He lowered her jeans just enough to get his hand between her legs. Warm and wet, his fingers slid over smooth, shaved lips. "Very nice."

His index finger delved, seeking the source of her sweetness. Kodiak pushed it all the way up inside, her tight, slick heat seemed to welcome him. He withdrew, only to push his way back in again, and she made that sound. "This what you wanted, Kelly?"

Biting her lip, her head frantically bobbed up and down.

"Want me to fill up this pretty little pussy?" Her lip between his teeth, Kodiak eased another finger inside her.

She moaned, the sound a long and drawn-out release.

"Want to be fucked, don't you?"

"Yes."

"Tell me. Ask me to fuck this pussy." He licked up the column of her throat. "And do it nicely."

"Here?"

"Right here, baby." The corner of his mouth ticked up, his thumb pressing on her clit.

"Fuck my pussy." Kelly clamped her fingers around his wrist. "Please, Kodiak. I need to know what it feels like."

Then sealing her lips with his, he fucked her with his fingers until she came.

Kodiak pulled his hand out from between her thighs. "Fix your pants before someone comes and sees you." Then he licked the deliciousness from his fingers. "Friends don't do this."

"Your friends do, don't they?"

She had a point.

Lowering her gaze, Kelly zipped her jeans. "I've been to the Red Door, remember? I know what y'all do in there."

The one place he was free. Kelly really had no idea, but she'd seen enough, he supposed. Did she get off watching him with Bo? Was she jealous seeing him and Dillon fuck a size queen's pussy together, slurping sweet cum from her gaping hole once they finished her?

"That's different."

"How so?" Blue eyes bored into his own.

*Because we all care about each other, dammit.* But he couldn't tell her that. She wouldn't get it anyway.

"It just is."

She stroked his cheek. "I'd like for us to be friends like that, Kodiak."

"Really now, why?"

"Because I trust you." She placed her hand on the hard bulge in his jeans. "I know you won't hurt me."

He was the last man on Earth she should trust not to do that.

"Oh, I'll hurt you, Kelly." He pushed himself into her palm. "Count on it."

"You feel good." She squeezed his aching dick. "I think I just might like it."

"Oh, yeah?" Biting her lips, he kissed her.

"Yeah."

"I guess we'll find out sometime."

Kelly smiled and she was beautiful. "Are we friends then?"

*We're friends.*

Opening his eyes, Kodiak looked upon the girl he'd loved from the moment she was born. She slept. He could do it now. He could keep his promise. The thoughts he once feared never came. Kissing his sister's cheek, he slipped out of her bed. "Goodnight, Linnea."

Yeah, he was better now.

# Five

High on dopamine after her lakefront interlude, Kelly swooped in the door to find Leo admiring his burgundy-painted nails. His head jerked in her direction, and eyeing her up and down, he grinned. "Nice walk?"

"You could say that, I guess." Containing a fit of giggles, she bit her lip.

What the hell was happening to her? The last time Kelly could remember ever feeling this way was when Kyle Donovan, only the most sought-after boy in school, invited her to senior prom. As it turned out, the dance sucked and Mr. Popular wasn't all that, but she could still vividly recall how giddy she felt when he asked her. It was like winning the lottery, Christmas morning, and zipping up a pair of jeans that were once a size too small all rolled into one.

Maybe it was just the first orgasm in two years she didn't have to give herself. *Right.* Who was she kidding? More like it was the *man* who gave it to her. And honestly, that surprised her.

She met Stacy after college. And *him.* It was at a ChiO sisters reunion party. Four years younger, Kelly hadn't known her when she was in school. Standing at the bar, someone hugged her from behind and softly kissed the back of her neck. She turned around to find the tall, stunning blonde smiling down at her.

An hour later, Kelly sat in silence on a sofa in Stacy's apartment. Heart popping out of her chest. Dry mouth. She'd never been touched by a woman before. Stacy ran her fingers through her hair, leaning in to kiss her. Their tongues met, and before she could even realize what was happening, Stacy slid her hand beneath her dress and gave her the most intense fingerfucking she'd ever had.

Until today.

"Mmhm." Cocking his head, Leo buffed his nails on his shirt. "What were you and that hard, wet dream of mine really doin'?"

"Nothing." Kelly did giggle then. "And you live with your dream man, remember? Or have you forgotten about him? Where's Katie-Kate?"

"Kevin came in. She went home." He dragged her over to him. "Now tell Leo everything. What kind of game are you playing, *mon cher?*"

"I'm not."

His eyes widening, he proclaimed, "You like him."

"We're just friends."

Leaning back against the counter, with a swish of his ponytail, Leo's arms crossed over his chest. "With benefits?"

"Maybe."

"You like him," he sing-songed, glossy lips breaking into a grin.

"I do not."

"Leo knows. You don't want to, *bebé*, but you do."

She did.

"That FWB thing almost never works out, you know." He pulled her close against him and smoothed her hair. "Feelings always get in the way. Someone falls in love…"

"I won't."

"…someone else gets hurt."

"That's not going to happen, trust me." Kelly put some space between them. "I know what I'm doing."

"Girl, you know how much I love you, but I don't think that you do."

Leo was right about that.

She didn't have a clue.

It was three days before Kelly saw him again. Friday night, just as Beanie's was closing, Kodiak strolled in carrying a jumbo-sized bag with familiar blue stripes. Garrett's popcorn.

"Is that Chicago mix in there?"

"Maybe," he teased.

Buttery caramel and cheesy deliciousness. "Gimme."

"Uh, uh, uh. Not so fast." Kodiak moved the bag just out of her reach. "I'll share my popcorn, but you have to take a walk with me."

"Not walking."

"All right then." He turned to go.

"Kodiak. Wait. I've been here since six this morning." He turned right back around. "I'm too tired, but I have a better idea."

"And what's that?" he asked, the corner of his mouth slowly creeping up.

"We can go upstairs. Watch a movie maybe." Leaning over the counter, Kelly peered into the bag, then smiled up at him. "I can put my feet up and you can feed me popcorn."

She didn't want it to look like she was trying too hard.

After opening a bottle of pinot and arming Kodiak with the remote, Kelly left him on the sofa to shower away sixteen hours of sweat and coffee grinds. She glanced at herself in the foggy bathroom mirror and throwing her hair up on top of her head, decided to forego the makeup. *Lash extensions and microblading. Best inventions ever.* Some tinted moisturizer and lip balm would do. An oversized Bears T-shirt and a pair of cotton boy shorts and she was ready.

He was sitting there, scrolling through his phone, Netflix home screen frozen on the TV, when she returned. "Didn't you pick a movie?"

"Don't know what you like yet." Shrugging with a smirk, Kodiak set his phone down and picked up his glass. He took a sip. "We should probably get to know each other better, being we're friends now."

"I suppose we should," Kelly agreed. Taking her seat, she reached for the popcorn and pulled her feet up. "God, I love this stuff."

"Kevin's not here?"

"No." She popped a handful of kernels into her mouth. "He's on a bus to Madison. Away game."

*It's a Netflix and chill night for Auntie Kelly.*

"Can I use your restroom?"

"Of course." She pointed him in the right direction. "Straight through there."

Kelly chugged down her glass of wine and quickly poured another. What was he doing in there? Besides the obvious, that is. Do guys do anything to get ready for sex? Freshen up the goods? Fix their hair? Pop a breath mint? Because they were definitely going to. Isn't that what getting to know each other better really means?

Wondering if she had enough time to down her second glass and pour herself a third before Kodiak came out of the bathroom, Kelly scrolled through the meager offerings on Netflix. She'd seen everything worth watching already.

Too late. The opportunity to not look like a lush passed. He stepped out of her room, looking much the same as when he went in. Rich chocolate waves flowed down to touch his waist. Longer than her own, he often pulled it back in a braid or a man bun. Not today. Thick and luxurious, it hung loose, just waiting for her fingers to run through it.

Pushing his sleeves up to his elbows, Kodiak showed off those veiny, muscled forearms of his and glanced her way. He smirked. "What?"

"I don't recall saying anything." Kelly raised her glass to her lips.

"You didn't have to." He sat down beside her, pulling her feet onto his lap. "Your face does all the talking for you."

*Shit.*

"You play a mean game of poker, don't you?"

"I suck."

He grinned. "I know."

"At poker." Laughing, she threw a piece of popcorn at him.

A moment of silence followed. Then Kodiak began rubbing her foot. Pressing his thumbs deep into the sole, Kelly closed her eyes, tipping her head back with a moan.

"Did you ever have a boyfriend, Kelly?"

"I did in high school…college," she said, fixing her gaze on him. "And then I didn't."

"What made you switch teams?"

"Stacy." Glancing up at the exposed ductwork in the loft's ceiling, Kelly shrugged. "I met Stacy."

He released his hold on her foot. "Did you love her?"

"She was what I needed at the time."

With a nod, Kodiak picked up the other foot and started rubbing. "Do you want kids one day?"

Were they playing twenty questions now? Because where on Earth did that come from? While she always pictured herself with a kid or two someday, she wasn't sure how to answer him.

"I don't know. Maybe." She pursed her lips, tilting her head to the side. "I could get artificially inseminated, I guess—if I ever decide I want a baby."

"You don't have to do that." He slid his hand up her calf.

"That's how lesbians get babies."

"You're not a lesbian." Sniggering, Kodiak squeezed her knee.

Rolling her eyes, Kelly tsked. "I was in a long-term relationship that would say otherwise."

"Then why do you have birth control pills in your bathroom?"

*Jesus, did you count the number of tampons under the sink too?*

Stammering, Kelly plunked her hand down on top of his. This conversation had taken a weird turn. There are plenty of other reasons women take the Pill besides the most obvious one, not that she could think of any now. And what difference did it make to him anyway?

Kodiak pulled his hand out from under hers. "Look, I've been with Bo. Doesn't mean I'm gay."

"Bi?"

"I don't think so. He was what I needed at the time." His lip curling into a smirk, he winked. "You shouldn't think of sexuality as being black or white, true or false, wrong or right. It's…fluid. And it's complicated, messy…sometimes it's downright frustrating."

"You sound like a shrink," she mumbled under her breath.

He laughed at that. "She'd be delighted to hear it."

"You have one?"

"Yeah." Looking down at his lap, Kodiak went back to massaging her foot. "Does that concern you?"

Not exactly, but she had to admit her curiosity was piqued. Now was not the time to ask, though. Kelly pushed her toes into his thigh. "No, unless you're some kind of psychopath who kicked puppies and drowned kittens when you were ten."

"Not even close." His index finger lazily swept along the tender arch. "You're safe."

*Said the spider to the fly…*

Just the way he said it made Kelly think she was anything but. Isn't that what she wanted, though? To get caught up in his web.

She wet her lips. "That's a relief."

"Have you ever wanted another woman?" Raising his head to look at her, his finger ceased its movement. "Besides Stacy."

"No."

Apparently pleased by her answer, Kodiak grinned. Then lifting her foot to his lips, he kissed it. "Maybe one day I'll put a baby in you."

"With your dick?"

"How else?" Brow lifted, green eyes aghast, the look on his face was comical. "A turkey baster? Not happening, Snicks."

Kelly tried to hold it in, but she couldn't do it. Rising from deep inside her belly, it came out of her nose in a snort. She sounded like a rhinoceros. Not that she knew what they really sounded like, but still, it was ridiculous. Pulling her knees to her chest, the thought made her laugh all that much harder. So hard, that her stomach was cramping, she couldn't breathe, and tears leaked out her eyes.

It seemed to go on forever, and try as she might, Kelly couldn't make herself stop. Every time she caught her breath, she'd burst into another fit of giggles. She glanced at him through watery eyes, swiping the tears from her face. He was grinning. "Wait. Snicks?"

"Yeah, like those cookies you're always feeding me." Releasing the tie from her hair, Kodiak brushed her lips with his and whispered, "Sweet cinnamon sugar."

"I know you like them." Her toes curled in his lap, rubbing over the placket of his jeans.

"Damn right, I do."

Then his fingers wound their way into her hair, pulling her down until her head landed on the sofa, cradled in his arm. He didn't just kiss her. Kodiak took her lips like he owned them. Tracing them with his tongue. Biting them. Cushioning them between his own. Where Stacy's kisses had been soft and sweet like cotton candy, his were a decadent dessert. A luscious gateau of Chiboust cream and caramel she'd been starving for.

He groaned, lips leaving hers, they skated along her jaw, down the column of her throat. Course denim pushed into thin cotton. God, his weight on her was glorious. Better than she imagined. Hard planes and angles demanding Kelly yield her softness, her body molded itself to his. She'd forgotten just how incredible it could be.

Her fingers, tangled in his long, thick hair, moved down his back to slip beneath his shirt. She wanted to touch his skin, the solid muscle, the heat of masculine flesh. His hand squeezed her bare breast. The hardness in his pants rubbed between her thighs. Sliding her hands inside his jeans, Kelly firmly gripped his ass, holding him to the place she needed to feel him the most.

"Fuck," he growled, pushing himself against her.

Kodiak lifted his chest, and sitting between her parted thighs, he gazed down at her. Fingers stroked her hair, and then he kissed her softly, before righting her rucked-up shirt.

"I don't understand. Don't you want…" Kelly stopped mid-sentence.

There was no need to ask. If Kodiak truly wanted her, which apparently, he didn't, she wouldn't have to. She wasn't desperate for his dick—okay, maybe a little—but she wasn't about to humiliate herself any further.

He took her hand and kissed it, then held it to his chest. "Oh, yeah, I definitely want you."

"Why'd you stop then?"

"We're friends, right?" His fingers laced with hers.

Fighting to keep her emotions from showing, she nodded.

Kodiak closed his eyes for a moment. "Well then, Kelly, there's a lot you don't know about me yet, and before you go letting me stick my dick into you, you should."

"Like what? You got herpes or something?"

"No, nothing like that. I'm clean." He softly chuckled, but there was no mirth in it. His expression turning serious, Kodiak shrugged. "It's just…I'm fucked up."

*That's okay. I am too.*

"And?" She smiled, then tugging on the ends of his hair, pulled him back down to her, and kissed him.

"And…" Kodiak whispered, his breath tickling her ear, "…I'm really looking forward to winning that bet."

"What bet?"

He winked. "Night, Kelly."

# Six

Maybe he was an ass.

Nope, there were no maybes about it.

Kodiak plopped onto his bed. He definitely was an ass. Instead of lying here alone, in the room his sister used to sleep in, he could still be there with Kelly. Tearing the clothes from her body. Sinking himself deep inside her. But no, he let his conscience get the better of him.

Anybody else, Kodiak wouldn't give two shits. *You wanna fuck? Let's go.* But this was Kelly, not another nameless face at the club. And she deserved to know him first. Really know him. Few actually did.

Let her see the ugly parts. Perhaps she'd find beauty in there somewhere. It was a risk, and a huge one at that, but if Kelly still wanted him afterward, it would be well worth it. Never mind his past, his upbringing, his transgressions, his flaws—and there were many. To be desired despite it all. Deemed worthy. Accepted. Isn't that what everyone secretly craves?

He was no different.

It was a tall order, though, and Kodiak knew it. He snickered to himself. There was just so much to unpack here. What should he start off with? His father? His sister?

*The whole truth, asshole.*

All of it. Every dark and dirty, nasty, twisted bit. Much the same as he'd told it to Babs. If he turned out to be the villain in Kelly's story, and he likely would, then so be it. Shame he couldn't just fuck her and not give a shit. Withhold the truth or tell her lies. It would sure be a helluva lot easier. But he couldn't.

Kodiak picked up his phone. Debating, he smacked it against his palm a few times before he gave in to the urge and called her. "I want a raincheck on that movie, Snicks."

He was met with silence, but he could feel her smiling on the other end of the line.

"And dinner," he added for good measure. "I want to take you to dinner. You ever give yourself a night off?"

"Um, sometimes," she stammered. "But I have to work them in around Kevin's football schedule. Katie's classes. Brendan wants her home in the evenings, and of course, Leo comes in early to do the baking every morning…"

"When?" Taking advantage of the pause, Kodiak tried to pin her down. "When is sometimes?"

"Thursday."

"Six o'clock, Kelly." He grinned into the phone. "Be ready for me."

She was.

He went to Beanie's first, only for Kevin to inform him his aunt wasn't there. "She left as soon I came in. Got herself a hot date or somethin.'"

"Oh, yeah?"

"Yeah." He nodded, the corner of his mouth lifting. "She had that look, you know?"

Raising his brow, Kodiak gave him a look of his own.

"Dopey grin and shit." Kevin winked. "Watch the eyelashes. If they get all fluttery, it's a done deal. You got 'em."

He pressed his lips together to stop himself from laughing. *Sure, kid.*

Shoulders exposed, Kelly answered the door in a sheer, flouncy blouse. Skintight jeans with rips in all the right places. Little suede boots.

*Sweet Jesus.*

Leaning in to kiss her cheek, he inhaled. Kodiak closed his eyes, sweet strawberries, a whisper of red apple, vanilla orchid, jasmine, and golden rum flirting with his senses. "Ready?"

"You said six, didn't you?" Taking a step back, Kelly smirked. "Just let me grab my purse."

A girl who actually understood the concept of time—how novel was that?

She returned, a sweater now covering the graceful slope of her shoulders. "Where are we going? Charley's?"

"Nah." He watched her close the door, making sure it was locked behind her. "I go there all the time. What do you feel like?"

"Um, anything. I'm not picky when it comes to food."

*My kind of girl.*

"C'mon. There's plenty of places to choose from on the way." Kodiak took her hand in his, and lacing their fingers together, they strolled along the avenue beneath the setting sun.

The evening breeze was mild, for late September anyway. It wouldn't last much longer, but for today, folks were taking advantage of it. Tossing a ball in the park. Grabbing a hot dog at a food cart on the sidewalk.

Kelly stopped, pointing to a restaurant up ahead at the corner. "Killer margaritas."

"You thirsty, Snicks?"

"No." She giggled, holding onto his arm. "Well, yeah, but Cesar's has killer Tex-Mex too."

"Guess that's what's for dinner then." His hand slipped around her waist. "We can save water and drink tequila."

Surprisingly, their patio was open. Kodiak was glad for that. With the place packed to the brim with happy hour and dinner patrons, he was hoping for a spot that was a little less boisterous. Where they could hear each other talk. A place where he could breathe. The hostess did him a solid, giving them a table on the rooftop.

"Is this okay? It's not too cold for you, is it?"

"Are you kidding? I love it up here." But she pulled her sweater tighter. "It's so nice out. We should enjoy it. God knows it could start snowing next weekend."

"Hush, you." He chuckled, taking the seat across from her. "You'll jinx us."

"Sorry, my friend, but summer's over." Kelly glanced up from her menu. "There's a cold front coming."

"I like the cold…the snow. Can't say I'm fond of shoveling it, though." Gazing back at her, Kodiak nodded. "I loved it in Alaska. Had dreams of building a home there once."

"Why'd you leave then?"

He swallowed. "Linnea."

Not the best place to start, he was grateful when she didn't press further. His relationship with his sister was complicated, and that was putting it mildly. He'd tell her everything when the time was right, once Kelly knew enough to hopefully understand.

The server brought them 'killer' margaritas and took their order. Kodiak clinked his glass with hers. "A truth for a truth."

"What's that?" She sat back in her seat, cocking her head. "Like twenty questions?"

"Kind of." Locking eyes with hers, he took a drink. Her pupils flared. "You can ask me anything you want to, and I'll give you my honest answer."

"Anything?"

"Anything."

Seemingly in thought, Kelly pursed her lips from side to side. "Okay, what's the catch?"

"Then I get to ask you one." A smile slowly spread across his face. "Fair?"

"I guess so."

Kodiak didn't notice when the server brought it by, but a platter with fresh tortilla chips, salsa, guacamole, and *esquites* sat on the table. He picked up a chip, dipped it into the creamy mashed avocado, and leaning toward Kelly, fed it to her. "I'll even let you go first."

"Hmm, this might be fun." She grinned, her tongue peeking out to swipe up guac from her lip. "Let's see, I should start with something easy…who in your family are you closest to and why?"

He sniggered. Easy enough. "That would be my sister. She's the only blood family I've got."

"Oh…I'm so sorry." Reaching across the table, Kelly took his hand. "What happened to your parents?"

*And so, it begins…*

With a slow exhale, Kodiak gave her hand a squeeze and let it go. He'd been toying with how to approach this from the moment he called her. His truths were triggering. The stories of his past stranger than fiction, even to him, and he'd lived them. So, like a book, perhaps it was best to deliver it in easier-to-swallow doses, one digestible chapter at a time.

"Linnea was a tiny baby when Grace died. She was…um… seventeen. Hanged herself." Taking a swallow of tequila, he grimaced. Nasty shit. He'd always hated it. "Her grandmother raised her."

*Fucking witch.*

Kodiak would never forget that day, the details of which still replayed in his head. He'd just sat down in front of the TV with a bowl of his favorite cereal to watch *Scooby Doo* until wrestling came on—*WWF Livewire*, never missed it. The phone rang, and the next thing he knew his father dragged him off the couch, Cap'n Crunch spilling to the floor, to get in the car.

No coat. Barefoot. Still in his pajamas. It was April. The Dairy Queen hadn't reopened yet. He could hear Linnea screaming her little head off when his father opened Catherine's front door. Jarrid tore up the stairs calling out for Grace, Kodiak coming in right behind him.

She was hanging there, swinging from a rope in her nightgown.

"Cut her down, will you?" Catherine just sat there, staring out the window. "And get that screeching thing out of my sight. I told you. She never should have been born."

"Take the baby, Seth," his father choked, steering him away from Grace's body. "Wait for me downstairs."

Linnea slept in her crib in his room for weeks after the funeral. Even as a ten-year-old child, he should've seen his father was just as horrible as Catherine, if not more so, for allowing a defenseless baby to return to the care of that woman. But he didn't know what true evil really looked like. Not then. That would come later.

Motioning for the server, Kodiak finished off his margarita and ordered a pitcher of beer. While across from him, pretty eyes wide, Kelly sat holding her hand to her mouth.

"We have different mothers, obviously, and don't bother asking about mine because I don't know shit about her." He rubbed the salt off the rim of his empty glass. "We're both estranged from our father."

"Why?"

"Simple answer? He's an evil bastard."

Balancing a large tray, the server returned with the beer and their dinner. She placed sizzling fajitas down in front of them, then quietly retreated.

"And the not so simple one?"

"Trust me, Snicks, you aren't ready to hear it yet." Small doses, right? Kodiak turned the tables. "That's three you owe me now."

"Three what?"

"Truths." And he grinned. "My turn."

"Okay, okay." Kelly smiled, her blue eyes twinkling in the lantern's light. "But our food's going to get cold, so can we eat first?"

They never did make it to the movies. Sharing fajitas and

stories and drinking beer, the hours spent up on the rooftop flew. He learned her favorite ice cream was strawberry, pineapples don't belong on pizza, and she wanted to be a veterinarian when she was six.

Walking home arm in arm, Kodiak asked her, "How'd you go from puppy shots to triple shot lattes?"

"Turns out I'm allergic to cats." Biting her lip, Kelly shrugged. "Most pet dander, really, but especially cats. Shame, because I always wanted a puppy."

"So, get one." His fingertips traced over her hand holding onto his arm. "There's hypoallergenic breeds, you know."

"I'm hardly ever home."

"Hire more people. Spend more time at home. Do whatever makes you happy." Having reached the alley, Kodiak stopped walking. Pulling Kelly with him, he leaned against the brick wall and tucked a wisp of hair behind her ear. "Life is too short to live it with regrets. Get the dog."

"Maybe someday."

"And one day, you wake up realizing you're all out of them." Lowering his forehead to hers, he gripped her shoulders. "Do it now."

"Once I get Stacy paid off, I can afford to hire more people. Then I can be home more and have a dog." Not waiting for him to respond, she ran her fingers through his hair and placed a kiss beneath his jaw. "Someday's going to be one day, okay?"

"When's your next sometimes?" Tightening his arms around her, he kissed the tip of her nose.

"Huh?"

"Night off." With a dip of his chin, Kodiak chuckled. "I still owe you a movie."

"Ohhh, that sometimes." Sinking her teeth into her lip, Kelly giggled. "I've got Kevin's game next Saturday, but my morning is free. How about breakfast?"

His mornings belonged to his sister. Linnea needed him, didn't she? But he wanted time with Kelly. Somehow, he'd make it work. "I like my eggs over easy, whole-wheat toast, and my steak medium rare."

"Guess you want me to do the cooking, huh?"

"Yup." Brushing the hair back from her face, Kodiak looked into her sultry blue eyes. "Truth for a truth, Kelly. You sure you want to be my friend?"

Long lashes fluttering, she smiled. "I do."

"Good." He smiled back.

Then he kissed her.

# Seven

He looked at the all-too-familiar address, and swiping left, deleted the email without reading it. *Fuck you.* Kodiak wasn't the least bit interested in anything the man had to say. Leaving his phone behind, he stepped out onto the sidewalk to stretch his muscles and set off on his morning run.

While he had yet to see a single snowflake, Kelly's prediction had come to pass. The October air had turned brisk. He could see his breath when he exhaled. A plume of white in the shadowy darkness. Moonlight giving way to the dawn.

His favorite time of day. It was the quietude of it. With most of the city still tucked in bed asleep, the only sounds to be heard were the leaves falling from the trees to skitter along the curb, the wind whirring past him, his heart pumping in his chest.

Third lap around the trail, the endorphins kicked in. A small measure of peace, he let them consume him. The email he'd deleted, and its sender, forgotten.

By the time he was finished, ribbons of pink unfurled in the eastern sky. Hands at his waist, Kodiak propped his foot up on a bench, stretching out his hamstring. He repeated the process with the other, then after paying equal attention to his quads and glutes, made the short trek home.

Any other day, he'd hit the weights set up in the spare room, but he was going to meet up with Kelly this morning, so he hit the shower instead. He was excited to see her again. This friend thing just might work, and dammit, he wanted it to. Needed it to. Sure, he wanted to fuck her. And he would. But his desire ran deeper than that.

Kodiak wanted to get inside that pretty little head of hers. To uncover every facet of Kelly Matthews. What parts of herself was she hiding from him? It didn't matter. Because little by little, he'd slice his way through all her layers. Just as eventually, he'd allow her to painfully peel away every last one of his.

Showered and dressed, he meticulously made up the bed, folding the sheet so the creases were neat and tucking the corners in tight. He'd found habits, like promises, were difficult for him to break. Deeply ingrained since childhood, and required during his years in the service, Kodiak kept his surroundings orderly and neat. Spic and span. And besides, who doesn't love the feel of a crisply made bed?

Picking his phone up from the night table, he glanced at the time. Half past seven. Being he wasn't meeting Kelly until nine, there was an hour left to kill. They were going to some trendy place over on Diversey with bottomless mimosas and an all-you-can-eat weekend brunch. Afterward, they'd go their separate ways. She to watch her nephew's football game, and he to check in on his sister.

Kodiak ambled down the stairs, running his fingers along the back of the camel leather sofa, on his way to the kitchen. A cup of hot tea would help pass the time. *And a joint. Thank fuck for Babs.* The state legalized weed for recreational use a few years ago, but since she gave him a prescription for it, he didn't have to pay the bullshit taxes that doubled the price. *Greedy motherfuckers.*

He opened his stash drawer to retrieve the vape pen and took it outside to the courtyard patio. Inhaling deep, Kodiak kicked back on the lounger while he waited for the kettle to boil. Its branches swaying, leaves of orange and fiery red rustled on the lone Japanese dogwood. Linnea loved that damn tree and said so every time she came by. He wondered what memories this place held for her. Many were of Kyan, he supposed.

Taking another hit off his pen, a chill passed through him. The ghost of the man was present everywhere. Slowly releasing the vapor from his lungs, Kodiak whispered to the tree, "She cries for you, brother. More than she ever cried for me."

*As it should be.*

He snickered to himself and closed his eyes, the cannabis taking effect. Sometimes his thoughts had a will of their own…sometimes his mind wandered to a place where they were happy together, blissfully unaware of the evil misdeeds perpetuated upon them, and she was still his. There was a time he welcomed going there.

The vision was fleeting, but so tangible he could almost touch it. Kodiak could see long blonde hair billowing out from behind her, chasing after a little boy on the grass. He forced his eyes open.

*You're a sick fuck, man.*

No.

No, he was better now. But still, there was this wrongness that dwelled within him, an unforgivable sin that could never be washed clean. It ran deep, embedded in his flesh, poisoning the blood that coursed through his veins.

And hers.

*I love you. I'm so fucking sorry.*

It would be a selfish act to taint someone else, wouldn't it?

He should call her. Come up with some excuse why he couldn't make it. The last thing Kelly needed was a friend like him.

The kettle whistled and his phone vibrated all at once. Dillon's name flashing on the screen, Kodiak answered it as he went back inside. Pouring boiling water into the teapot, he let the aromatic leaves steep. Apparently, Monica succeeded in getting Linnea to leave the house. His sister had plans to go to some arts and crafts show in

Long Grove, so he made plans to meet Dillon for coffee later that afternoon. Without Linnea to fuss over, the poor guy didn't know what to do with himself.

"She needs this, bro." And the doorbell rang. "Someone's here. I'll be there at two."

*Who the fuck?*

Some bible peddlers, no doubt. *Been there. Done that. Never wanna go back.* Opening the door without looking, he droned, "Whatever it is you're selling, I'm not the least bit interested."

"You sure about that?"

*Shit.*

Kelly stood on his stoop, a large, eco-friendly, reusable shopping bag in each hand. She smirked, long loose waves framing her exquisite face. Tight faded jeans. Snakeskin ankle boots. The black sweater she wore reached her calves and bared her shoulders. "I got T-bone steaks."

"I thought…" Shaking his head, Kodiak grinned. He relieved Kelly of the bags, and holding them both in one hand, hooked an arm around her neck. "Get in here."

Mischievous blue eyes glanced up at him. "I know we were going to go out, but I figured we'd be more comfortable here or at the loft. But since Kevin hasn't left yet and Katie's working downstairs, so, yeah, um…" She took a breath. "You did say you wanted me to make you breakfast, didn't you?"

"I did." Setting the bags down on the island, Kodiak tugged Kelly to his chest.

Damn, this girl was something else. Except for Linnea, he'd never had a woman who *wanted* to cook for him. Not that he needed or expected that from anyone, he was perfectly capable of fending for himself, after all. But that Kelly made the gesture, made him feel some kind of way. He refused to put a name to it, though.

Running his fingers through her silky waves, Kodiak gripped the hair at her nape and lowered his lips to hers. He kissed her. With the air leaving his lungs, a feel-good chemical cocktail released into his bloodstream.

More potent than a runner's high.

More calming than cannabis.

She'd become an addiction if he wasn't careful.

Kodiak let go of her hair, smoothing it down her back. He turned his attention to the shopping bags and began unpacking them. "What do we have in here?"

"Besides steak?" With her teeth pressing into her bottom lip, Kelly grinned. "Um, you know, breakfast stuff."

"Uh-huh." And smirking, he held up two bottles of champagne. "I can see that."

"There's orange juice to go with it. Where's your glasses?"

"Right over there." Tipping his chin, Kodiak peeled the foil off one of the bottles. "Second cabinet on the left."

"Nice place you've got here," she said, retrieving two crystal flutes. "I love it."

"Thanks." He popped the top. Champagne erupted, flowing over his fingers. "It was Linnea's until she and Kyan moved over to Park Place."

"Really?" Kelly held out the glasses.

"Yeah." Kodiak filled them. "Cheers."

"Cheers." She smiled and stepped over to the French doors, peering through the glass at the courtyard patio. "Pretty tree. You're so lucky. The only place I can sit outside is the fire escape."

"I come out here a lot." He threw his arm around her shoulders. "Tell you what, I'll grill the steaks, you make the eggs, and we can have breakfast out here if you want."

"It's a bit chilly, don't you think?"

"Nah." Squeezing her to his side, Kodiak smiled down at her. "I'll keep you warm. Promise."

While the autumn air was crisp, the sun shining down on the patio made it pleasantly so. After searing the steaks, he pushed up the sleeves of his Henley and switched the fire table on. Hell, he could sit out here on the coldest January day with that thing going, and he had. She'd be fine.

Kodiak poked his head into the kitchen. Kelly had plated their food, arranging it on a tray, as she sipped on a mimosa. "Steaks are about done."

"Perfect timing." She set her glass down and smiled. "I was just about to take everything outside."

"I've got it." Reaching for the tray, his fingertips brushed her skin. Her lips parted and he watched her cheeks pinken. "Bring the champagne."

Side by side, each tucked into their breakfast. He dipped whole-wheat toast into a perfectly prepared over-easy egg. She cut into her steak. "You know how to grill. This is really good."

"And this is fantastic…" Savory home-fried potatoes, fresh fruit drizzled with honeyed yogurt, and Leo's famous banana-nut muffins. "…better than any restaurant."

"Thanks," she said, cozying up against him.

"You warm enough?"

"Yeah, I'm good."

"There's a blanket if you need it." Turning toward her, Kodiak tucked her hair behind her ear. "I did say I'd keep you warm."

"So, you did." Picking up the bottle of champagne, Kelly topped off his glass and handed it to him. "Bottle's empty."

She didn't have to ask. He peeled back the foil and opened the other. Its contents sprayed, bubbling over the neck. With a burst of delightful laughter, she caught the wine on her tongue, then sucked it from his fingers.

And his dick twitched.

"Truth for a truth, Kelly." He traced her lips with his thumb. "Tell me what you want."

"You."

Taking her hand, Kodiak pressed it to the hardening bulge in his jeans. "When's the last time you touched a cock?"

"At the club, with you."

He liked that answer.

Gliding his fingers around her neck, they slipped into her hair. Kodiak pulled her closer, kissing along her jaw, he burred into her ear. "And when's the last time you felt one inside you?"

"Ohhh…a long time ago."

"How long?"

"Does it matter?" Shaking her head, Kelly pulled away. "College."

A decade? *Jesus Christ.*

Kodiak tugged her back. "You want me to change that?"

Sultry blue eyes locked with his, she wet her lips. "Yes."

"Say it."

"I want…" Slipping her hand inside his jeans, Kelly held onto his dick and squeezed. "…to feel you inside me."

His lips quirked up. "I win."

# Eight

"Y**ou win?"**

"I win." Reclining against the arm of the sofa, Kodiak took Kelly with him. His nose skimming along hers, he whispered softly against her lips, "Our bet."

"I don't recall any—"

He took her mouth, sealing off her words. Enfolded in his strong, muscular arms, Kodiak kissed her. Soft and warm and breathless. Tasting the wine on his tongue, Kelly inhaled the hedonistic scent of his skin. Bergamot, hot cocoa, and a light air of incense wrapped around her senses while a burgeoning need began to pull at her belly.

And she was so fucking glad for it.

She hadn't felt this way with a man for so long, she feared she never would again.

But with his hands kneading her ass, Kodiak pressed her pliant body to the hardness in his jeans. "Oooh," Kelly gasped. Yeah, no mistaking that. She definitely felt it.

He groaned into her mouth, their kiss turning deep and hungry. His fingers thrust into her hair, grasping it tightly at the nape. Then holding onto her ass with his other hand, he lifted them up from the couch. Her legs encircled his waist, and with his lips never leaving hers, Kodiak walked them back inside.

Up the stairs.

Ten paces down a hall.

And when her feet finally touched the floor, he was still kissing her.

He released her hair, fingertips sweeping down her spine. Succulent kisses along her jaw. Staggered breaths. Spectral eyes of the softest green, the pupils burning black, stared straight into her soul.

Goosebumps sheeted her skin.

Kodiak couldn't know that, yet the corner of his lips turned up in a smirk, seemingly pleased with himself for the effect he was having on her. Hands dipped beneath her sweater, grazing bare skin along the way. He raised it over her head and let it drop to the floor.

Kelly stood still, cheeks heating, her chest heaving with every breath. Fingertips swept her collarbone, slowly brushing across her breasts. Quivering flesh confined in translucent, sorbet silk.

"So beautiful," he whispered, awestruck as if seeing her for the very first time.

Maybe, in a way, he was.

Landing on top of it, his Henley joined her sweater. Defined ridges, ink, and smooth, golden skin. Fine, dark hair dusted his chest, narrowing into a trail down his stomach. Kelly reached out to feel it, surprised at its softness.

His hand covering hers, he held it against his pec and sat down on the bed. Then inhaling her, Kodiak pressed a kiss to her belly and popped the button on her jeans. Warm lips pressed to her skin, he pulled them down.

It was getting harder to breathe.

Clad in just her underwear, Kelly closed her eyes. She felt his exhale through the silk, hands traveling up inside her thighs. They parted, a finger gliding over the wisp of fabric that covered her clit.

*Zing.*

Eyes snapping open, she clutched onto his hair. And with a soft chuckle, Kodiak slipped those panties to the side, spreading her open with his thumbs.

Humming against her pussy, his fingers toyed at her entrance. She sucked in a breath, holding it, anticipating that first glorious sweep of his tongue, the moment he'd fill the hollow space inside her. Unable to wait any longer, pulling on the chocolate waves in her fingers, Kelly bucked her hips.

He growled, lips and teeth clamping down on her clit. Kodiak sucked. Hard. He ate her with expert precision, flicking the bud pulsing between her legs, spearing her with his tongue, lapping the evident desire that flooded her core.

Kelly bit down on her lip, trying to squelch the sounds that eked out of her. Stacy likened them to that of a hyena. *A squeaky chew toy.* In her shame, she learned how to silence herself.

But any attempt was futile with this man. Kodiak wouldn't allow it.

"Give it to me," he commanded, thick digits penetrating her.

She whimpered through her teeth. Thighs trembling, Kelly widened her stance, fisting his long hair tight. Kodiak fucked her with his fingers, the onslaught fervent, just as she knew it would be.

"More." He scissored them, stretching her, his thumb pressed up against her clit. "I want everything."

Her lips parted and the sounds broke free.

"That's it, baby." A wave of warm liquid rushing out of her, Kodiak gentled the movement of his fingers. "You're perfect."

Then his mouth was back on her cunt. Tonguing her clit, he fucked her slowly, the lull a devilish trick. With every drag of his tongue, every measured push and pull of his fingers, the sensations in her body amplified.

As did the sounds.

Kelly screamed his name, her knees giving out from under her.

But Kodiak held her, lapping up every drop she gave him. It was all she could do to hold on.

He laid her down on soft linen bedding. Raking her teeth over her lip, she watched him unbutton his jeans. This was really happening. His pants hit the floor and her gaze went right *there*.

*My God…*

Glancing up, Kodiak caught her looking. He smirked, and coming closer, hooked his fingers in the waistband of her ruined panties. They sailed to the floor.

"You're not going to regret this later, are you, Snicks?" Sitting down on the bed beside her, his fingers ran through her hair.

"Of course not," Kelly implored, fingertips tracing his lips. "I want this…you."

"And I want this off." With a flick of his fingers, Kodiak unclasped her bra, the cups giving way. His hand squeezed her breast, the thumb brushing over her nipple.

That zing sweeping through her body, he pulled her onto his lap and took her lips between his. Fingers sank into her bottom. Kneading the ample flesh, Kodiak pushed up between her slippery thighs, but he didn't try to enter her.

Straps of silk slipped from her shoulders, and freeing her of the annoying garment altogether, he held her breasts. Sucking and biting on her nipples, before dragging his teeth up her neck to take her lips once more.

"My *queen*," he rasped into her mouth. "Get on your throne."

Kelly reached beneath her, and gripping the thick, rigid length, held him poised at her entrance. Could she ever be that girl again? *You're safe with him. He won't hurt you. Not like that.* Closing her eyes, she licked her lips and took in a fortifying breath.

*Holy fucking hell…*

She could feel her flesh split open as she took him inside her, one slow and delicious inch at a time. God, how he filled her. Kelly's hand squeezed his pec, the other holding onto the headboard, and she rocked. Tentatively at first. Because when had she last ridden a man? And for that matter, had she ever?

"Open them." His hands pressed up her back, fingertips moving along her spine. "I want those pretty blues on me when we fuck."

He nipped her nipple and she complied. Finding her rhythm, Kelly leaned over and kissed him. Licking his tongue. Sucking on it. Her hips began to move faster. Confidence growing, along with her momentum, she sat up straighter. Kodiak moved with her, the change in angle driving him deeper.

*There.*

*There.*

*There.*

*Yes, right fucking there.*

Her gaze focused on those hypnotic greens, he hit the spot again and again until her vision went black. A myriad of colors burst behind closed lids and her jaw went slack, his cum bathing her insides. Out of air, her body crumpling, he kissed the life back into her.

Because he wasn't done.

Kodiak turned her over, and with strong hands bracing her belly, the small of her back, he held her still. She listened to the groans from between her legs as he feasted on the mess they'd made together. His tongue dragged through her swollen pussy, up the split of her ass, lingering at the forbidden place where no one had ever been.

She whimpered.

Chuckling low, his teeth sank into her flesh, and with a parting lick, Kodiak nudged her onto her knees, placing her hands on the headboard. Kissing her nape, his chest grazed her back, rich chocolate tickling her skin. He notched his dick to her cunt that still throbbed, then anchoring his hands on the wood rail beside hers, slammed himself inside.

*Ooff.*

The solid power of a single thrust forcing the air from her lungs, she couldn't make a sound. Glancing back at him, her fingers curled around his bicep. The intensity of his gaze tore through her, along with his cock. And in that moment, Kelly knew she'd never be that girl again.

This. Man.

Sweeping her hair to the side, lips pressed to her temple, he fucked her. Heavy breaths. Fingers clenching her throat, Kodiak kissed her crown. *"My queen."* Pulling her head back, his mouth found hers. All-consuming. Voracious. Primal.

With every kiss, every caress, every solid thrust from behind, he changed her.

They fucked for hours. Kelly couldn't say how many, but right now she'd happily stay in this bed with him forever. Replete. Satiated in a room that smelled of sex, she languidly traced the ridges of muscle lying beneath his skin.

Reaching over her to the night table, he kissed her brow. Kodiak settled back into the pillows, and draping his arm around her, pulled her snugly against him. He drew on the pen, holding the vapor in his lungs. Glancing down at her, he slowly released it. "Want some?"

"No, thanks." Not that she was at all opposed to it. "Just makes me sleepy…and hungry."

"Pretty sure I can keep you up, Snicks." Kodiak took another hit, and shotgunning the vapor into her mouth, he kissed her. "And I like you hungry."

"Uh-huh." She giggled, playing with his beard. "I just never understood what everyone else seems to get out of it."

Sucking off his pen, he shrugged. "My shrink gave me a script."

"For what?"

"Stress." He exhaled. "PTSD."

"From the army?" Kelly asked, stroking his beautiful hair. "Were you deployed?"

"No." He snickered, tossing the pen to his side. "The army was my escape, my refuge."

"From what then?"

"Hell."

Jesus, what on Earth could that mean? As much as Kelly wanted to know, she was almost too afraid to ask. Searching his eyes for the answer, she tenderly kissed his lips.

"I can tell you all about Hell." Fingers absently strummed

through her hair, his gaze fixed on the ceiling. "And whatever you're imagining, it's worse."

"You can talk to me…if you want to, that is," she added, treadling lightly. "That's what friends are for, right?"

"Is that what we are, Kelly?" Turning his gaze toward her, he squeezed her pussy. "I promise I'll tell you everything, and it's a lot. But not today, okay?"

"Okay." She blinked. The afternoon sun poured in through the bedroom window. *Shit.* "What time is it?"

"Two," he replied, checking his phone. "I'm supposed to be at Beanie's meeting Dillon for coffee."

"I'm supposed to be at Kevin's game."

"Bad Auntie." Kodiak tsked. "Afraid you missed it, my *friend*."

"Yeah, what happened?"

He nuzzled her neck, sliding his fingers inside her. "We did."

And she smiled.

*It's me. I win.*

# Nine

Today was going to be a wretched day, and not because today was Monday. Once school days, church days, and army days were behind him, one day just blended into the next. Weekdays were no different than weekends. A perk of being self-employed, he supposed—or perhaps not. Considering how he liked to have a sense of structure, an order to things, sometimes Kodiak missed the delineation of his days.

But no, Monday had nothing to do with it. A quick glance at the calendar reminded him, not that he needed one, not only did he have a Zoom session with Babs scheduled for this morning, but it was also Linnea's wedding anniversary.

*Two years. Damn.*

The day he gave her away to another man.

Shaking the thought away, Kodiak ambled into the kitchen to make himself a cup of coffee. The aroma of it a pleasant reminder of Kelly. He smiled to himself. Kind of. *Snicks.* That girl just might be his undoing—or the answer to his prayers, all right. If Kodiak still prayed, that is, which he didn't.

Maybe he'd stop in at Beanie's later. That would make today less wretched. But he had to get through this chit-chat with Babs first, and those were always fun—not. He loved her, but the woman infuriated him sometimes. She always knew which buttons to push. Course, he's the one who handed them to her.

And then, Linnea. *Christ.* How he dreaded having to see her cry.

Grabbing his coffee, Kodiak got settled in front of his Mac. He logged in, vacantly staring through the glass while he waited. A squirrel, looking for crumbs to nibble on, scampered across the courtyard, and finding none, climbed up the dogwood tree. Clinging to a branch, the creature stood on its hind legs, beady eyes looking back at him, then was gone.

"Morning there, Kodiak." With a yawn, Babs lit a cigarette on the screen.

"That shit'll kill you, you know."

"Hasn't yet." She shrugged. "Besides, I only allow myself one a day. In the morning with my kombucha to get me going. The damn birds aren't even awake here yet."

"You picked the time, Barbara, not me."

She huffed out a plume of smoke. Her wiry, graying red hair in disarray, a strand went up in the air with it, only to land in her face. Poor Babs looked like she'd been up all night, and knowing her, she probably had been. "So, how've you been since we talked last?"

"All right," he replied. Kodiak schooled his features, attempting to maintain an impassive expression. The woman could read him like a book.

"Any more dreams? Nightmares?" Writing away on her notepad, she wasn't looking at him.

Kodiak tucked his tongue in his cheek. *Hmm…not exactly.*
"No."

"And how's your sister?" She stopped her scribbling to take a drag from her cigarette and glanced up at him.

"How do you think?" He bit out, head half-cocked. "Today would've been—"

"I know what today is." She smirked, picking up her pen.

"Jesus, Babs. Is everything on your little notepad there?"

"You know it." She chuckled, stubbing out her cigarette. "Any more emails?"

He pursed his lips, and pulling at his beard, Kodiak nodded.

Her drawn-on eyebrow quirked. "Have you responded to him?"

*Stupid question.*

"Fuck, no." He sniggered. "Don't even read them."

"Why not?"

Not deserving of an answer, Kodiak hit his vape pen instead.

"Ignoring him won't make the past go away," she said. He'd heard it a million times before. "Close the circle."

"I didn't open it," he seethed, the words gritting through his teeth.

"Doesn't matter," Babs countered, wagging her finger at Kodiak through the screen. She tapped on her chest. "You're holding onto it all in there somewhere. The psychological weight of that adds up. And what of Linnea?"

"What about her? The man is as good as dead to both of us. I just need to forget…"

*…everything.*

He couldn't, though.

"You need to forgive yourself too."

He couldn't do that either.

"Are we done here?"

"For today." She lit another cigarette. "Close the circle."

"Is this a bad time?"

Bo sat at the piano, fingers hovering over the keys. "Never." He swung his legs around the bench, that endearing grin on his face.

"Just playing around while I wait for Emmy to wake up from her nap. Everything okay?"

"Yeah," Kodiak assured him, planting his ass on the sofa in Bo's music room. "Going to Linnea's. Thought I'd pop by and see you first."

"How's our girl?"

He shrugged.

Chewing on his lip, Bo nodded. "And what about you?"

Not sure how to answer that, Kodiak lifted his brow, then dropping his shoulders, he exhaled.

"Talk to me, man." Taking a seat next to him, Bo yanked on the ends of his hair. "That's why you're here, isn't it?"

"I got another email from Jarrid."

"The fuck?" He cocked his head, wrinkling his nose. "Delete that shit."

"I did," Kodiak assured him.

"What the hell does he want? And why now all of a sudden?"

*Don't know. Don't care.*

"No idea." He sniggered. "Barbara thinks I should speak to him."

"Well, I'm no shrink, but Barbara hasn't met his crazy ass. She doesn't know what the fuck she's saying."

"Psychobabble bullshit."

"Don't do it." Bo emphatically shook his head, long blond hair flying about his face. "Made it out of there by the skin of our teeth last time. I thought he was gonna kill you."

With a chuckle, Kodiak smirked. "Got what I went for, though, didn't I?"

The portrait of Linnea and Grace.

Kyan was right about one thing, its rightful place was with his sister. But he was going to be the one to go get it for her, not him.

A friend of Bo's lent them a car, an old Ford Taurus so they could blend in. Prayer meetings were held on Wednesday nights, so his father would be occupied across the street—or so Kodiak thought at the time. They'd go in, take the portrait from the wall, and get out. It was his only chance. He was leaving for Cali next Wednesday.

"I'm not sure this was such a good idea." Bo gnawed on his lip, thumping out a beat on the steering wheel. "This place gives me bad vibes, man."

They were parked outside of the Dollar General waiting for the gray November sky to darken. Nothing good ever came out of Crossfield. *Except her.* "We won't be here long. I have to do this."

"Why? It's just a fucking picture."

Because it was for him to do. Not Kyan or anyone else. *He* knew her mother. *He* loved Linnea from the moment Catherine put her in his arms. *He* was her knight in shining armor. *But you failed her.* She was *his*, dammit. God's promise. *And after everything, you lost her.*

*Burn in Hell, you motherfucker.*

Because it was the only thing he could do for her. His parting gift. Because Wednesday, after he kissed her one last time, he'd never see her again.

"I just do."

Looking back, maybe he should've stayed gone.

When Kodiak boarded that plane to California, he never planned on coming back here. Figured it was better that way. For her. Linnea had Kyan to love and protect her. Bo would look out for her too.

And since he no longer could, it was best for *him.*

After six months of listening to Babs every day, Kodiak bid goodbye to his room with the kitchenette and a view of the Pacific Ocean and returned to Alaska. The one place where he felt peace. Content to live out the rest of his days there, alone with the wrongness inside him.

But no, Linnea wouldn't let him. Despite it all, she naïvely loved him still. Begged him to come home, to be there for her wedding. She had no idea what she was asking, how dearly it cost him. Kodiak made a promise, though, one he vowed to keep. And besides, he loved her first.

It was almost noon by the time he left Bo's music room. Kodiak called out to his sister, but she didn't answer. An album of wedding photos sat open on the coffee table; a video paused on the big screen. Linnea and Kyan frozen in the steps of their first dance.

He turned off the TV.

She was in Kyan's office when he found her. Sitting on the floor, cardboard tubes strewn about all around her, Linnea unrolled a large sheet of vellum, the tears he'd been dreading silently streaming down her face.

*I can't bear to see you cry, little one.*

Kodiak got down on his haunches behind her. He squeezed her shoulders and letting go of the paper, she grabbed onto his hands and began to sob. "Shh…" He kissed the top of her head, holding her back against his chest. "…I got you."

And rocking with her on the floor, he let her cry.

"I'm sorry." Tucked beneath his chin, Linnea wiped her face on the cuff of her sweater. "I told myself I wouldn't…"

He stood. Helping her up from the floor, Kodiak pulled her to him and rubbed her back. "It's okay. You needed to."

"I hate this."

"I know." With a kiss on her forehead, he gave her back one last pat and let her go. "Today's a tough one."

"Yeah." She nodded. Glancing around the room, Linnea swiped beneath her eyes. "Why did I come in here?"

"C'mon." His arm went around her shoulders. "I'll make some tea."

"Okay."

Steering his sister into the kitchen, away from the album on the coffee table, the memories that hung on the walls, Kodiak put the kettle on the stove. Linnea sat down at the island, and looking up at him, a tremulous smile appeared on her face. "Come quick. Give me your hand."

She held it to her belly.

Beneath his fingertips, Charlotte made her presence known.

A gentle ripple. He closed his eyes to it. Remembering. Once, there was a time he'd dreamt of this, but he couldn't allow himself to dream those dreams anymore.

*"Close the circle."*

# Ten

A thin veil of clouds parted, just enough for a blast of sun to come pouring through the storefront window, momentarily blinding her. She blinked, adjusting her vision to the intensity of the light, only for it to disappear as quickly as it came. Kelly glanced at the time, returning her gaze to the screen. Fifteen minutes until cutoff time. She had to get this supply order in now if she wanted a delivery here tomorrow.

From apple pie bars to pumpkin snickerdoodles, Leo had come up with an entirely new menu board of goodies for fall. *And don't forget the cupcakes. Jesus.* He'd heard it on the down-low, the Lebanese place next door wasn't renewing their lease—God, she missed their falafel already—and suggested they snag it and expand Beanie's.

It wasn't a bad idea.

Leo could have a whole case of fucking cupcakes. And they could use the extra space. More often than not, the place was packed.

But that would require talking to Brendan, which she'd rather not, and capital. Lots of it. Renovations, equipment, more employees, higher rent. *Ugh.* Until she finished paying Stacy off for her half of Beanie's startup, Kelly couldn't even begin to dream of it.

Too late. The seed was planted now.

Maybe she could get a loan for enough to fund the expansion *and* get the high and mighty bitch off her back. She'd been open for business, and profitable, for more than a couple years now. Beanie's was a sound financial investment. *Wouldn't hurt to try.* At the very least it was worth a shot.

After confirming her order, with barely a minute to spare, Kelly submitted it, and snapping her laptop shut, got up to join Katie and Leo behind the counter. "I'm gonna go for it."

"Go for what?" her niece wanted to know.

She didn't get a chance to answer because Kodiak, looking every bit as delicious as the chocolate espresso buttercream cupcake in Leo's hand, came walking in with Bo carrying his little girl behind him.

"Mmhm, if I was you, *ma chérie*, I'd be goin' for that, too." His pink tongue peeking out, Leo licked the frosting off his cake.

"But…but…but…" Doing a poor imitation of her, Katie wrinkled up her nose in distaste and giggled. "…he owns a penis."

"I know." Leo grinned, swiping buttercream from his lips. "*Succuleux.*"

"Shut. Up." Glaring at the two of them, Kelly turned on her heel and smiled. "Hey there, pretty girl. I bet you'd like a cookie."

Emery looked up at her father, who grinned, and she nodded.

"I can do better than that, *ma belle fille.*" Leo blew the drummer and his daughter a kiss, giving the toddler a cookies 'n' creme cupcake. "For you."

"What do you say, darling?" Smiling, Bo kissed her on the head.

Taking the Oreo off the cupcake, she grinned. "Thank you." But it came out 'dank you' as she stuffed the cookie into her mouth.

Kodiak leaned across the counter. "Hey, Snicks."

"Hey," Kelly softly murmured, suddenly feeling shy. Well, she knew they had an audience and it felt like she had *'Yes, I fucked him'* written all over her face. "What can I get you?"

His eyes slowly traveling her body, he smirked. "Americano."

"Make that two," Bo chimed in. "And a hot chocolate for Emmy."

"I got it," Katie called out from where she stationed herself at the espresso machine.

Seizing Kelly's hand, Kodiak dipped his head, lips skimming along her skin, he whispered in her ear, "Why you blushing like that, baby?"

Luckily for her, he let go before she could answer. Not that she had one.

"You bringing Ava to the masquerade ball, Bo-Bo?" Katie asked, handing him his order.

"I didn't get my kiss, coffee girl." Taking it from her, he smacked his lips to her cheek. "Sorry, we're going to have to miss it. Carving pumpkins at Monica's this year."

Sticking her bottom lip out, she made a pouty face. "You're going, aren't you, Kodiak?"

"Wouldn't miss it." But he was looking right at her when he said it. "How 'bout you, Kelly?"

Katie pushed the coffee into his hands. "My aunt? Are you kidding? God forbid, she does anything…"

"Yeah, I'll be there."

"…fun."

Dead silence.

Making a mess out of her cupcake, Emery giggled.

Kevin came out from the back. Tying on his apron, his gaze flicked up to his sister. "Where the hell has Ava been? I never see her anymore and I want to ask her to homecoming."

Looking at Bo, Katie winced.

Venery's drummer leaned up against the counter and winked. "Ava's with me."

*Oh, dear.*

"You knew I liked her, Katie," Kevin lamented once they'd gone. "You should've told me."

"Months ago," she scoffed with a snigger, rolling her aqua eyes. "And just how many rah-rahs have you banged since then, bro?"

*Judging by the dwindling supply of condoms in his room? I'm thinking plenty.*

Shooting her a confounded look, Leo asked, "What's a rah-rah?"

"Cheerleader," Katie supplied, turning toward her. She smirked. "And just what are you up to, Auntie?"

"Don't know what you mean."

"Just yesterday you said you'd never go back…" Pausing mid-sentence, that smirk became a grin. "Ohh, I get it."

"Get what?"

*For fuck's sake, leave it alone, Katie.*

Kelly knew she wouldn't, though. It ran in the family. She could be just like Kristie, but then she was her sister's daughter, after all.

"It's Kodiak." She sing-songed like she was back in high school, which for Katie, wasn't that long ago, "You've got a thing for him, don't you?"

Leo snickered.

"We're friends," she insisted, glaring at him.

"Was he the hot date you had a couple weeks ago?"

"What date?"

*Thanks, Kev.*

Repeating herself, Kelly raised her voice, "I said, we're *friends.*"

"Right." Folding her arms across her chest, Katie giggled. "When have you ever been *friends* with anyone who has a dick?"

And she turned to Leo.

"Don't be lookin' at Leo, *bebé.* I don't count."

"Oh, Brendan is going to die when I tell him this."

Her eyes widening, Kelly shook her head. "Seriously, Katie. Don't."

"He's my husband. Why not?"

This time, she shouted, "I told you, we're just friends."
*And I'm not ready for the whole damn world to know it.*

He told her he'd come for her at eight. They could grab some dinner at Charley's on their way to the club. But since she had to close up shop first, Kelly couldn't make it until ten.

Knowing she'd been hard at work since early this morning, Kodiak wanted to make sure she was fed. He was here at her door, takeout in hand, half an hour early.

Clutching a robe tightly at her chest, beautiful as ever, Kelly let him pass. She followed him inside. "I'm not quite ready yet."

"Plenty of time." He pulled out a chair for her. "Eat."

Kodiak watched her devour the burger. She'd seemed—he wasn't sure, exactly—uncomfortable, perhaps, with his attention that afternoon at Beanie's. He wanted to know if she had been, and if so, why. "Truth for a truth, Kelly…"

"Again?" With a cute little laugh, she wiped sauce from her lips with a napkin.

"Always." He smirked, tipping his head to the side. "You never did tell me what made you blush."

Her brows drew together.

"At Beanie's, when I stopped in with Bo—remember?"

"Ohhh." Nodding, Kelly rubbed her lips together. "Yeah, I do. Was I blushing?"

"Like a cherry tomato."

"I was probably imagining…" Flush darkening her cheekbones, she lowered her gaze. "Everyone was watching us and…"

"And?" he prompted when she didn't continue.

"Look…" She glanced up, blowing out a breath. "We're friends, but that doesn't mean everyone needs to know we're fucking. Actually, I'd prefer that they didn't."

Laughter bellowed from his throat. "I don't think…"

"Katie already thinks it."

"Does it matter?"

Fingers fidgeting in her lap, Kelly worried her lip.

*Apparently so.*

"It's not what you're probably thinking." Taking his hand, those blue eyes looked into his. "This is all new to me, okay? I don't know what I'm doing, and I don't need Katie, her husband, your friends… everybody…looking at me like some kind of oddity…watching us, dissecting our…friendship."

"They would never. You know that."

"Maybe not." She scrunched her shoulders. "But at least for now, I'd rather we keep things private."

"Okay." He got up from the table. Leaning over the back of her chair, Kodiak kissed her crown. "Finish getting dressed. I'll clean up."

*Fuck.*

She came out of her room in a little black dress. Boned bodice. It laced up the back, molding to every alluring curve. Thigh-high stiletto boots.

Mesmerized by the sight of her, he crooked his finger. "Come here."

"What?" Kelly stepped over to him. Wearing a sly, little smirk, pools of hypnotic blue looked up at him from beneath a fan of black lashes.

He didn't answer. Threading his fingers into her silky hair, his thumb swept across her cheek. Kodiak grasped her nape, and pulling her luscious mouth to his, he kissed her.

If Kelly wanted to keep this between them, so be it. He'd take what he wanted now. And later, with her lips swollen from his, every pulse of her clit inside the club would remind her just who she was fucking with.

Fingertips tracing the way, his kisses followed. Down her neck, her chest, between her breasts. Cupping the creamy swells that threatened to spill from her dress, he squeezed. Then he reached around her back, and lifting the hem, sank his fingers into the smooth, bare skin of her shapely ass.

"No panties?" It wasn't a question. She obviously wasn't wearing any.

Kodiak dropped to his knees, pushed the dress up her thighs, and spread her legs apart. His tongue touched her clit. Flicking at it with the tip. Dragging the flat of it through her lips. And when her hips began to squirm, and panting whimpers could be heard, he thrust his fingers inside. Hot honey flowed. He sucked on her swollen clit, then he gave it a kiss and pulled away, licking her from his fingers.

He stood. Righting her dress, Kodiak studied her face. Lips parted. Skin flushed. Needy and so close to coming. She looked beautiful like that.

Opening her eyes, glazed with desire, Kelly flashed him a look of confusion.

Pulling her flush against him, his hard, throbbing cock pushed into her soft belly. Kodiak chuckled, his nose running alongside hers, and slipping his tongue inside her mouth, he kissed her.

"But..."

*I know, baby.*

He held out her coat. "Time to go."

And closing the door behind them, he grinned.

# Eleven

odiak held her hand, making chitchat about some case he was working on, as they walked the single block. Like his tongue hadn't been buried in her pussy just five minutes ago. She was about two seconds away from a delicious orgasm too, and then poof. *Time to go—really?* What the hell?

Determined not to let him see how much he'd gotten to her, Kelly schooled her expression to appear unaffected. But she totally was. Slick with need, cool night air drifted up her dress, accentuating the incessant pulse between her thighs, as if she needed the reminder.

Two hulking goons stood guard at the club's entrance, and with a nod to Kodiak, the red doors opened. His arm slinking around her waist, he held her against him and ushered her inside. Sweeping the hair away from her neck, his head dipped. Warm lips brushed her skin, and he murmured, "I'm not done with you."

Like bubbles in a champagne glass, the tingles between her legs popped. Her heart took flight, soaring to the top of the enormous entryway along with her gaze. Unsure of how to respond to that, Kelly wet her lips.

He chuckled low, warm breath tickling her ear. "C'mon."

This place was indescribable, words inadequate. She'd only been here once before. The night she met him. And that was the night Kelly decided if she ever took a chance on a man again, it would be for him.

Kodiak led her from the lobby, down the wide, darkened corridor, toward the main club floor. The purple uplighting she remembered from last time was absent, replaced by a haunted forest that lined the walls. Trailing vines suspended from overhead. Murky mist swirled at her feet. Brendan spared no expense for the ball, apparently, but then she'd heard people paid an obscene amount of money to be members here.

He stopped at the discreet stairway that went up to the VIP level. Placing a palm on her riotous belly, Kelly drew in a breath. *They* were all up those stairs and she was in uncharted territory here. "You go ahead. I need to…um…use the restroom first."

"There's nothing for you to be nervous about, Kelly."

"I'm not nerv—"

His fingers firmly gripping her nape, Kodiak's mouth came crashing down on hers. He owned her with that kiss. Cupping her breast, he squeezed. The plump flesh escaped the daringly low-cut bodice, exposing her nipple.

Her eyes snapping open, she gasped. Half-naked people milled about the corridor. Nobody looked their way. Not one even batted an eyelash.

"It's okay, baby." His cadence hypnotic, Kodiak toyed with the stiffened peak. "Every part of you is beautiful. Let them see."

Kelly lowered the bodice, in plain sight of anyone who happened to come by, offering her breasts to him. Reverently, he stroked her nipples with his thumbs, and this powerful feeling washed over her. She owned him too.

"Yes, that's my girl," he crooned. "You're free here. Show them what I get to touch. To taste…" Kodiak kissed her lips, then bent his head, sucking a nipple deep into his mouth.

Grabbing onto the doorframe, she cried out at the exquisite sensation of it. Electric desire coursed through her veins, weighing heavy between her thighs. People stopped to watch, but surprisingly she didn't care. Quite the opposite, in fact. Tangling her fingers in his hair, Kelly held him to her breast. Right then, she wanted everyone to see the pleasure this man was able to give her.

"Please…God…"

"He's not here, sweets." His tongue flicking at her nipple, a hand slipped beneath her dress. "I am."

Two fingers penetrated her. "Fuck," Kelly whimpered with relief. She needed to come.

"I know," he soothed, pumping in and out of her.

Slipping closer to the edge of the volcano, hot lava flowed down her thighs. She bit down on her lip and closed her eyes tight, readying herself for the fall.

"Open." His tone commanding, green eyes bored into her own. "I want you looking at me."

*I see you.*

He plunged inside her again. And again. And again.

*Almost there.*

One more second. Maybe two.

*For God's sake, don't stop.*

*Please…*

But just as he had before, Kodiak abruptly withdrew, slowly licking the copious wetness that glistened on his fingers. Then he smirked, and with a devious chuckle, he kissed her on the lips. "Patience, Snicks. You'll be thanking me later."

*Think so, do you?*

"If you'll excuse me." Hastily, Kelly pulled up the top of her dress. "I'm going to the restroom now."

She pushed open the door to the private lounge. Expelling a breath, she surveyed the opulence around her. *Fucking hell.* Black marble. Crystal. Sumptuous fabrics. An ornate armoire housed a warming drawer with cleansing cloths and towels, lotions and oils. Kelly snickered to herself. "Anything you might require to freshen up the kitty, eh?"

Her nether regions a dripping mess, she made use of the amenities.

A quick glance in the mirror told her she was none the worse for wear after her public tryst. Kelly touched up her lips, finger-combed her hair, and put the silly lace mask on. She was glad for it, though. A veil of protection, it gave her something to hide behind, a sense of security, false as it may be.

This was not her scene, and everybody out there knew it—her niece, especially. She wasn't stupid. Katie knew why she was here. Bracing herself for the scrutiny that was sure to come, Kelly took a deep breath and ventured out into the hallway.

Except for tiny flickers of candlelight, the club was pitch-black. She peeked over the railing to the main floor below. No music. No chatter. Nothing but darkness until a single beam of murky light hit the fog-filled stage. Kelly tiptoed along the railing, sidling past Chloe, Jesse, and Taylor, to get to Katie over at the bar.

"What are you doing here, Auntie?" With a saucy smirk, her niece planted a kiss on her cheek. "Your *friend* is over there."

Snickering, Brendan choked on his whiskey.

"Please, Katie-Kate." Subtly turning her head, Kelly spotted Kodiak on the big U-shaped sofa between Sloan and Dillon's girlfriend. *Ugh! Forgot about him.* "Not now."

No way was she going over there to sit with them. She'd stay right here with Katie. *And her husband.* Kelly wrinkled her nose. "I need a drink."

Pushing a glass of champagne into her hand, Brendan winked.

She tipped her chin in thanks and downed it in one swallow.

He handed her another.

Kelly couldn't make out what they were saying, but things looked heated, and not in a good way, between Dillon and what's her name—Kelsey? Yeah, she was pretty sure that's what it was. Only met her once at the funeral. The chick's ponytail whipped back and forth, smacking poor Kodiak in the face.

Dillon got up and left her. The girl just sat there, her mouth hanging open, before she followed him over to the railing. Kelly traded a look with Kodiak. He shrugged.

Katie leaned into her ear. "I have a feeling this is going to be quite entertaining."

A low, drawn-out snarl echoed throughout the club. Kelly couldn't tell which direction it was coming from and glanced to the big screen. A girl's eyes darted about as she scrambled to find a place to hide amidst the trees that covered the stage.

"Isn't that the point?"

Then sidling up next to Kelsey, Matt growled loud enough for everyone to hear, "Run, rabbit, run."

"I didn't mean the hunt," Katie said, giggling behind her hand.

Kelly watched Dillon's girlfriend leave the railing in a huff, Dillon chasing after her.

*Oh, got it.*

"Wait. Hunt?"

With a giggle, Katie tipped her chin at the Jumbotron screen. "You'll see."

Following her gaze, Kelly saw the nubile, barefoot girl, just as she crouched beneath some branches. The set design, realistic and elaborate, was like something out of a movie. Menacing trees draped with moss, bushes, and boulders all shrouded in mist.

Looking down at the stage itself, she couldn't see a thing. *Night vision camera, maybe? Must be.*

She heard it then, and goosebumps sheeted her skin. As if they were a warning, eerie growls, long and deep, reverberated from every direction. Four men, wearing pants and wolf masks with glowing eyes, their muscled torsos bare, appeared at each corner of the stage.

Kelly chanced a look toward the purple couch to find everyone's gaze riveted to the screen. All except for Kodiak, that is. Lip turned up in a devilish smirk, his sights were set right on her.

A lone howl pierced the air, and the pack of snarling beasts set off. They sniffed along the forest floor like dogs, foraging through the mist to hunt down their prey. She'd never heard of a game of hide-and-go-seek being played quite like this one.

The girl, her knees drawn tightly to her chest, curled up into a ball. It was just a matter of time before one, if not all of them, got to her. But then, that was the object of the game, wasn't it? Nevertheless, the anticipation of when was downright palpable.

His eyes still on her, Kodiak's tongue skimmed across his teeth. Kelly wished now that she hadn't been such a self-conscious idiot. Fuck Dillon Byrne and all the rest of them. Aroused as she was, she'd much rather be snuggling with him than standing here with her niece and Brendan, because honestly, this was kind of awkward.

A scream ripped her gaze back to the screen. One of the beasts had reached the girl. He pulled her out of her hiding place by the hair, and straddling her tiny waist, ripped the sheath from her body with his teeth. Naked, she thrashed beneath him. Having conquered her, the alpha of the pack lifted his head to the spotlight shining down on him like the moon, and he howled.

Kelly reached for Katie's hand to squeeze it. Except it wasn't her niece who now stood beside her. So mesmerized by the primal tableau playing out before her, she hadn't noticed when this tall, masked stranger, the devil himself, took her place. "Who are you?"

Raising her hand to his lips, he kissed it. "Lucifer."

*Course you are.*

She wanted to laugh. Maybe it was the way he carried himself, his commanding presence, because the man oozed sexual dominance. Whatever it was, just as surely as Lucifer was not his real name, she got the distinct impression he was not someone to cross. "Kelly."

With a slow up-down perusal, he released her. "Lovely."

His eyes feral, Kodiak appeared none too pleased. She shrugged, and gazing again at the stage, watched as the wolf, his engorged cock jutting out in front of him, savagely claimed the girl for all to see.

*Fucking Christ…*her jaw dropped.

As if that wasn't exactly what Kelly wanted. To be taken. Ravaged. Loved so fiercely…

She glanced at Kodiak.

The house lights came back up.

And everything went to hell.

He held Kelly tight, her back to his chest, as their breathing slowly returned to normal. His cock, happy in its home inside her, was softening. Even so, Kodiak didn't pull out. He didn't want to leave the solace of her body just yet.

Tonight, hadn't gone at all how he'd wanted it to, thanks to Dillon's girlfriend. *Make that ex.* Because he was pretty sure after the shit that went down, Kelsey no longer had the title. His brother-in-law couldn't get the girl out of there fast enough.

Kelly came over to him then. She tucked herself beneath his arm like she had every right to be there, which she did, and looked up at him. "I think the ball's over."

She wasn't wrong. Kelsey had effectively killed the vibe. So, he took her home to his place, his bed, to finish what he'd started back in her loft.

And he did.

More than once.

His fingertips languidly strumming bare skin, he kissed her hair. Kelly sighed. Rolling over to face him, his cock slipped free of her warmth. Kodiak mourned the loss. He wanted to stay there inside her.

Snuggling into his chest, she kissed his pec. With her arm draped over his side, she traced the scars that lay hidden beneath the ink. Her breath catching, she whispered, "Kodiak, what happened?"

Not ready for this, he sat up and reached for his vape pen on the night table. He took a long draw, inhaling deep, and held it in his lungs.

Her palms running over the tattoo that covered his back, Kelly laid her head on his shoulder. "Please, talk to me."

He exhaled.

"Who hurt you? Your father?"

"Those scars didn't come from him." With a shake of his head, he sniggered. "Not by his own hand anyway."

The scars Jarrid Black left behind couldn't be seen and ran so much deeper than the physical ones he bore. He'd rather take a thousand lashes than to have to relive any of it again, but Kelly needed to know all his truths.

*Those who choose to forget the past are condemned to repeat it.*

*Here goes nothing…*

"The summer I was seventeen, my father sent me to camp." There was no way to ease into it really. His hand rubbing her thigh, Kodiak took another hit from his pen. "The belts they used to beat us with had names."

And they used them. Unmercifully. Every goddamn day.

"Jesus." Her head shook in disbelief, honey-blonde tresses whipping side to side. "What the fuck kind of camp was it?"

"The pray away the gay kind." He sniggered. "My father…I'm not sure where or how to begin. It's pretty fucked up. My father is the pastor of…I guess you'd call it a Pentecostal church."

He could hear her intake of breath, see her deep blues widen in the semi-darkness. Her hand came down on his and squeezed. "Most folks in Crossfield call it the crazy church, and me? Well, I'm the son of the crazy preacher."

"Why do they say that?"

"Think Jim Jones, David Koresh, or any cuckoo nut televangelist you've ever seen on TV. He cavorts like he's God himself, and worse than that, his congregation believes every word as if he truly is. But it's all lies. He's a fake. An evil, manipulating motherfucker.

"Anyway, I haven't mentioned Jonathan, have I?"

"No."

"He was my best friend, my brother, and I loved him." Kodiak closed his eyes, unshed tears burning behind them. "He's dead because of me."

"What?"

"My father witnessed the one and only time we were together.

Fucker was spying on us through the window. He didn't say a word about what he'd seen to me, but he told Jonathan's parents everything. He sure enjoyed it too." Seeing Kelly gazing up at him, the tears he could no longer hide slid down his face. "I didn't find out until the next day after Jonathan parked behind the football field and blew his brains out."

"Oh, my God," she choked.

"He ain't real, baby." Kodiak angled his head, and stroking her hair, he smiled. "But Hell is, that I can attest to."

# Twelve



*Seth, seventeen years old.*

Staring vacantly out the window, he didn't care where his father was taking him. Seth didn't care about anything much at all, really. Except Linnea and getting them both far the fuck away from here. He was already working on a plan to do just that.

One more summer.

One more year until graduation.

He'd spoken with a recruiter from the United States Army who came to his high school on career day. Seth would have signed up right then if they'd have let him. He could wait until January. He'd be eighteen then and wouldn't need Jarrid's permission for anything anymore.

Course, he'd have to leave his little one behind for a while, being she was only seven. And that was the only fault in his plan. It worried him, but what other choice did he have? *None.* He'd come back for her, but he couldn't stay here.

The day Jonathan took his own life, a big piece of Seth went with him. He lost everything. The boy he loved—his best friend since he was five. The cheerleader he'd been fucking. Football. Friends. Freedom.

And it was all his own doing.

He'd broken his promise.

*The Lord giveth and the Lord taketh away.*

For the past seven months, he'd done everything he could to atone for his sins. Ignoring the whispers at his back, Seth went to school and studied hard. Every other waking moment was spent on his knees, in prayer, for Jonathan's soul, and his own, begging God to forgive them.

The only respite he was afforded was when his father and Miss Catherine allowed him to take Linnea to the playground or to get an ice cream cone at the Dairy Queen. They encouraged him to, actually, and he did so willingly. Gladly. Anything to see that smile light her face.

*No one will take your joy from you.*

And Linnea was all he had left.

His head jolted. Seth turned away from the window as his father swerved onto a narrow dirt lane. In the middle of fucking nowhere, sad, scraggly-looking trees lined one side, barren fields stretched as far as the eye could see on the other.

"Where are we?"

Without bothering to answer, Jarrid lit a cigarette. He took a couple drags, tapping his thumb against the steering wheel as if weighing his words. "You must repent, boy. The devil has his hooks into you. We need to cast him out."

*Only devil I need to cast out is you.*

Isn't that what he'd been doing every fucking day since Jonathan died? And he'd likely never stop. No one was sorrier than Seth was. Sorry, he'd forsaken his vow. Sorry, he couldn't save him somehow. But he'd never be sorry that he loved him. Loving someone could never be wrong, and there wasn't anyone who could convince him otherwise.

Seth knew better than to tell his father that, though. To survive he had to keep up with the facade of being the preacher man's good, obedient son. Hell, he'd been doing it for most of his life.

*One more year.*

Bowing his head, he groveled, "Yes, sir."

"This place came highly recommended by an associate of mine." Taking another drag of his nasty cancer stick, his father turned his head to look at him. "It's a camp for youth who've lost their way, like you have. They'll put you back on the righteous path."

"Camp?" *Christ, you gotta be shitting me.* "You're sending me to summer camp?"

Jarrid grinned. "I am."

Seth wasn't dumb. There'd be no singing "Kumbaya" around the campfire or roasting s'mores where he was going. "Dad, I told you, it was just that one time. I'm not gay."

He wasn't.

"I know, son. You like fucking girls too." He sniggered, crude signs of wood, bible verses painted on them, coming into view. "But I gotta make sure of it, see? We must rid you of these sinful urges and wash you clean. Can't have you tainting her."

*I won't.*

His father had nothing to worry about. Jonathan was dead. It could never happen again, and he would keep his promise.

They brought him to a dingy wood cabin, of which there were two—one for the girls and one for the boys. The camp lodge was in the middle. Jarrid went no farther than the porch, dropped his duffel bag at his feet, and patted him on the shoulder. "Forty-two days, my son. I'll be praying for you."

*Sure, you will.*

It was just an act for the benefit of the camp's director, Reverend John. A cursory glance was all Seth needed. Rotund belly. Skin, sallow and pockmarked. Dark hair dripping in greasy pomade. The fetid odor of cheap whiskey and stale tobacco clung to his clothes. He was certain this vile, middle-aged man was no Christian.

The musty cabin contained four sets of bunk beds, eight lockers, a desk, and a door which he presumed led to a bathroom. A framed print of the Sacred Heart of Jesus hung over the desk, the paper brittle and yellowed with age, a water stain in the corner.

"I'll leave you to get acquainted with the others. They can explain the rules to you," he said, tipping his chin toward a couple of blank-faced boys sitting together on a bunk. Turning to leave, the reverend paused. "Be ready to get dirty and lie in blood, because some sins don't wash away with water and prayer."

*What. The. Fuck?*

"He ain't kidding. You'll find out soon enough." Lanky, with wiry copper hair and freckles, the boy's long arms reminded him of limp pool noodles. He looked like the type of kid who wore checkered button-ups to school and used a pocket protector. "Name's Jeffrey."

*Figures.*

"Seth."

"Daddy's a twisted individual." The soft voice decidedly effeminate, Jeffrey's bunkmate extended his hand. "Casey."

Seth shook it. "Daddy?"

"Yeah, that's what he insists we call him," Jeffrey supplied with a roll of his buggy blue eyes.

Taken aback, he scoffed, "Not me. I won't do it."

"Oh, trust me, honey." Casey rubbed his fingers along Seth's thigh. "You will. He's your mother, father, and God while you're here. You'll obey unless you want…"

"Sadistic motherfucker." A burly dude with the body of a linebacker came out of the bathroom. Fastening his pants, he glanced up. "Who's this?"

"This is Seth, Austin," Casey informed him. "Now we have an even four."

Lumbering over to his locker, he grunted. Raised welts, angry and red, crisscrossed his back. Austin reached for a clean shirt and closed the door.

That's when he noticed it. Three of the lockers had a glass jar on top of them, filled with exactly what, Seth couldn't say. The goop inside resembled pasty, rotten chocolate pudding.

*Wait, are those maggots?*

He pointed. "What the fuck is that?"

"Shit," Austin replied, matter-of-factly. "They make you go in a jar as a reminder of how gay men have sex."

"That's disgusting." Seth thought he might puke.

"That's the point." Austin nodded. "Aversion therapy."

"I'm not gay."

"None of us are, baby." Casey winked, and unzipping Austin's pants, he pulled him to his mouth.

*Jesus Christ.*

Jeffrey cleared his throat. "Rules."

"And what are they?"

"Be a good boy. Never question him—like never ever. Do everything Daddy says and tell him what he wants to hear." Wagging his finger, Casey saucily grinned. "You know, play the game."

"Cleanliness is godliness," Jeffrey added.

"We watch each other's backs in here, so no snitching. Get me?" Taking a seat next to Casey, Austin kissed him. "And this pussy is mine, but I might share if you ask me real nice."

*No, thanks.*

Jeffrey crossed his pool noodle arms over his chest and sighed. "Better clue him in on Friday nights."

"Daddy likes to watch us jerk off to porn—the straight kind." Grabbing hold of his knee, Casey wrinkled up his nose. "Don't let him catch you with a boner looking at the homo stuff, though. It's a test."

Seth swallowed down the bile rising in his throat. "What happens if he does?"

"C'mon, we can talk more later." Jeffrey tugged on his arm. "Dinner's at six. We get ten if we're late."

"Ten what?"

Glancing at Austin, he slammed his fist into his palm. "The belt."

"And which one he uses depends on the mood he's in."

Hell.

He was definitely in Hell.

But then maybe he deserved to be here.

How long had he been here now? *Three weeks, I think.* Seth wasn't entirely sure. Each torturous day blended into the next. Wake up at four. Morning prayers followed by breakfast at five. Then the boys were sent out to clear fields, haul rock, or dig ditches until noon, while the girls scoured pots and slaved in the kitchen. He liked the hard labor, actually. Focused on a task, it was the only time he didn't have to think.

After lunch came the daily devotionals. That's what the reverend called it anyway. They were mind fuck sessions if you asked him.

"Pray until you can see yourself up on the cross with Jesus, hanging, dying, and bleeding with Him. Cry and weep, boys and girls. The Lord, through Daddy's hand, will change you."

Then the slimy sonofabitch would get his belt out.

Seth received his share of beatings.

No one was spared. They all got them.

If his jollies were satisfied enough in the afternoon, he usually let them be come supper. He'd send them back to their cabins with instructions to reflect on their unhealthy affliction and to beseech God to cure them of it. Single file the boys went left, and the girls went right. That's when the asshole retired to his room and drank himself into a stupor.

And for a short while, they could breathe.

Being there were only four of them, each of the guys had a bottom bunk. He and Jeffrey watched out the window—just in case—while Austin plowed into Casey's ass behind them. Those two went at it any chance they got and judging by the ever-present marks on Austin's back, the reverend likely knew it.

"Why do they keep us separated from the girls, you think?" Seth had been pondering this for a while. "Seems kinda silly, considering."

"Considering what?"

"They think we're not into them."

"I'm not," Jeffrey confessed. "But that's our secret."

*Trust me, Jeff. That is so not a secret.*

"Well, I'm definitely into them." Settling back in his bunk, Seth clasped his hands behind his head. "Not the ones here, though. I'm promised to a girl back home. We're getting married as soon as she's eighteen."

"So? That don't mean anything." Snickering, he shook his head. "You love her?"

"I do." A smile coming to his face, the first one in weeks, Seth nodded. "From the moment I saw her."

"How'd you end up here then?"

*Shit.*

He'd said too much, and the smile vanished.

"I had a friend…I loved him too…and then he died. Shot himself." Tears he didn't try to hide fell. "My father is the pastor…"

"Say no more." Jeffrey came over to his bunk and sat down beside him. "I get it. I have a girl. Wedding's in May, right after I finish my degree."

"You're in college?"

"Yeah, engineering major at ISU."

*Figures. Bet you do wear checkered shirts and use a pocket protector.*

"You look so young."

"Everybody says that." His cheeks turning as red as his hair, he blushed. "I'm twenty-one."

"So, how'd you get here?"

"Ready for this?" With a click of his tongue, Jeff nodded. "I asked to come."

"The fuck, why?"

Gnawing on his lip, he lowered his gaze to his lap. "Because Amy deserves more from me."

"You love her?" Seth asked, nudging his arm.

"She's a great girl. Teaches Sunday school, volunteers at church…my parents love her."

"That's not what I asked, man. Do *you* love her?"

Jeffrey got up. He wouldn't look at him. "She's a great girl."

He was quiet after that. All week Jeffrey went through the motions, deflated as a day-old birthday balloon. Seth—hell, Austin and Casey, too—were concerned. Maybe he'd done too much reflecting and realized, try as he might, he couldn't fit a square peg into a round hole.

Friday night came around. Once again, after supper was finished, the girls were seated at their desks on the right side of the makeshift classroom. There were six of them. They outnumbered the four boys on the left—go figure.

The reverend handed each of them a laptop, his pre-selected-for-you 'test' already loaded and ready to go. Seth hated Fridays. Everyone else did too. Sick fucker did this for his own twisted, voyeuristic pleasure, he was sure. Though he claimed otherwise, and said it was for their own good.

Seth clicked on play, releasing his breath as a man and woman appeared on-screen. He got a straight one. Not that he cared all that much, but it made it easier to perform for the sick fuck and his minions—make that counselors—who monitored the room.

Casey didn't lie. Daddy liked to watch. Brownie points were given to anyone who passed their test to his satisfaction—translation got themselves off. But heaven help the camper who failed. The almighty himself wouldn't be able to save them. It seemed to him, the sadist enjoyed that even more.

Seth tuned everyone else in the room out. Eyes on the screen, he got down to business. The quicker he could make himself come, the faster this would be over with.

"Fuck," Jeffrey whispered under his breath.

Flicking his gaze, Seth could see him in his peripheral.

He sat at the desk next to his. Unfortunately for Jeff, he got gay porn—and an erection. Daddy was up front, watching. He grinned. Then he started walking over.

*Jesus, Jeffrey, you dumb fucking fuck.*

This was bad. Very, very bad.

Pretending not to notice, Seth kept his head straight and his hand inside his pants. To do otherwise could put him in the line of fire. No matter how much he wanted to, he couldn't intervene. Any attempt at all would be suicide.

"Are you all right, Jeffrey?" The reverend poked at the bulge between his legs with the handle end of a riding crop.

"I'm fine."

"No, boy." He tsked, smacking the crop against his palm. "If looking at a man suck another man's dick arouses you, you are *not* fine. What would Amy think if she could see you right now, hmm? She'd be repulsed by you, wouldn't she?"

*Whack.*

Jeffrey screamed.

Seth didn't dare look. He didn't have to. The reverend always struck where it would hurt the most.

"Just as God is repulsed by you. You're weak. And sick…still so sick. I'm disappointed in you, boy. We all are."

As Jeffrey sat there whimpering, Seth heard the snap of the sadist's fingers. "Bring me Bertha."

Seth's eyes snapped up to the collection of leather belts hanging on the wall. There were twelve, and each one of them had a name—Judy, Betty, Mama. But Bertha was the thickest, heaviest one of them all. She wielded the greatest amount of pain and inflicted the most damage.

"No, Daddy. Please, I'll try harder," Jeffrey pleaded to no avail.

Squeezing his eyes shut, Seth winced at the sound of the first strike. And the godawful sounds kept coming. Sick to his stomach, he fought the urge to vomit.

Then a hush fell over the room. Thick and pungent, the metallic scent of blood assaulted him. He opened his eyes to see Jeffrey on his knees beside the desk, his bony back an oozing bloody mess.

With tobacco-stained fingers, the reverend unzipped his pants. "You like sucking cock, boy?"

"No." The word was barely audible.

"What'd you say?"

"No, Daddy."

*Jesus Christ, leave him alone.*

But Seth knew that he wouldn't.

Laughing, he shoved his dick in the boy's face.

Jeffrey vomited, puke spewing everywhere.

"Get this worthless little fuck out of here," he bellowed at his minions. Then he looked at the nine of them sitting there, horrified at what they'd just witnessed. "The rest of you can clean up this stinking mess."

No one spoke a word. Knowing Jeffrey would need to be tended to, they hurried through their task. The six girls went with them to their cabin. Opening the door, Seth expected to find him writhing there in pain. Instead, they found his bunk empty, the mattress bare.

Austin went to his locker. "His stuff's gone."

Even his reminder jar was missing.

"Where the fuck is he?" Seth paced the cabin floor. "Where'd they take him?"

"Maybe they put him in the cage," one of the girls supplied. Isolation was another tactic the reverend liked to employ.

"Or took him to a hospital," said another.

"Doubt that." Austin pounded his fist into the locker. "The cops would come and shut this hellhole down if they knew the shit that goes on here."

"Think they don't?"

They knew, and their parents probably did too. A bible and a belt. Who was going to interfere with God's work? And no one gave a shit about them, really. They were an abomination, after all.

Every day Seth waited for Jeffrey to come back, or some word that he was okay, but his name was never spoken of again. *I should've done something…why didn't I help him?* Guilt gnawed at him, and he was already drowning in it.

When Friday came again, they filed into the classroom after supper, just like they always did. The desks had been pushed to one end of the room, an old gym mat laid out on the floor. Seth looked over to Austin and he shrugged.

"Have a seat, boys and girls," the reverend instructed like they were in kindergarten. "Make a nice, big circle."

*What, now we're gonna sing Kumbaya? Have story time?*

Whatever. Seth welcomed the reprieve. At least he wasn't making them watch videos, right?

"I have failed you all, and I am sorry," his hand on his heart, he spoke. "I'm going to amend that. Right now. Satan will not win."

*Damn right, you won't, asshole.*

He walked over to one of the girls, and stroking her mousy-brown hair, he asked her, "Tell us, daughter. Why did our heavenly Father send you to me?"

Her eyes nervously flitting around the room, the muscle played in her throat. Trick question. No matter what she said, she was fucked.

"Please, I didn't do anything."

"Men with men and women with women are indecent acts that offend God," he responded, patting her on the head.

"But I've never been with *anybody*." Choking up, tears rolled down her face. "Me and…well, neither one of us had ever been kissed by a boy. We just wanted to know what it felt like."

Crossing his arms over his barrel chest, the reverend chuckled.

"I swear!"

"The Lord has entrusted me to show you the way, to teach all of you a lesson." He snapped his fingers. "Seth, come here."

*Oh, shit. Oh, shit. Oh, shit.*

"Rachel needs to know the kiss of a boy." He smirked. "I think you're man enough. Kiss her."

*Phew…okay, I can do that.*

Leaning forward, Seth chastely kissed her lips.

"C'mon, you can do better than that, boy."

He kissed the girl again.

"Now lie with her." And turning his back to them, he addressed the others, "Male and female, each for the other, as God intended. He ordains Seth and Rachel to come together in the physical union. Look at them. This is a lesson for you all."

Dumbfounded, Seth shook his head. "No, I can't…I won't. It's wrong."

"Sticking you're dick in another boy's ass is wrong."

The reverend retrieved a belt from the wall, he thought it was Judy, and smirking, came to stand behind the girl.

Rachel's eyes grew big and wide. She looked absolutely terrified.

*I failed Jonathan and Jeffrey, but I won't fail you.*

"You need to hit someone, asshole? Hit me."

But the leather came down on her back.

"Please," she begged him, tears staining her cheeks. "For God's sake, just do it."

He nodded, laying her down on the old gym mat.

Violence cleanses evil. It purifies the heart. People think it's the flames that make Hell unbearable, but it's not. It's the absence of love.

*No one will take your joy from you.*

Drawing a breath, Seth entered her.

"I'm so sorry."

# Thirteen

K elly tossed the stack of papers onto the coffee table. Personal financial statements. Profit and loss statements. Income. Cash flow. Projected balance sheets. *Jeez, what else are they gonna need—a blood sample? The soul of my firstborn?* The list of documents required just to apply for the loan made her brain hurt, along with the football game Kevin had blasting on the TV.

She couldn't focus anyway. Pulling her feet up onto the sofa, Kelly got comfy and opened Google on her phone. Kodiak's story was stuck in her head. She had so many questions, but she didn't dare ask him. First, she was almost too afraid to know the answers. More importantly, though, she didn't want to cause him any more pain.

He'd already endured more than a lifetime's worth.

What he'd shared with her was just the tip of the iceberg, sanitized for her consumption, she was sure. Hidden beneath a bear tattoo, scars laced his back. She'd felt the raised ridges, tracing her fingers over each and every one. There had to be more.

*"I've done horrible things, Kelly. Unforgivable things."*

Kodiak was the victim here. She understood that. Why didn't he?

Settling back against the cushions, Kelly entered some search words and clicked go. She didn't have to scroll very far. It was so much worse than he'd told it. So very much worse.

Seven years after Kodiak left that godforsaken place, Reverend John was arrested outside a mini mart in Missouri. Maybe the police and the parents had turned a blind eye, but an investigative reporter did not. He exposed the things that had been going on there for *decades*. And the beatings, the Friday night 'tests', the reminder jar—all under the guise of therapy—were the least of the horrors.

The reporter took a camera crew to film the now-abandoned camp where Kodiak had spent one terrible summer. Run down, desolate, and overgrown with weeds, the faded wood signs with bible verses remained. A closet they'd lock a transgressor in for days— no light, no water, no food—the door hanging off its hinges. Desks, covered in layers of dust, sat empty.

Kelly quietly wept, gazing upon the very floor where Jeffrey knelt and was beaten. Where Kodiak had been forced to take a girl's virginity to save her from an even worse fate at the hands of that twisted bastard. *Corrective rape.* She hadn't known there was an actual name for it. Right, like forcing people to have sex with the opposite gender would 'cure' them.

*How is this even legal—like how?*

Because the government is not allowed to tell a *church* what it can and cannot do, especially if people like Jeffrey consented to it, or parents gave permission to save the souls of their children from eternal damnation by any means necessary. Ain't that some outrageous level of fucked uppery?

At least the fucker was in prison where he belonged. *Bet you're someone's bitch now, Reverend. How's it feel?* An old man, it was likely he'd never walk free again. But there were others just like him still out there. Taking place in church basements, secluded camps, and weekend retreats all around the globe, conversion therapy, with all its lasting repercussions, continued.

Somehow, with sheer will and his own fortitude, her Kodiak had survived it. Scarred, and a little bit broken, maybe, but then Kelly was too. She had this urge to wrap him up in a fuzzy, warm blanket, keep him safe, and heal all his hurts.

Swiping beneath her eyes, she sniffled. *And since when did you start thinking of him as yours?*

By her own design, he wasn't, but nevertheless she did.

"What's the matter with you?"

"Nothing." She closed out the app on her phone. Typically, Kelly was *not* a crier. Kevin must be thinking she'd lost her damn mind. "Hungry?"

"Aren't I always?"

*Yup.*

Kelly got up, speaking as she sauntered over to the kitchen, "I'll fix us something."

"Mom keeps asking if we're coming for Thanksgiving."

"Can't. Black Friday is only the busiest shopping day of the year." *Need to show the bank all that positive cash flow.*

"Cool with me." Stretching his arms out over his head, Kevin's gaze returned to the TV. "We're not gonna get out of Christmas, though."

"I know."

"So, are we going to Kit's with Katie and everybody?" He grinned. "I hope Ava's there."

"Would you just forget about Ava?" Rolling her eyes, Kelly took sandwich fixings out of the fridge. "And yeah, I told her we more than likely would."

"I shall confirm," he said, tapping away on his phone. "Katie says to make the Brussels sprouts…"

*But I hate Brussels sprouts.*

"…and your spoon bread."

She shrugged. "Okay, I guess I can do that."

Thoughts of Kodiak weighed heavy on her mind. In her heart. The man had foraged his way inside and taken up residence there.

*"That FWB thing almost never works out, you know. Feelings always get in the way. Someone falls in love…someone else gets hurt."*

Leo could very well be right about that. Only two months into their *friendship*, Kelly was already emotionally invested—perhaps too much. How had she ever thought it would be possible to remain somewhat detached?

But then Kelly hadn't anticipated the way he'd look at her with those mesmeric eyes of pale green. How the slightest brush of his fingers would bring goosebumps to her skin. A kiss that brought her to her knees. The sound of his smooth whiskey voice in her ear.

She was fucked, wasn't she?

Because it didn't matter if Kelly was falling in love or ended up being the one who got hurt. Either option scared her shitless.

Sipping on her kombucha, Babs scrutinized him from her side of the screen. She looked somewhat rested this morning. Up in its usual twist, her hair was combed at least. "How's the weather over there in Chicago?"

*Planning to come for a visit, Babs?* The get right down to business type, she wasn't one to make small talk.

"Cold." Gray. Dismal. Same as most other days in November. "And how's it in Santa Barbara, Barbara?"

"Warm." She smirked. "The forecasted high is a balmy seventy-two degrees."

"I'll be breaking out the shovel by this afternoon."

If WGN-TV chief meteorologist, Tom Skilling, was to be believed, and he was seldom wrong, there'd be a few inches of white stuff on the ground come nightfall. That was okay with him. Other than having dinner with Dillon and his sister, Kodiak had no plans for tonight.

"You have fun with that." Notepad at the ready, Babs picked up her pen. "Everything going all right?"

"It is."

"Any dreams?"

"Nope."

*Truth.*

Not the kind she was interested in hearing about anyway.

"Has your father made any more attempts to contact you?"

"No."

It had been more than a month since he deleted the last email. Maybe Jarrid finally got the hint. Never mind the damn 'circle'. Kodiak had no intention of speaking to him ever again.

Period.

Amen.

End of fucking story.

Brow raised, her lips pursed to the side, Babs looked at him oddly. "Hmm."

"What?"

"Nothing." She lit a cigarette, talking as she exhaled, "Is there something you want to share with me? I can read you like a book, you know."

He snickered. "When have I ever *wanted* to share anything?"

"Never." As if it was of no consequence, she shrugged. "But I have a way of getting it out of you, regardless. It's your dime and your time, let's not waste either, shall we?" Tipping her head to the side, Babs plastered a grin on her face. "So, spill it."

Kodiak pulled at his beard. He wasn't sure he was ready to have his relationship dissected. The litany of questions. Because that's what shrinks do. "I've been…uh…seeing someone."

"You have a girlfriend?"

Why did she look so surprised? Never mind. He knew exactly why. Unless that cheerleader he was banging back in high school counted, and she didn't, Kodiak had never had one. Meaningless encounters, yes. Of those, he'd had plenty. And technically, he did have a wife once, course he couldn't count her either.

"Well, she is a girl, and she is my friend," he reasoned. "So, yeah, I guess you could say that."

"Is that what you think of her as?"

Did he? Kodiak wanted Kelly to count. They were both kidding themselves, playing it safe with the 'we're just friends' bullshit. He wasn't sure if she was afraid, or embarrassed, or ashamed, or what, but she was holding back something, of that he had no doubt. And no one understood those feelings better than he did. Time is what she needed, what both of them needed. He could be patient. Because to him, she counted.

"I do, yeah."

Glancing up from her scribbling, Babs smiled. "What's her name?"

"Kelly." He couldn't help but smile back. Just saying her name, his muscles seemed to lose some of their tension.

"How long have you been seeing each other?"

"A couple of months, but we've known each other a while. Her niece is married to Kyan's cousin."

"I see." Her pen went back to the paper. She began writing. "And you're communicating well?"

"Yes, Barbara."

"Good." She nodded without looking at him. "That's good."

"There's so many things I wish I didn't have to tell her. I don't want her to know that part of me." He held up his hand. "And before you even say it, I know that I have to."

"Have you shared anything with Kelly at all?"

Blowing out a breath, Kodiak plowed his fingers through his hair. "Yeah, she knows about Jonathan…what came after. Not much else."

*Not yet.*

It was still too soon, their time together too new. Why Kelly didn't bolt for the door after he told her about the camp, Kodiak had no clue. But she didn't. And that gave him some semblance of hope.

"I know it's not easy for you to talk about, but…"

"And it won't be easy for her to hear," he countered, picking up his vape pen.

"Nothing worthwhile is, right?"

"Right." Kodiak inhaled. "Look, I told you. I'm going to be

completely honest with Kelly, but I'm not dumping all my trauma on her either."

"I would never suggest that you do." She lit up another cigarette.

*Chain-smoking now, Babs?*

"Trauma dumping—oversharing—is a manipulation tactic. It's one-sided and done impulsively. We commonly see it in clients with narcissistic personality disorder, and that's not you. Is it sympathy you're looking for?"

"No."

"Didn't think so." She leaned in closer to the screen. "An ongoing, mutual exchange of sharing your stories over an extended period of time, an open dialogue, transparency—all of that builds intimacy between you and Kelly. It's learning about each other. You're in the discovery phase of a new relationship."

His laugh brisk, Kodiak scoffed, "She's got a lot to discover, doesn't she?"

"That she does," Barbara conceded. "But it's where you've been, what you've experienced, that's made you the man you are today. And you, Seth, are a good man."

Not quite.

The wrongness in him would always be there.

Because he couldn't undo what he'd done.

# Fourteen

Every year on Thanksgiving, the Park Place enclave prepared a feast and came together just as any family would. Because no matter by blood or by choice, that's what they all were to each other. Family. And they'd adopted him as one of their own.

Kodiak couldn't understand it, honestly. If anything, they should despise him, but they didn't. *Yeah, but what if they knew the whole truth? What then?* At the lowest moment of his life, they saved him. Cared for him. Maybe it was because they all loved his sister, or because Bo wouldn't have it any other way, regardless, he was welcomed into the fold.

The love, the warmth, the genuine camaraderie—the dynamic in this room was a thing he might've envied once. But then growing up as he had, Kodiak never knew it existed. He was grateful to know it now.

Surveying the assemblage from Kit's funky sofa of bright purple velvet, Kodiak took it all in. Bo, missing his Ava, sat on one side of him, Kelly on the other. That she did so, pleased him. It was where she belonged and right where he wanted her to be.

Planted on the opposite end, Dillon watched the game. Well, kind of. Fighting to keep his eyes open, he succumbed to the tryptophan coma. His belly stuffed full, Kodiak was feeling the after-effects of turkey and all the trimmings himself.

He looked on. Linnea's fingers in her brother-in-law's hair, she casually stroked the shaggy mop on his head as he snoozed. This was the first holiday gathering without Kyan, and his absence was keenly felt by everyone, but even more so by his sister and his friend. Being with them every day, he saw first-hand how much they were hurting. Those two comforted each other in a way that no one else could, and he couldn't help but notice how good they were together. Smiling to himself, Kodiak saw a future for them, even if they didn't see it yet, and knew with the passing of time they'd both be okay.

With a toss of her head, Kelly tsked. Distracting him, he followed her gaze. Kevin, still miffed he'd lost out on his chance with Ava, steered clear of Venery's drummer, instead attaching himself to baby Declan, his sister, and her husband. Deep in conversation, it was obvious the kid idolized his brother-in-law, just as it was readily apparent his aunt did not like that he did.

For as long as he'd known her, Kelly barely tolerated Brendan— or Dillon either, for that matter. Seemingly on guard, she'd tense up in their presence, making no attempt to hide her disdain. He'd witnessed it on several occasions. Bo and the Venery boys she was okay with, but not them. He didn't get it. As far as Kodiak knew, there was no good reason to warrant it.

"Going to the restroom," she clipped. "Be right back."

"Okay." Without thinking, he kissed her cheek.

Bo chuckled under his breath.

"What?"

"You…" His fingers waving between him and Kelly's retreating backside, Bo's face split into a grin. "…and the ice queen?"

"Shut up, Bo-Bo." Kodiak gave him a good-natured elbow to the ribs. "And don't call her that."

"I should've known something was up when you dragged me to Beanie's," he said, slapping his thigh. "Does Linn know?"

"There's nothing for her to know, and until there is…"

His brow raised, Bo shot him a look.

"It's complicated, all right?" And he wasn't about to explain it now. At least not here.

"I get it, man."

Nursing his Glenlivet on the rocks, Kodiak chanced a glance down the hallway. Chandan and Elliott chased after Emery, who went crashing into Kelly the moment she emerged from the bathroom. The rambunctious tykes halted in their pursuit. Not bothered in the slightest, she picked the stunned little girl up from the floor and soothed her, combing Emery's hair back into place with her fingers.

Bo looked over at Kelly holding his daughter. The corner of his mouth quirked up, and with a shake of his head, he chuckled. "Nope, never woulda thunk it."

Loving how she looked with a child in her arms, Kodiak smiled. "That's because you don't know her like I do."

Gently depositing Emery on her father's lap, the grateful tot rewarded Kelly with a kiss for her efforts. Lacing her fingers with his, she returned to her seat beside him. "What a sweet, little girl. I sure hope when…"

He squeezed her hand, urging her to continue. "What?"

"Nothing."

"It was something." Kodiak turned her chin in his direction. "Tell me, Snicks. What is it you're hoping for?"

"Fine." Releasing a sigh, she rolled her eyes. "*If* I ever have a kid, I hope she's like her."

"When." He grinned. "You said, *when*."

Maybe she hadn't meant to say it, but she did. Still, his offer stood. When Kelly wanted to have a baby, he'd be more than happy to give her one. *No turkey baster required.*

Kodiak didn't get to tell her that, though. Kit brought out some old photo albums. The bright purple couch becoming crowded, they slid over, squished together against the end.

Chloe turned the pages. She came upon an old image, taken in what looked to be a basement, of the Venery boys as teenagers.

"Look, Emmy." Bo pointed to his bare-chested self seated behind a drum kit. "That's Daddy when he had nice hair."

Even then it was down to his waist.

Hooking his arm around the drummer's neck, Kodiak ruffled his locks. "Aww, Bo-Bo, it's still pretty."

"I don't know, man," he said, running his fingers through it. "Seems thinner to me."

*Fuck's sake.*

Rolling his eyes from where he sat on the floor, Sloan quipped, "Better start the Rogaine now then, dude. David Draiman, you ain't."

Covering his daughter's eyes, Bo flipped him the bird.

"Oh, that's Courtney." Four heads snapped up, each member of Venery turning their gaze toward Kit. "My wife."

"Damn," Bo mumbled low. "Can't believe he kept a picture of her."

Leaning across Kodiak, Kelly whispered, "Why?"

The three of them huddled together, Bo didn't answer until Kit left the room to put the photo albums away. "He took her to our eighth grade dance. First girl he ever kissed, and as far as I know, she's the *only* one."

*The hell?* Now *that* was news to him. He'd seen Kit with a lot of women, and usually a couple of them at once. At the club, the guy spent most of his time downstairs in the playpen, but come to think of it, Kodiak couldn't recall ever seeing him kiss a single one.

"They were glued to each other all through high school," Bo continued. "We all warned him not to do it, but Kit refused to listen. Married her right after graduation. Didn't last a year. She did him dirty—like real dirty. It was bad, man."

"How bad?" Kelly wanted to know.

"Bad enough. Kit hasn't so much as breathed her name ever since."

Once football was over, for the most part, Thanksgiving was too. Dillon saw his sister home. Chloe and Katie stayed behind to help Kit. Kevin opted to go hang out with Brendan, much to his aunt's chagrin. And with the late evening air cold and damp, Kodiak kept Kelly close, bundling her to his side.

"It smells like snow."

"When doesn't it?" Sniggering, he entered the code into the keypad. "I think it's supposed to." *Again.*

She held onto his arm with both hands as they began their stroll through Coventry Park. "I wonder what happened."

Not following, Kodiak angled his head.

"With Kit and his wife."

"Ex-wife," he corrected her.

"Everyone seemed so surprised he was married—everyone except the guys, that is." She gazed up at him. Even in the darkness, her blue eyes sparkled. "Did you know?"

"No, but I didn't know him then."

"True, but don't you find it…I don't know…odd?" Her shoulder did this quick up-down thing underneath his arm. "He's never mentioned it. No one has."

"Maybe it's too painful," Kodiak reasoned. "People usually don't like talking about what hurts, you know? It's probably best forgotten."

"Is that why you don't talk about your wife?"

He stopped in his steps. Kelly wasn't anywhere close to being ready to hear this chapter of his story—at least not all of it. More than that, knowing he'd probably lose her once he did, he wasn't ready to tell it.

"Yes and no." Pulling her to stand in front of him, Kodiak kissed her forehead. "You haven't asked about her, so I wasn't sure you wanted to know."

"I'm asking, unless it's too painful, of course."

*No, not painful. It only crushes my soul.*

"Was it bad?" she asked, searching his eyes for the answer.

He resumed walking. "Yes."

"What happened? Did she do you dirty, like Kit's wife?"

His laugh brisk, Kodiak scoffed, "No, that would be my father."

Apparently confused by his statement, Kelly pulled her brows together. Her tongue peeked out, wetting her lips, and then she rubbed them together, as if to stop herself from speaking.

"You have to understand how things were inside that church." Not that she ever really would. No one could unless they'd lived it. He held her closer against him. "His congregation didn't go to Sunday service to worship God, you see. They went to worship my father—their savior here on Earth. *His* word was gospel. No one ever dared to question him. He made up the rules and we obeyed them."

"Sounds like a cult."

"Yeah, I guess you could call it that. Course, I didn't see it for what it was back then." *Because it was all I knew.* "Anyway, he decided who married who, and when." Kodiak snickered, adding, "It was God himself who ordained him to do so."

Realizing where this story was going, he saw her eyes go wide.

"Being I'm his son, I was made to be an example. The ceremony was quite the spectacle. There, on an altar of lies, I was betrothed to my future bride, the girl God had chosen for me when I was sixteen." *A daughter shall fall for a son.* "She was six."

Her jaw dropped. Literally.

"And you married her?" Kelly asked like she didn't quite believe it.

"On her eighteenth birthday. Fucked up, ain't it?"

He knew now that it was, but then? To spend a lifetime with her was everything Kodiak had waited for, suffered for, paid penance for. His heartache, his salvation, and his only hope.

"I was stationed in Alaska at the time, and she was still in high school, so it was by proxy, but yeah, we were married. There was a big wedding planned for when I came home on leave, but it never happened."

Leaving the park, they stepped out onto the empty sidewalk.

Kelly was quiet, and strangely enough, so was First Avenue. Not a single car drove by.

She looked up at him, the wind carrying the soft sound of her whisper, "Why not?"

"When I got there, she was gone."

"What do you mean, gone?"

Funny, he'd said those very words when Jarrid told him she'd fled. Disappeared without a trace. Permanently etched into his memory, Kodiak could see him sitting there, that smirk on his face, as he nonchalantly relayed the mind-numbing news as if he were reciting the weather.

And he *knew.*

The soulless motherfucker knew that after everything, this would cripple him. Devastate him. His father knew, without a doubt, he could endure anything, except losing her. Because for as long as Kodiak could remember, he'd made it so.

"Upped and left town. No one knew where." His throat tightening, he choked on the words. "My father said it was *my* fault. I had displeased God. He was punishing me for my sins."

*Jonathan.*

And by then, Bo, too. Except Jarrid didn't know about that. Riddled with guilt all over again, Kodiak believed it. He didn't deserve her, and the only one he could blame was himself.

"You found her, didn't you?"

*Of course, I did.*

"It took a while, but yeah, I found her," he said, behind her on the stairs. "We...uh...had the marriage annulled."

Kelly unlocked her door and turned to him. "I'm so sorry."

She meant it.

He could see it in her shining blue eyes.

"Trust me, baby, I don't deserve the sympathy."

And he didn't feel like talking anymore.

Pushing her up against the wall, his hands came to rest on either side of her head. Kodiak watched the pulse beating in her neck quicken and traced it with his tongue. Her fragrant skin, sweet beneath his lips, incited him. Sucking the delicate flesh into his mouth, he scored it with his teeth.

"Yes…" Kelly whimpered, reaching for his belt. She unbuckled it. "…you do."

Already open and raw, he made no attempt to contain himself. Abruptly switching places, Kodiak leaned against the wall and pulled her back to his chest. Sliding his hands inside her sweater, he stretched out the neckline, ruining it, and exposed her breasts.

Kelly brought his fingers to her nipples. He pinched and pulled on the pliant nubs, then needing them in his mouth, he turned her around, biting them while he rid her of her clothes.

She tugged at his pants, rubbing over the hardness in his boxers.

With a growl, his hand went to her throat. Kodiak pressed in, and yanking her to his chest, his fingers slid down her belly, seeking that sweet, sweet pussy.

"Oh, fuck," Kelly cried, widening her shaky thighs, as he sawed his fingers in and out of her. "Make me beg for it."

*So perfect.*

Biting the tender lobe, Kodiak rumbled his praise in her ear. She squeezed his dick. And except for his thumb on her clit, his movements stilled.

Tracing circles on the swollen nub, he watched her nails sink into her thigh. Her head falling back on his shoulder, Kelly bit on her lip, sucking in air through her teeth. She was so beautiful at that moment, naked and trembling like a newborn fawn in his arms.

"Please," she squeaked, her head thrashing back and forth.

His fingers hooked in the opening of her pussy, he held onto her, tapping her clit with his thumb. "There's my girl."

"I need…"

*I know, baby.*

Pressing his thumb into her clit, Kodiak pushed his fingers up inside her. And he didn't stop until her wild cries ceased. Then collapsing to the floor, he just held her. Kissing her lips. Stroking her hair.

She palmed his cheek, his weeping dick throbbed against her thigh. "I did say when."

He smiled.

"One day…"

He didn't deserve Kelly either.

But that didn't mean he wouldn't do his damnedest to keep her.

# Fifteen

All belly on her slender frame, Linnea waddled around her kitchen like a penguin on speed. She seemed not to notice him standing there, breakfast sandwiches along with Leo's renowned banana-nut muffins in hand, as she rifled through the cabinets.

"What in the hell are you doing?"

"Looking for the cookie cutters." On a mission, she didn't even bother to look up.

Setting their food down, Kodiak picked up a Ziploc bag filled with metal objects. They sure looked like cookie cutters to him. "What are these?"

"Those are the Halloween ones," she answered, finally turning around. "I need Christmas."

Glancing around the house, there wasn't a Christmas decoration to be seen, save for a snowman cookie jar on the counter. Maybe she was trying to keep busy, a trait he and his sister both seemed to share, to keep her mind from dwelling on the fact that her husband was dead. The baby was due in a few weeks, and this was her first Christmas without him.

Or maybe she just wanted to fill up her sad, empty cookie jar.

"I brought breakfast." Brooking no argument, he pointed her to a chair. "Sit."

"So bossy." Pressing a hand to the small of her back, Linnea complied.

"When I have to be." Kodiak smirked, taking a seat across from her. "And only because I love you."

"Yeah, well, I love you too." Biting into her fried egg sandwich, she licked the runny yolk from her lip. "So, what are you up to today?"

"Oh, a little of this and a little of that."

Kelly left early this morning to spend Christmas with her family, not that she seemed to be thrilled about it. And thanks to Leo, he had an agenda.

"Jesus, Seth, you're exasperating sometimes." Linnea sighed, a strand of caramel hair blowing out of place. "Can you ever just answer a question?"

"Christmas isn't the time to be asking any." He chuckled, popping Leo's muffin into his mouth.

She let go of her sandwich, and with a slight grimace, Linnea sat up straighter in the chair, her hand on her back.

"You okay?"

"I'm fine." She waved her hand, pooh-poohing his concern. "I just can't seem to get comfortable anymore. She's heavy, you know."

His throat tightened, a sudden wave of melancholy washing over him. Fleeting thoughts of the dreams he once had, what was supposed to have been. Uncomfortable with where his mind was taking him, Kodiak got up to leave.

"Not much longer now, little one." Kissing the top of Linnea's head, his hand rested on her belly. The baby kicked his palm. "I've got to go."

"Where do you have to go?" She looked funny with her head cocked to the side.

He responded with a soft chuckle.

"You'll be back for dinner, right?"

"Not tonight," he said over his shoulder, strolling toward the door.

"Tomorrow?"

"Christmas Eve with you and Dillweed?" Grinning, Kodiak snorted. "Wouldn't miss it."

*I'm better now.*

He reminded himself of that. They came without warning sometimes. The thoughts. The heaviness in his chest. Something seemingly insignificant could trigger it, like just now. Chrissakes, he'd had breakfast with Linnea almost every day and been fine, so why was today any different?

In the beginning, the thoughts bombarded every dream, every waking moment. And not wanting to let them go, Kodiak was glad for it. Babs assured him this was normal, and that with time, reflection, and therapy, their impact would shrink. She'd been correct in that regard.

Walking through Coventry Park, he inhaled the frosty air and slowly let it go. And with each step he took, his unease lessened. After almost thirty-five years, Kodiak was finally at a place in life where he could envision a future of his own making, with a partner of his own choosing.

The little brass bells on the door announcing his arrival, Kodiak stepped inside Beanie's. Coffee beans, mocha, and snickerdoodle cookies. His eyes went to look for Kelly, even though he knew she wasn't there. Ava and Emmy, mugs of hot chocolate in front of them, waved to him from a table in the corner.

Greeting the toddler, he ruffled her silky blonde hair. "Hello, little princess."

"Unkey Koko," she exclaimed in her sweet baby voice, little arms wrapping around his leg. "Santa is coming!"

"So I've heard." With a kiss to the top of her head, Kodiak chuckled. "Have you been a good girl this year?"

Emery turned to a beaming Ava, who nodded. "Mommy says yes."

"Hey, Ava." He leaned over to kiss her cheek. "Bo's not with you?"

"No, I left him in the basement with Chester. He's cursing at assembly instructions." She winked. "I figured it was a good time to get Emmy out of the house. Do a little last-minute shopping."

"Gotcha," he said with a snigger. "Tell him to call me if he needs any help with that. Merry Christmas, Ava."

"Merry Christmas."

Looking particularly festive, Leo tapped his red-lacquered fingernails behind the counter. A wide headband, bedazzled with jingle bells, held back his waist-length, bleached-blonde waves. Green cropped sweater, with 'Merry & Bright' embroidered on it, showed some skin and his pierced navel. Tight red pants. Silver boots.

*Good Lord.*

"She here yet?"

"No." Leaning over the counter, Leo planted a kiss right on his lips. "Koko, *bebé*, I'm so nervous."

"Why?" he asked, wiping red lip gloss off with his thumb.

"Kelly's gonna be mad."

"Maybe…for about five minutes." Smirking, Kodiak shrugged. "Ask forgiveness, not permission. Think about all those cupcakes, sweet stuff. You want that expansion, don't you?"

"I do."

And Kelly wanted it too. The bank approved her loan, but not for the amount she wanted. She could either pay off Stacy or do the expansion. Not both.

Kodiak wanted to make her happy. For her to have everything she dreamed of. A dog. A baby. Even if it wasn't with him.

"Then you're in?"

Grinning, Leo held up a certified check. "I'm in."

They were going in together, splitting it fifty-fifty, to buy out

Stacy so Kelly could use the loan proceeds for the expansion. Kodiak overheard her and Katie talking one day—she was disappointed, but decided using the loan to pay off Stacy was the best course. Kelly didn't want to be indebted to her anymore. That's when he and Leo came up with a game plan of their own.

She wasn't at all what he was expecting. Older than he'd thought—mid-thirties if he were to guess. Stunning and statuesque, with salon-perfect highlights, the woman was a dead ringer for Cindy Crawford. But she couldn't hold a candle to Kelly Matthews.

Her gaze darted between him and Leo, paying them each a brief up-down, before the three of them sat down. Kodiak already decided he didn't like her and wanted to make this brief.

Phil drew up the documents for him. "It's a simple transfer of your interest in Beanie's to us."

Stacy signed.

And Kelly was free of her.

*Boom.*

Done deal.

Leo got up and left right away, but Stacy made no such move. Leaning forward, she planted her elbow on the table, rested her chin in her hand, and smirked. "So, just who are you to Kelly?"

"A friend."

"Right." She sat back, folding her arms over her chest. "That's a helluva lot of money to hand over for a *friend.*"

"It's just money." He shrugged.

"Uh-huh." Nodding her head, Stacy swiped her tongue across her lip. "I've got to say, I'm rather surprised."

"Why's that?"

"You're not Kelly's type."

The woman was blunt. She certainly didn't pull any punches. He'd give her that much.

"And you are?"

"As it turned out, no," she conceded with a snicker. "But then I think I always knew that. I'm glad she's okay now."

"What do you mean?" Kodiak asked, keeping his expression neutral.

"I've got to get going. My wife is waiting on me." Stacy rose from the table, extending her hand. "It's been a pleasure."

*Yeah, well, alritey then.*

With his business at Beanie's concluded, Kodiak figured he'd do a little Christmas shopping of his own. He saw it hanging in a shop window on Maple Street while walking home. The moon and stars. A sun-catcher made of crystal.

"Swarovski," the white-haired old lady said.

The name meant nothing to him, but Kodiak knew in his gut, Charlotte was supposed to have it.

He wrapped it up in pretty pink paper and was tying it off with silver ribbon when his phone vibrated on the table.

"Hey, my man. What's up?"

"You need to get over to Illinois Masonic. Linn's in labor. She needs you."

She was slow dancing with Dillon in her hospital room when he quietly opened the door.

"Seth?" Her strained voice sounded whisper thin.

"I'm here, little one."

He held her head to his chest, and gently rubbing the skin on her back, they swayed on a linoleum floor. Reminded of the first time he held her, Kodiak closed his eyes. God, he'd loved this girl for her entire life, and he always, always would. His heart, his soul, and his blood. He couldn't simply unlove her.

And that wasn't 'the thoughts' talking. It was just fact.

"It hurts." Linnea looked up at him, green eyes like his own, tired and glassy.

"Shh, you know it kills me to see you cry." Kodiak kissed her forehead, whispering in the most soothing voice he could muster, "Remember when you were little, and we'd go to the park? I used to push you on the swings."

"Yeah."

"Close your eyes now." He glanced to Dillon, who stood behind her, pressing his fist into the small of her back. "How high do you wanna go?"

"As high as the sky."

He couldn't see Linnea's face, but he felt her smile on his chest. She remembered. "And you'll get there. I'll help, but you've got to do your part."

"Pump those legs."

"That's right." Smiling, Kodiak closed his eyes once more. "Imagine the wind blowing through your hair, the sun warm on your face."

And gently, he placed her in Dillon's arms.

*I love you, sweet sister, forever and always. You were worth every sin.*

Just after midnight on Christmas Eve, Charlotte came into the world. Kelly was the first person that he called.

It was time.

A time of miracles and new beginnings. For Linnea. For Dillon. And for him, too.

# Sixteen

She sat in her sister's family room, swirling ice cubes in her glass with her finger. Looking outside, past blinking multi-colored lights, snow softly fell, dusting the stark landscape in white. As a young girl, Kelly loathed this place, and she still did. Stagnant and stifling, its small-town charm held little appeal. Certain there was something better out there just waiting for her, at eighteen she moved to Chicago and had been there ever since.

Thirty now, life hadn't turned out exactly as she'd planned it, but then, does anybody's? Kelly never anticipated the curveballs that would come her way. Once naïve, innocent, and far too trusting, she'd made a lot of mistakes. *So fucking many.* And some mistakes? Well, they can last a lifetime.

Sipping her watered-down Baileys, Kelly glanced over at her niece. Katie was just like her. Being only ten years apart, they'd always been close—as close as sisters. It wasn't surprising to anyone, least of all her, when Katie followed in her footsteps. Lord knows, she'd tried to protect her, to keep her from making the same terrible mistakes that she had, but she failed.

*Miserably.*

Katie sat across from her, all pretty and prim, under her husband's wing. It seemed as if he always had to be touching her in same way, like she might disappear if he didn't. Hell, she was cuddled up in his lap half the time, Brendan petting her like a puppy. *Weird.* Her niece thought it sweet. At least they were keeping the PDA to a minimum, playing the respectable married couple—no doubt for the family's sake.

*If they only knew.*

Katie's father would have a coronary.

Kelly's sisters would have a field day.

Living vicariously through others, as if they didn't have lives of their own, Kristie, Kim, and Kara thrived on idle chatter. Offering up their unwanted opinions. Sticking their noses where they didn't belong. As the youngest of the four, Kelly had been putting up with their tiresome meddling her entire life.

Luckily for Katie, Brendan, with his authoritative charm, won them over. Everyone except her, that is. But then Kelly wasn't young and dumb anymore. She knew better.

Barely twelve hours into this holiday gathering, and already she wished it was over. The liqueur coating her tongue made it fuzzy. *Gross.* With *Miracle on 34th Street* playing on the TV, Kelly left them to their movie, tossing what remained of her drink down the sink.

"Auntie, your phone's going off."

She glanced back over her shoulder. Katie held up her phone, a wide grin on her face, Kodiak flashing on the screen.

"Give me that." Snatching the phone from her niece, Kelly returned to the kitchen. "Hey, you. Miss me already? It's late."

"Sorry, did I wake you?"

"No." *And even if you had, I love hearing the sound of your voice.* "Everything okay?"

"Oh, yeah, everything's fine. I'm at the hospital. Linnea just had the baby…"

Kodiak told her all about Charlotte, and she listened. How beautiful she was. How much she weighed. While his pride in becoming an uncle was evident, there was a note of sadness in his happiness.

"I just needed to tell you." A long pause followed. "Oh, and Snicks?"

"Yeah?"

"I miss you."

*I miss you too.*

With a smile plastered to her face, Kelly returned to the family room. Her three sisters expectantly stared up at her. "What?"

"Just friends, huh?" Her niece giggled, breaking the silence.

Kevin snorted.

"We are."

"That's what she says…" Turning to her mother, Katie kept going. "…but trust me, there's more to it than that. Right, Kev?" Not that she waited for an answer. "Come on now, a guy who's…" She threw up air quotes. "… *'just a friend'* wouldn't be calling at one in the morning—"

"Katelyn." Squeezing her knee, Brendan put an end to it.

"Linn had the baby," Kelly announced to a captive audience. Raking her teeth over her lip, she nodded. "And I'm going up to bed. Goodnight."

Peeking through the blinds, Kelly watched Kim and Kara climb into their truck and drive away. *Oops, was it something I said?* She snickered to herself, the taillights receding in the distance.

A gentle tap sounding on her door, Katie poked her head in. "I'm sorry."

"You know how they are." Kelly shook her head. "The last thing I need are my sisters weighing in on my love life."

"So, you are more than friends." Then coming all the way inside, her niece took a seat on the bed.

"Not officially."

"I like Kodiak." Katie took her hand, urging her to sit beside her. "Never would have imagined it, honestly, but I think the two of you are good together."

"Thanks. I didn't know I needed your approval."

"You don't." Smiling, her head tipped to the side. "And I didn't need yours either, but you have it anyway. Never mind my mom and the aunts."

"I can hear Kim already. What, did she change her mind? I thought she was a lesbian," imitating her sister's grating voice, Kelly wrinkled her nose in distaste. "You know that's what they're thinking."

"Is that what's bothering you?"

*Maybe.*

She shrugged.

"You don't owe an explanation to anyone." Katie hugged her. "It's your life, your choices. That man is the one who makes you happy, so fuck what anyone else might think."

"How'd you get to be so smart?"

And she winked. "You."

Linnea tenderly laid the baby in his arms.

"She's so tiny." Just one week old, Kodiak gazed in awe at his sister's daughter. "I don't remember you being quite as small."

"Well, you were just a kid yourself."

"I was ten, Linnea." Feeling Charlotte's wispy curls, soft beneath his fingertips, he took in her newborn smell. Raised up as he was, even at that age, he'd felt ancient.

"Perception, brother."

*Yeah, maybe.*

"I was so afraid you'd break," he murmured, chuckling softly at the memory. "You feeling okay? Can I do anything for you?"

"I'm sure I don't look it, but I'm fine."

Hair a tangled bird's nest on top of her head. An old, faded sweatshirt. No makeup to hide the circles under her eyes. "You're beautiful."

Her delicate fingers unfurling, Charlotte squeaked. His smile broadening, Kodiak touched a finger to her tiny palm. The baby grasped it, and the muscle in his chest squeezed.

"She loves her uncle already." Linnea beamed. It was so good to see that smile on her face. "Here, let me take her, and you can make us some tea, yeah?"

"Chamomile?"

"Perfect."

Returning with the tea, he found Charlotte suckling at her mother's breast. Kodiak held his breath, waiting for the wave that would surely come. Relieved when it didn't, he released it, handing a cup to his sister. "Got it?"

"Yeah," she assured him, adjusting herself on the sofa. "I'm getting good at this multi-tasking thing."

He nodded once, and picking up his tea, noticed the screen light up on his phone. Right there on the coffee table. In plain sight. A quick glance and she'd see it. An email notification from their father.

*Fuck off and die, why don't you?*

So as not to draw attention to it, Kodiak slipped the phone into his pocket.

"A little birdie told me Chloe is having one of her little parties tonight. What does she call them?"

"A soirée." Linnea puffed out a sad excuse for a laugh, none the wiser. "And who might that little birdie be? Let me guess, Bo?"

"You would be right." *He misses you. Everyone misses you.* "I think you should go. Be with your people."

"I already told Chloe I'm not coming."

"You can change your mind," he offered.

"I could, but I'm not going to," she affirmed with a shake of her head, then lifting Charlotte to her shoulder, Linnea rubbed her back. "You're going to the club, aren't you?"

"Thought I might."

"Good. Promise me you'll make sure Dillon has a good time."

Kodiak raised his brow. "I'll, um, do my best."

"It's his birthday, you know."

The baby burped.

"Yes, Linnea, I'm aware."

"And be sure to have some fun yourself."

He grinned.

*Oh, I'm planning on it.*

Kelly was sipping on champagne, waiting for him in the greeting area, when he got there. As beautiful as ever. Slinky black dress. Strolling over to her, Kodiak kissed her cheek and grinned. "Wore that for me, did you?"

"You remember it?" She seemed surprised.

"How could I forget?"

It was *the* dress, after all. The very one she was wearing the night they met.

"I'm rather impressed." Her bottom lip disappearing behind her teeth, Kelly smoothed the lapels of his jacket. "Didn't think you'd notice."

"You should know by now. Nothing slips by me, Snicks." Threading his fingers in her hair, Kodiak brought her close. "Especially when it comes to you."

Her lips were right there. His for the taking. Tasting strawberry champagne on her tongue, he kissed her.

"Now, do you want to tell me why you're down here all alone?" he asked, surveying the cavernous two-story lobby. "Where is everyone?"

"Upstairs, I guess." Pursing her lips to the side, Kelly shrugged. "I ditched them."

Drawing his brows together, his voice took on a serious tone, "Why?"

"Just because." She tipped her head. "Besides, I wanted to wait for you."

*Bullshit.*

But he wouldn't press her. For now, anyway.

"I don't want you wandering around here without someone with you," he said, clasping her shoulders so she knew he meant it. "Understand?"

Kelly nodded.

"Say the words."

"Yes, I understand."

"Thank you." Slipping his arm around her waist, Kodiak squeezed her hip. He tipped his chin to Axel, walking her up the stairs to VIP.

With half their usual crew not here, the private space felt rather empty. Matt, Kit, and Sloan were the only ones sitting on the big purple couch—for the moment, at least. Before too long a harem of eager females—model types, starstruck wannabes living off Daddy's trust fund—would come sniffing around.

Dillon stared out at nothing, sipping whiskey at the bar. Taking hold of Kelly's hand, Kodiak went over. "Happy birthday, Dillweed."

"Just another day, Klondike." He poured himself another shot and kicked it back. "But thanks."

"What's going on with you, brother?" Kodiak turned Dillon to face him, Kelly slipping around them to get to Katie. "I promised Linnea you'd have a good time tonight and she's going to hold me to it."

"That's the thing, man." He slammed his hand on the bar top. "I can't. 'Cause I want *her*."

Seeming startled that he'd said the words out loud, Dillon's head shot up. He plowed his fingers through his hair, and picking up the bottle of Glenlivet, refilled his empty glass.

Kodiak already knew that, of course. And he'd known it for a very long time, not that Dillon ever said as much. He didn't have to. From the day he carried Linnea out of his apartment all those years ago, he'd known it. Saw it. Understood it. With every cell in his body, just as he did, Dillon loved Linnea. And yeah, he was more than good with that.

"Easy, man," Kodiak warned him. At this rate, he was going to drink himself to death before the clock struck twelve.

From the other side of him, Kelly tapped on Dillon's shoulder. "You wouldn't want to miss out on all your birthday kisses, would you?"

Raising his brow, he glared at her. "No kisses."

"Isn't that a rule?" Kelly retorted.

The look on her face said it all. Pure ice. *There's my queen.*

Getting Dillon out of the line of fire, Brendan stepped in between them, while Kodiak pulled Kelly away from the bar. "What is it with you two?"

She shrugged, her gaze cast down to the floor.

"Why are you always tossing jabs at him? Did something happen I'm not aware of?"

Lifting her chin, stormy blue eyes bored into his own. "I know what they call me behind my back."

*Ice queen.*

Though he couldn't say she hadn't earned the title.

*You melt for me.*

"They've got it all wrong, Snicks." Running his fingers through her hair, Kodiak tucked a strand behind her ear. "You're *my* queen."

And just to show her the truth of his words, he kissed her.

# Seventeen

Honey-blonde hair fanned out on the pillow behind her, Kodiak rubbed it between his fingers. Running them down her back, he gently traced her spine, the curve of her hip. Kelly turned over with a bottle of champagne in her hand and a wicked gleam in her eyes. "Happy birthday."

Kodiak glanced at the clock on the nightstand. Most people didn't have them anymore, but he did. Habit, he supposed. "Not for another twenty-seven minutes."

Birthdays never meant much to him—not his own anyway. Unless one of the church ladies happened to bake one, there were no birthday cakes. Though, the year he turned eight, Grace was at the house and made him brownies. When Jarrid got home, she lit a candle, and they sang to him.

Grace would've been fifteen then. Thinking back now, he wondered if his father was already fucking her.

Kelly pressed a kiss to his lips, pulling him out of his thoughts. "Close enough."

*Thirty-five. Damn.*

Why did it seem so much older than thirty-four? If he lived to see seventy, half his life was already over. Wasted. Years spent chasing promises, lies, and unanswered prayers.

No matter how many years he had left, Kodiak wasn't about to waste another single one. Kelly was his answer, his truth, his friend, and more. *So fucking much more.* Whatever was left of his battered heart was hers, all she had to do was take it.

Kodiak took the bottle of champagne from her hand. "C'mere then."

She straddled his lap, and he popped the cork. The wine sprayed, christening them both. It bubbled over his hand, dripping off his elbow onto the sheets.

"Oops." And delighted, Kelly giggled, licking champagne from his fingers. "You made a mess."

He raked his lip with his teeth, carnal thoughts amping his blood to lava. Gripping her chin, he filled her mouth, and watching the muscles move in her throat, she took every last drop.

Kelly licked her lips and grinned. She leaned in, and kissing him, slipped the bottle from his hand. Smooth glass to his lips, she poured wine into his throat. Down his chest. Onto his cock.

"And who's made a mess now?"

"Me." Her pupils flaring, she thrust the bottle back in his hand. "But I always clean up after myself, so…"

Starting at his neck, Kelly, his ice queen-turned-fiery siren, licked her way down his body. Flicking at his nipples, nibbling on them. Tracing every ridge of his abs with her tongue. And she wasn't quick about it.

No, she made him wait.

Anticipating the moment those luscious lips would kiss his dick, when he'd fill that hot, little mouth, Kodiak gathered up her hair. He twisted it, fisting the silken tresses in his hand. Her smoldering blues peeking up at him, she smiled.

"I'll be watching you, Snicks." He tugged on her hair. "Just to be sure you do."

Then she swallowed him whole.

Fingernails scored his abs, and raked his balls, as Kelly traced the veins, engorged with blood, that laced his thick shaft with her tongue. It swirled around the head, flicking at his frenulum, the little flap of skin on the underside of his cock that she knew made him go feral.

Fire licking up his spine, but not near ready for this to be over yet, Kodiak flipped the script. Yanking her up from his dick, he rolled Kelly onto her back, then drenched her in champagne.

"Good job, baby." The bottle in one hand, his fingers trailed over soft, slick skin with the other. "Very, very good."

Heady. Drunk on her, he lapped up every square inch of flesh. Her arms. Her sides. The divot at the hollow of her throat. Those beautiful breasts. Sucking on her nipple, Kelly released a moan. So consumed he could eat her alive, Kodiak clamped down with his teeth. And with the taste of her blood on his tongue, he indelibly marked her as his.

Fuck that body and blood of Christ bullshit.

This is how he prayed.

Kelly his holy communion.

With a desperate need to devour her, his tongue swept up her wine-soaked slit. He latched onto her clit, and she cried, "Oh, God."

*That's right, baby. Scream for me.*

No mercy.

Kodiak worked that clit, licking, and laving, and sucking, and nipping like he couldn't get enough.

Because he never would.

Falling in love was never part of his plan, but then she gave him a bag of cookies, and holy shit, he blew it.

Because he did.

Her hands flying to her breasts, Kelly squeezed her nipples. Then she reached for the bottle still clutched in his fingers, and parting her lips like the holiest water, Kelly inserted it inside herself.

*Goddamn.*

Mesmerized at the sight of green glass moving over crisp, white sheets, Kodiak sat up beside her. With her teeth pressed into her bottom lip, it was the most erotic thing he ever saw. "Does that feel good?"

She answered with a moan.

"You're amazing, baby." He reached for her nipple, pressing a finger to her clit. "Yeah, get that pussy ready for me."

Then he leaned over, and licking her clit while she fucked herself, Kodiak drank in all her sweetness.

And after she came, the bottle tossed to the side, his spent dick deep inside her, he understood the depth of the gift she had given him. Naked and vulnerable, wild and wanton, completely uninhibited, Kelly splayed herself open. For him. Gave not just her body, but her whole, true self. To him.

Maybe she loved him too.

*Happy birthday to me.*

After thirty-five years without it, the idea alone gave him reason to start living again.

Only stopping in briefly to wish Chloe a happy birthday and to say hello to Bo, Kodiak left the club's Eros party to walk the short block to Beanie's. Kelly had no desire to attend, not that he blamed her. Brendan and Katie were taking the stage tonight, so, yeah, he was taking her out for a romantic dinner instead.

Flowers.

Champagne.

Smiling at the thought of it, he opened the coffee shop door to see Leo, tapping his fingers on the bar in front of him. Garbed all in red, a light-up heart blinking on his chest, the dude looked positively smashing. And nervous?

"Where's Kelly? She ready?"

"Oh, she's ready, *bebé,*" he said, dramatically, leaning in for the kiss. "And she's mad."

"Mad? Whatever for?"

"Damn right, I'm mad." And as if on cue, there she was. "Why'd you do that?"

"Told you so," Leo muttered under his breath.

"Do what?"

Of course, Kodiak knew exactly what. He figured she'd find out sooner or later. Except he'd been hoping for later. Or better yet, never at all.

Kelly popped out her hip, planting her hand on it, with a toss of her honey-blonde waves. She looked so damn cute when she got angry. "Don't play dumb. It doesn't suit you."

"Can we talk about this after dinner, maybe?" *Not doing this here, Snicks.* "We have reservations."

"Fine." Snatching her purse up, she headed for the door. "Let's go."

"Good luck, man," Leo bid with a snigger.

Following her outside, he feared he just might need it.

While the Uber ride was quiet, Kelly didn't seem altogether mad. The driver exited Lake Shore Drive onto Michigan Avenue. A smile lighting her eyes, she turned in her seat. "We're going downtown?"

He just smirked.

The car came to a stop at the Hancock building. Taking her hand, Kodiak held it as they walked across the plaza, Kelly glancing back longingly at the Cheesecake Factory as they passed it. He snickered. Did she really think that's where he'd bring her on Valentine's Day? Maybe he wasn't the most romantic guy in the world, but even he knew better than that.

Slipping his arm around her waist, they entered the magnificent lobby. Travertine and black granite. An icon of the Chicago skyline, the skyscraper housed one hundred floors. Kodiak led her to an express elevator that would bring them straight up to the ninety-fifth.

"The Signature Room?"

She looked positively giddy.

The corner of his mouth ticked up. "Unless you'd rather go to the Cheesecake Factory."

"No. No, I would not rather."

*Didn't think so.*

The award-winning restaurant, almost as iconic as the building it was in, was classically elegant. Dramatic views of the city and shoreline. Seated at a table for two by the floor-to-ceiling windows, just as he'd requested, Kelly picked up the red rose resting at her place setting and brought it to her nose. "This is lovely, Kodiak. Thank you."

"So, you're not mad at me?" The Moët sat chilling in a silver bucket tableside. Filling them each a glass, he handed her one.

She pursed her lips and snickered. "Oh no, I most certainly am."

His timing perfect—not—the server appeared with the first course of lobster bisque and pull-apart French bread. Kelly slathered two slices with grass-fed butter, topped them with roasted garlic, and gave him one, before tucking into her soup.

While he'd been hoping to postpone this conversation until after dinner, being Kodiak had more important things to talk to her about, he decided it was probably best to clear the air first. "Why? You wanted to do the expansion and now you can."

"And now I'm obligated to you instead of Stacy."

*Is that it?*

He chuckled. "No, you're not."

"But you paid her off."

"Technically, Leo did." Taking a bite of his bread, Kodiak shrugged. "My name's not on anything."

His motives purely altruistic, that's the way he wanted it.

"Still…"

"Look, Snicks, it's no big deal. Leo wanted the space next door, and so did you. We went in together to make it happen, all right?"

"But why?" she asked, softly resting the spoon on her plate.

He drained his glass of champagne and poured another. "Why what?"

"Why'd you do that?"

By now, didn't Kelly know? Her happiness mattered to him, and so did she.

"Why do you think?"

She didn't get the chance to answer. The server with impeccable timing brought out their entrees. And then it was the white and dark chocolate mousse cake. It wasn't until after dinner, halfway across the plaza, when he paused mid-step and pulled her to stand in front of him.

"Truth for a truth, Kelly." His fingers clutching the lapels of her coat, Kodiak looked into her eyes. "Do you really think we're just friends, you and I?"

"No," she whispered, slowly shaking her head.

"That's good."

And those blue eyes gazed back into his.

"Because I love you."

# Eighteen

On top of the world, Kelly and Katie spun around together in the middle of the empty space that was once the Lebanese place next door. Having just signed the new lease with Brendan, it was officially theirs now. He and Leo stood off to the side, chuckling at their childlike antics, Declan squirming to get out of his arms.

Dizzy, she stumbled to the floor, taking her niece down with her. Kelly sat up, laughing, and leaning back onto her elbows, surveyed the newly acquired space. There was so much work to be done here, but even with the scent of *za'atar* and olive oil still lingering, she could already envision what this place would become.

Brendan let his son down, the ginger-haired toddler running to his mother's waiting arms. Kelly ruffled his hair, pointing to where his father and Leo still stood. "We'll have to knock out that wall, redesign the kitchen…maybe we should leave it open, so the customers can watch you bake magic. What do you think, cupcake?"

"Yesss, *ma chérie*, Leo likes that." His head did this shimmy thing, pink curls bouncing. "Mmm, all those delicious smells blending together."

"Can we get a fireplace now?" Katie chimed in. "Every time that door blasts open in January, I feel it in my bones. The one they have in Charley's is so cozy."

The expression on Brendan's face turned wistful.

Kelly swiveled on her bottom to look at the opposite wall. "A fireplace would look amazing here. I wish that was brick."

Beanie's was an end unit, so it had an exterior wall, the exposed brick giving it texture, merging the past and present within the space. Not so the case here.

"You can make it brick," Brendan offered.

"But it wouldn't be the same."

"Yes, it could be." He winked. "Reclaimed Chicago brick. We get it for projects all the time. I know a guy…and if you'd like, we have all of Kyan's drawings—there's a ton of them. Maybe you can make one work for you. He designed Charley's, you know."

"Yeah?"

"Yeah," he answered with a single nod.

"I'd love to be able to do that."

"Come by the office. We can have a look." His smile reaching his eyes, Brendan tipped his chin to his wife. "Katelyn, are ready to go home, sweet girl?"

"It's time for your nap, isn't it, baby?" Katie cooed to her son, but she just as easily could've been talking to her husband. Helping Declan into his jacket, her head shot up. "You know, you should think about rebranding while you're at it. Beanie's won't be just a coffee bar anymore."

"True, but everyone knows the name. I don't think changing it would be a good idea."

*That would be like starting all over.*

"You don't have to change it altogether, silly." Giggling in that cutesy way of hers, she handed Declan off to Brendan. "Just add to it."

"I'm not following, KK." She rolled her eyes.

"Sugar Beanie's Bakery & Coffee Roasters." Before Kelly could protest, Katie threw her hands up in the air. "Wait, now hear me out. You're just adding two words. The blue cups and logo can stay the same. Just add 'sugar' in all caps behind it—a block font in light pinkish-taupe would look nice."

*Hmm…maybe.*

"Ohh, Leo likes it!" Grabbing Katie by the shoulders, Leo smacked his juicy, pink lips on hers. "I'm sugar." Then, in a bad Joe Elliott impression, he started singing, "That's me, hot and sticky sweet, from my head to my feet."

"Oh, God." Kelly snorted, and giving in, she shrugged. "It's actually not a bad idea."

"Chloe can update the logo for you," Brendan said as if it were a done deal.

But then it was, wasn't it? *Change is good.* And it made sense.

"Okay. Why not? Let's do it."

After Katie and her family departed, she and Leo remained. Sitting together on the floor, they gazed at the bare walls surrounding them. He grabbed hold of her hand, and raising her fingers to his lips, he kissed them. "Told you so."

"Told me what?"

Smirking, he let her go. "That friends-with-benefits thing never works out."

"Yeah, well…" Laying her head against his shoulder, Kelly smiled. "…I'm glad that it didn't."

"Me too, *chérie*," he said, stroking her hair. "That gorgeous hunk of man sure does love you."

Two broken pieces somehow mended and made whole together, she loved him right back.

"I know."

His fingers sliding through her hair, Kelly lay tucked beneath his arm. Kodiak loved the smooth, silky feel of it, the warmth of her skin, and how perfectly her body molded itself to his. Almost as if they were made for each other, they fit.

The TV was on, but neither one of them was watching it. After closing up shop, Kelly came straight to his place as she often did. He fed her dinner. They fucked on the couch. Content, just by being with her, Kodiak listened as she talked about her day.

"Sugar Beanie's, huh?" Smiling, he kissed her crown. "Yeah, I like it."

"I hope we can have construction completed by summer. I want to have our grand re-opening the first week of July—that's Beanie's third birthday."

"If anyone can make it happen, it's you," he said, squeezing her a little tighter.

She craned her neck, those pretty blue eyes looking up at him. "I love you."

"Say it again."

"Why?" Kelly giggled, suddenly sounding shy.

Because the words were foreign to him. In all his life, only two other people had ever spoken them—his sister and Bo. Not even his own father. Not once. And Jonathan never had the chance.

Tipping her chin up, Kodiak kissed her. "Because I like the way it sounds."

"I love you."

Stretching his arms out wide, Kodiak returned the sentiment, "I love you too, baby, as far as my arms can go." Then he wrapped them around her, stroking her skin. "Everything is different now. Even Linnea noticed. She keeps asking me if I met someone."

"Oh?" Rolling onto her side, she glanced up at him.

He met her gaze. "It's about time I told her, don't you think?"

"I think she won't be too happy about it." Rubbing her fingers on his chest, Kelly worried her lip.

"Yes, she will be. Why the hell would you think that?"

Shooting him a look, her features hardened. "Dillon, for starters. He does *not* like me."

*Truth.*

"Linnea likes you." Strumming her skin, he kissed her lips. "I know my sister, and if I'm happy, then she'll be happy."

"And Dillon?"

That was a tough one.

Resignedly, Kodiak sighed. "He's like a brother to me, Snicks, so I hope one day you guys can kiss and make up."

Wrinkling up her nose, Kelly made a face.

*Guess not.*

He sniggered. "Set aside your differences, at least? I'd like for the two of you to be friends. If not, next Thanksgiving's going to be all sorts of interesting."

"I can try."

"That's all I ask." Kissing her on the forehead, Kodiak covered Kelly with a throw. "I got Linnea one of those jogger strollers for her birthday so she can take the baby and run with me. Be good for her to get out of the house, you know?"

"She's so lucky to have a brother like you."

Now perhaps, but she sure wasn't then.

Of course, Linnea didn't know her Seth was, in reality, the big brother she always wished for. And Kodiak had no idea she was his father's daughter. Though, looking back, maybe he should have.

He remembered that day, the day he made promises to a God that didn't exist, as clearly and as vividly as if it happened only yesterday. Linnea's sixth birthday. Nineteen years ago, tomorrow. He could still smell the beeswax of candles burning on the altar. The Murphy's oil soap used to shine the pews. And her.

Sweet and innocent, in a pretty white dress, she smelled of baby shampoo. Beaming up at him, Linnea put her little hand in his, Jarrid pontificating to his congregation how God spoke through him. He declared them betrothed. Her six-year-old self probably thought it was all for her birthday.

And twelve years later, the day she turned eighteen, the deed, and their further descent into Hell, was done. Married by double proxy, though unbeknownst to him, he became his sister's husband, and she his lawful wife.

Once the marriage had taken place, and the license filed, his father called him with the news. His chest bursting with emotions Kodiak couldn't describe, the heavy weight he'd been carrying lifted from his shoulders, and the dark cloud he'd been living under vanished. Through it all, Linnea, the only good, pure thing he'd ever known, had become his lifeline by then.

Despite his past transgressions, after years of waiting and countless letters, she was really, truly his. He wished he could call her, but Catherine wouldn't allow a phone in her house. Soon, though, he'd be able to go and get her out of there. *God's promise.* At last, he could keep his. And at that moment, everything he'd gone through beforehand became worth it. Because he had her to protect and to love.

That's what he believed at the time anyway.

While Kodiak was certain his father never intended for them to learn of it, his greatest sin was still to come. The darkness hadn't left. It was right there, hovering over his head, he just didn't know it yet.

"Let's go, Linnea." Leaning down into the stroller, Kodiak tucked the blankets in tight. "You're ready, aren't you, Charlotte?"

"Jeez, I told you I'm coming." Pulling her hair back, she ambled down the stairs in the running gear he'd gotten for her, from the beanie on her head to her new Brooks shoes.

He'd be lying if he denied being just a little bit nervous. And oddly enough, guilty. Linnea had been the only woman in his life for so long—the only woman ever, actually—that introducing her to Kelly as the woman he was in love with almost felt as if he were betraying her in some weird, fucked up kind of way.

In his head, Kodiak knew that he wasn't.

But that jagged hole in his battered heart didn't seem to agree.

If there was anything he was good at, it was compartmentalizing things. A coping mechanism, as Babs explained, that had allowed him to function, enabled his ability to survive. His brain put Kelly in one box, and his sister in another. And right now, as much as

Kodiak wanted to, needed to, the thought of integrating them felt rather awkward. Uncomfortable. By doing so, he would cut the only remaining thread of a fragile cord that never should have been woven in the first place.

They walked at first, only increasing the pace to a light jog when they reached the park trail. "How's it feel?"

"Like I'm starting over, but it feels good."

"We'll take it nice and easy for a while." Tapping her shoulder, he ran a few steps ahead, glancing behind him. "You'll get back on track in no time."

"Easy for you to say," she shot back, sounding a bit winded. "Look at me, I'm already breaking a sweat here."

"You're also pushing a stroller." In a swift maneuver, Kodiak grabbed the handle. "Here, let me take the baby."

Linnea hadn't gone on a run in months. Not since Kyan, at least. He didn't want to push her too hard, too fast, but he wasn't going to let her slack either. She needed this. Exercise, fresh air, and endorphins were not only beneficial for the body, but a soothing balm to the soul.

"Better?"

"Yeah." She smiled, finding her stride.

"So, did you have a nice birthday?"

"Yes." Seeing the smirk on his face, Linnea grinned. "I knew you were up to something."

"Just helping out a friend who happens to love my sister a whole helluva lot."

"I...I...I love Dillon." And eyes filling with tears, her feet stopped. "With all my heart, I truly do, but I don't think I'm ready for that."

"Take your time, little one. He's not going anywhere." *I'm not either.* Wrapping her in his arms, Kodiak kissed her crown. "All I want for you is to be happy again."

"That's what I want for you too, you know."

And much like the day he said goodbye to his wife, holding each other, they swayed.

*Cut the thread. Now.*

*Cut it.*

*Cut it.*

*Cut it.*

He swallowed past the lump forming in his throat.

"I am happy." Gently stroking her cheek, Kodiak let her go. "More than I have a right to be."

"Don't say that, Seth. You have every right."

*No, I really don't.*

Linnea wiped the tears from her face and smiled. "You *are* seeing someone, aren't you?"

"Yes."

"I knew it."

And he smiled too. "Kelly and I have been together about six months now."

"Kelly?" Her eyes widened. "Katie's aunt?"

"Yeah." His smile growing wider, Kodiak nodded.

"Is it serious?"

"I love her," he answered without hesitation.

"It is then. Gosh, Seth, I'm so happy for you." She hugged him, then biting her lip, her head peeked up from his chest. "Does she know?"

"About us?" He exhaled with a shake of his head. "Not yet."

"You're going to tell her?"

"I have to."

*It was my sin, not yours, sweet sister.*

Her lips pressed together, Linnea nodded. "I know."

# Nineteen

A year ago, if anyone had told her this would be her life now, she would've laughed right in their face. Seriously. Not that it was horrible. It wasn't. In fact, life had been going pretty darn good, considering. Kelly just couldn't have imagined then that she would have more, that it would be better.

But then one day, she took a chance and made a friend.

Then she took another, and another, and another…

It's funny how life changes then.

Two short weeks from now, once they got through the summer festival, the bigger and better Beanie's—make that Sugar Beanie's—would be ready to open. The blue plastic tarp serving as a temporary wall could finally come down. Kelly was tired of looking at the hideous thing—and the mess behind it.

*"Patience, Snicks."*

That man. She could hear him in her head, but then Kodiak was on her mind every minute of every day. Yeah, life sure is funny because Kelly never would've imagined loving him a year ago. But she did, despite the fact he owned a penis. Then again, maybe she loved him because of it.

*Well, it is a nice one.* Restocking the pastry case, she giggled to herself.

"Something funny down there?"

She looked up, her face splitting into a grin. "Penis."

And getting off her haunches, Kelly popped a snickerdoodle into his mouth. "It's a funny word."

Linnea snickered behind her hand.

Chewing his cookie, Kodiak looked at her like she'd gone and lost her mind. He swallowed. "Call it what you usually do then."

"And what's that?"

He leaned in close, warm breath tickling her ear. "God."

"Only you, baby."

"Damn right," he breathed, then straightening he winked and took another bite of his cookie.

Muscles pumped from running, each and every one of them defined, sweat glistened on his skin, sending a wave of tingles through her body. If they were anywhere but here, she'd be pouncing on him. Licking the salt from his pulse. Scoring her nails down his abs.

But they were here. His sister, with the baby in her stroller, at his side.

Turning to Linnea, Kelly wet her lips and smiled. "Coffee?"

"Yes, please." Her smirk a little too all-knowing. "I'll take an americano, iced, and a water. It's hot out there today and your beast of a boyfriend here thought an extra lap was a good idea."

"That's what brothers are for. Someone's got to push you." Playfully, Kodiak swatted her bottom. "Got three miles out of you, didn't I?"

"Yeah, yeah." Linnea rolled her eyes.

Chuckling, he leaned over the counter to kiss her. "Can you make one for me too, Snicks?"

"Well…" Kelly pursed her lips and grinned, pretending to think about it. "…I suppose I could."

"How's it looking next door?" Linnea asked, taking Charlotte out of her stroller.

"It's getting there." Snapping the lids on their drinks, she handed them off to Kodiak. "Want to see?"

Lifting the flap on the makeshift wall, they followed her inside. A long glass case, still covered in protective paper, fronted the open kitchen. It would flow seamlessly into the coffee bar once they were done. The gas fireplace, its mantel and surround made of old Chicago brick couldn't have been any more perfect.

"They're installing the new doors next week. The pastry case on the other side is coming out, so we can move the beverage station there. That way there'll be a dedicated space for when we have acoustic sets, poetry readings, and such."

"Wow, I can see it…stunning. Speaking of…" Linnea turned to her brother. "Do you want to tell her, or shall I?"

"Tell me what?"

Linnea was helping her with the grand re-opening. Chloe rocked out the updated logo—Katie was right, the pinkish-taupe SUGAR looked flawless—then she outdid herself, designing signage, business cards, flyers, and even their new shirts. Those Park Place girls got their hands in everything, not that she was complaining.

Slinging his arm around her shoulders, Kodiak reeled her in tight. "We talked to Bo."

"Venery is going to play an acoustic set for you on opening day." Bouncing on her heels, Linnea placed the baby in her arms.

"Here?"

*Get. The. Fuck. Out.*

"Surprise!"

"My queen." Kodiak kissed her lips, then the top of Charlotte's head. "I'm so proud of you, baby."

Yeah, it sure is funny how life changes.

*God, and to think, it all started with a bag of cookies.*

"I love you."

First Avenue was a jam-packed clusterfuck. Clamoring with festival goers from one end to the other, Kodiak ducked into the alley and entered through the back door. Cleaning up at the counter, Kelly didn't see him behind her. He snuck in closer, and wrapping his arms around her front, kissed the tender skin beneath her ear.

"Ready to go?"

"I'm exhausted." She sank back against his chest, then turned herself around. "But yeah, I'm ready."

"Ninety minutes until showtime." Holding her close, he kissed her forehead. "If you're a good girl, I'll take you to ride the Ferris wheel on the way."

"Oh, yeah?"

"Yeah, c'mon."

With dusk settling in, the June breeze tousling her hair, Kodiak wound his arm around her waist, and they walked toward the midway. Kelly wanted to personally thank Bo and the boys for agreeing to play at her grand re-opening, so he was taking her to see them before the show. Maybe they'd stay for a bit of the concert too.

"How long have you and Bo been friends anyway?"

"Oh, a decade at least." His fingers skimming up and down her hip, Kodiak chuckled. "Met him up at Richardson, of all places, before he was famous."

"Really?"

"Yeah." He peered down to see pretty blue eyes looking up at him. "Venery was playing a gig at some dive off base, and we've been tight ever since."

Kodiak remembered their first glance at that bar in Anchorage. Drawn to each other instantly, that feeling he had with Jonathan came over him again. Fifteen minutes later they were in a bathroom stall. Bo's beautiful cock down his throat.

"Yeah, keep sucking me, baby. Just like that," Bo crooned, rubbing his fresh buzz cut. "You gotta place we can go?"

"Yeah, I've got a room off base."

"Good." Bo filled his mouth with cum, then pulled Kodiak up from his knees to kiss him. "I want to fuck."

"Yeah?"

"Oh, yeah."

The pull between him and Bo wasn't purely physical, though. It was something else, something more. That they even met at all was kismet. It was as if the universe put them in each other's path for a reason. Most folks don't understand that kind of thing.

"So, Linn met him through you then?"

*If catching me sucking Bo off on a tour bus counts, then sure.* In this very park. At this very festival. Almost four years ago to the day.

"Is that how you both ended up in the city?"

"Err, not exactly," he said, rubbing the back of his neck. "Linnea and Bo became friends on their own."

Her brow arched, Kelly looked at him, obviously confused. Kodiak wished he had his pen with him, or a beer because this wasn't the best time or place to have this conversation. And quite honestly, he'd been dreading it.

He took a breath and blew it out. "When I left for the army, Linnea and I lived worlds apart for a very long time. While I was waiting for my future bride to grow up, I did a lot of things I shouldn't have."

"Like Bo?"

His throat tightening, Kodiak nodded. "After Jonathan, I never had the desire to be with another man. Until him. There was something about Bo. Can't explain it. We've gotten each other through some rough shit over the years." Pausing, his fingers plowed through his hair. "He saved my life."

"What do you mean?"

They'd reached the beer garden at the entrance to the midway, and now, he definitely needed one—or two. And likely, so would Kelly. Kodiak ordered two in the large souvenir steins—thirty-two ounces, easy. Handing her one, they continued walking.

"You know Linnea's grandmother raised her."

Swiping her tongue across the foam on her upper lip, she nodded. "Yeah, you mentioned that."

"Well, when Catherine died, she left Crossfield and came here." He took a long pull and swallowed. "I did too."

Kelly was smart. She'd figure it out now. It might be easier that way. Then he wouldn't have to say the words. Swallowing, Kodiak prepared himself for the abject reaction that was sure to come.

"And that's when we found out it was my father who impregnated her mother when she was just sixteen years old."

It took a minute before the words sank in, then she gasped. "Wait…all those years you didn't know you had the same father?"

*Ding, ding, ding.*

Still, she hadn't quite connected all the dots yet.

"He and Catherine kept it a secret from us. That's what finally broke me."

Not Jonathan.

Not Jeffrey, or Rachel, or even Reverend John.

It had all been for nothing. By gaining a sister, he'd lost everything.

They stopped walking and looking into her eyes, he tucked a wayward strand of silky hair behind her ear. "And Bo knew it. He flew with me to California and made sure I got the help I needed."

"Jesus." Reaching for him, Kelly stroked his face.

She looked at him with love and concern. Not revulsion or horror, or least of all, pity. It would come, though. And she wouldn't love him then.

The Ferris wheel rotated high above them, bright lights flashing across its spokes reflected in her eyes. Rubbing his palm over her fingers, Kodiak held her hand to his cheek. Kelly loved him today, and he was going to hold onto that for as long as it lasted. Lowering his forehead to hers, he softly kissed her lips.

"Told you, Snicks, I'm fucked up."

*But I'm better now.*

"C'mon." Lifting his gaze to the top of the wheel, he smiled just for her. "I promised you a ride."

# Twenty

There's something about the smell of a coffee shop. And a bakery. But put the two together and it's something else entirely. Sweet, aromatic nirvana.

Opening day and the place was mobbed with a line out the door that wrapped around the corner. Not an empty seat to be had. The stage set for Venery, folks crammed themselves into any available space, waiting for them to appear.

Leo, in heavy wing-tipped liner and a platinum-blonde ponytail, passed out mini cupcakes for customers to sample, while Katie cranked out one latte after another. Catching Kelly's eye, Kodiak winked at her. She looked so happy.

Except for Dillon—no surprise there—everyone was here. Kelly's sisters even took the train into the city for the occasion. Much to Brendan's delight—not—they were staying with him and Katie for the weekend. After spending six hours with them last night, helping Kelly and Leo put the finishing touches on Sugar Beanie's,

Kodiak could sympathize. Opinionated and unfiltered, they were…
well, they were a lot.

Even now, they debated the merits of the Venery boys amongst
themselves. "I think you should go for the drummer—he's hot. I
danced with him at Katie's wedding," Kim advised her younger sister.

Kristie, the eldest and Katie's mom rolled her eyes.

"You go for him then. I want the guitar player." Kara squealed,
fanning herself like a teenager with the latest issue of *Tiger Beat*
magazine.

"Taylor's married." Smiling from beside him, Linnea leaned
into his ear. "How old are these women?"

"Uh, late thirties, I think," he whispered with a shrug.

"See? Go for the drummer. He smells hella good too."

"Bo is taken, ladies," Kodiak informed them.

"That's okay, and I know the inked-up one is married. I want
the other one."

"Which other one?"

*Never gonna happen.*

It's not that Kara wasn't attractive, an older version of Kelly,
she was. But if there was one thing that turned these guys off, it
was fangirling. A groupie might luck out when they were on tour,
only to be forgotten the next day. Here at home, though? No way.
Besides, out of respect for Katie and Brendan, hooking up with either of them was out of the question.

"Forget it, Kara." Giving him his juice, Kristie adjusted Declan
on her lap. "You're too old for any of them anyway."

"I. Am. Not," she seethed, turning to her sister. Then with a
flip of her hair, and in the haughtiest tone, she said, "I'm a cougar."

*Oh, dear.*

Kodiak about choked on his coffee.

His sister, however, apparently having swallowed the wrong
way, sputtered into a napkin. Linnea put Charlotte in his arms, and
waving her hand in front of her face, tried to catch a breath and keep
herself from laughing. Looking up at him with her bright blue eyes,
the baby pulled on a handful of his hair and grinned.

He grinned right back. Bringing her up eye level with him, Kodiak rubbed her button nose with his, making her giggle. She had the cutest little laugh.

"You look good with a baby," Kristie commented, tipping her chin at him. "Are you and Kelly planning on having any?"

*I hope so.*

"She's not getting any younger, you know."

Rude. Not to mention, their plans were none of her business. As much as Kodiak wanted everything with Kelly, it was very likely she wouldn't feel the same once she learned what he'd done. His unforgivable sin.

*Your sister forgave you.*

She did, but then Linnea could hardly remember it.

Brendan, Jesse, Chloe, and Ava, their little ones in tow, appeared, saving him from Kristie's meddling. The buzz grew louder, and that could only mean one thing. He glanced up, Bo and the boys were taking their places on the tiny stage, and just as the din began to calm, Kara stood up and excitedly pointed. "Him."

*Oh, shit.*

"I want that one."

Everyone in the place heard her.

Taking it all in stride, Matt blew her a kiss.

Venery played a thirty-minute set. After stopping to sign autographs and take pictures with fans, slowly, they made their way over. Chloe letting him go, Chandan flew to his father. Bo kissed Ava, Emery tipping out of her arms into his.

And Matt?

Sitting his ass down on the arm of the sofa, the rhythm guitar player draped an arm around Kelly's sister. Then he laid one of his boyish grins on her. "Hello, pretty."

Frozen, her eyes bugging out, it appeared that Kara had ceased to breathe.

"Now's your chance." Kristie snickered. "Cougar."

Whispering something in her ear, Matt played with Kara's hair and kissed her on the cheek.

Kodiak stopped paying attention to them then, because Kelly was coming their way, and he only had eyes for her.

Following his gaze, Bo elbowed him in the ribs. "You looking to wife up, man?"

"Are you?"

"I'm fixing to ask her," he murmured low, so Ava wouldn't overhear. "Yeah."

If only it were that easy. Get a ring. Pop the question. Get married. Pop out a couple of kids. His own happily ever after was so fucking close, he could almost touch it. Only one thing stood in his way.

"I couldn't be happier for you, brother. Congratulations."

It was clear to him. Kodiak couldn't put it off any longer. He had to tell her.

Up on the roof above Kelly's loft and Sugar Beanie's below, much like his stomach, he twisted his hair into a knot at the back of his head. It was just him and her. Everyone was up at the lake house for the Fourth. Even Kevin had taken off with some girl. With the sun making its descent behind him, First Avenue came ablaze in fiery hues of orange and pink and gold. People walked toward the park, hefting cumbersome lawn chairs and coolers, to watch the fireworks. Grateful, at least he didn't have to mess with that, Kodiak readied the blanket.

He had a bottle of pinot.

The Garrett's popcorn that she loved.

And a story.

The last easier-to-digest chapter, only this one was the most difficult of all to swallow.

Kodiak didn't know how he was going to tell it. It's not like he had the words. Except for Babs, he'd never confessed all his sins to anyone. Not even Bo, and especially not to Linnea.

But he was in love with Kelly, and for reasons he couldn't

fathom, she was in love with him too. If Kodiak wanted to share his life with her, and he did, there couldn't be any secrets between them. *They always have a way of coming out, don't they?* And of all people, he knew just how quickly lives could shatter once they did.

*Those who choose to forget the past are condemned to repeat it.*

Her back to his chest, she sat between his legs on the blanket. Munching on popcorn, and sipping on wine, they watched the lights burst up in the sky. His arms folding around her, he kissed the spot beneath her ear. "I love you, Kelly."

"I love you too."

He took a breath. "I just need you to know that."

"What's wrong?" Twisting her neck, pretty blue eyes sought his own.

Maybe she detected a change in his tone, the hesitancy in his voice. Kodiak wished there was a way to ease into this, to make it palatable, but he couldn't think of one.

"Nothing." Stroking her arms, he kissed the top of her head. *I just needed to hear you say it one more time.*

"Truth for a truth, my man." Turning around to straddle his lap, Kelly pulled the tie from his hair. "What is it?"

"You know everything else there is to know about me, so I think you're ready to hear it now."

*At least I hope so.*

"Hear about what?"

"My wife." His gaze cast downward, he gave her a tremulous smile. "Although, technically, she never really was."

*God, where do I even begin?*

Gathering his thoughts, Kodiak rubbed his lips together. In a silent bid for him to continue, Kelly squeezed his hands.

Nodding, he inhaled. "As far back as I can remember, my father told me that since I was his son, God had promised to give me a most precious gift. They put her in my arms when I was ten years old, then I promised to love and care for her all my life when I was sixteen."

Confused, her eyes searched his. Kelly knew this part. At least, she thought she did.

"I promised to marry her, give her babies, and bring them up to serve my father and his church. Then Jonathan and all the rest happened, so I had to go. Not just for me, but to save *her*. She didn't understand, though, and was crying so hard when I left. *That's all I ever did, make her cry.* I promised to come back, and I always keep my promises. We'd get married, have babies, but fuck my father, somehow, I was going to get her out of that godforsaken place. Live a peaceful life somewhere far away from there, you know?"

Remaining silent, Kelly nodded.

"But when I came back for her, she was gone. And I got angry. Lost my mind for a while. It's hard to put into words but see, she was the only good thing I had to hold onto my entire miserable life, and without her I didn't have one."

She reached up, stroking his face with her fingers. "What did you do, baby?"

"I went back to Alaska. Finished out my enlistment. I had planned to re-up, build us a house there, but…all the while, I was looking for her."

"And you found her." The muscles in Kelly's throat twitched as she swallowed.

"You know I did." Kodiak couldn't help it, his lip curled into a smirk. "I moved into an apartment around the corner from where she was living. She wasn't the little girl I left behind. All grown up, she was beautiful. For a year, I watched her from a distance, just waiting to see who came sniffing around. And that was my mistake, you see."

"Why?"

"Because eventually, someone did come. And I snapped." Chewing on the inside corner of his lip, he shrugged. "Though considering what happened later, it was the best mistake I ever made."

Her brows drawing together, she pulled her head back. "What happened later?"

"I talked to her, several times, and she didn't even recognize me." His laugh sardonic, Kodiak shook his head. "Imagine that? My own wife had no idea who I was. That only made me angrier. With her. And him. Then an opportunity came my way, and I took it."

"Opportunity?"

"To get my wife back." He took Kelly's hand, rubbing his thumb along hers, just so he could feel her skin. "There's no excuse for what I did. No matter how you look at it, and believe me I have, my actions were unconscionable."

"Tell me." Her voice was a borderline plea.

"She was running like the devil himself was chasing her. Crying. You know, I always hated seeing her cry." Closing his eyes, Kodiak was back on Ash Street. Four years ago, now, but he could still see her. Louboutins in her hand. Mascara running down her face. "I was just going to walk her home, but then she fell. Hurt her foot something awful. Toe all bloody. So, I carried her to my apartment instead."

"And?" she prompted him.

Opening his eyes, he inhaled. "I tended to her foot. Made her some tea, added a little GHB, and we got to talking." Briefly pausing, Kodiak watched her, waiting for his words to register, for the moment she would recoil. And when she didn't, he continued, "Talking led to kissing. Touching. I came so close to fucking her. Would have too, until she called me by his name, thinking I was him."

Her face blank, Kelly just stared. Kodiak couldn't tell what she was thinking, or if she was thinking at all. *Disgusted by the sight of me, no doubt.* Not that he could blame her. And he hadn't gotten to the worst part yet.

"She passed out. I guess I should be thankful she doesn't remember any of it. The next morning, I reminded her who I was. Who she was. Her husband. My wife. All those letters she'd written…nothing but lies because she didn't want me. She cried for him." And to be honest, that still ate a hole in his heart. "Then they all showed up at my door to rescue her from the evil monster—me— and Kyan dropped the biggest bombshell of them all. Linnea couldn't be my wife because she was my *sister*. My father…our father…that sonofabitch…why the fuck would he do that?"

It wasn't Kelly's head that was shaking, it was her entire body.

"I fell apart. Died right there and then. It was Bo who put me back together." His voice softening, he reached for her hand again. She let him take it. "After DNA tests confirmed it, I filed for the annulment. Went to Cali for six months. Got therapy. Then Alaska. Never planned on coming back here, because for a very long time, I didn't care if she was my sister. I mean, how do you learn to unlove somebody you've loved your whole life?"

Tears ran down Kelly's face.

"But Linnea was getting married, and she wanted her brother to give her away. So, I came back." Swiping beneath her eyes, Kodiak touched his lips to her brow. He couldn't take seeing Kelly cry either. "And then, on New Year's Eve, I kissed the most beautiful girl in the world, and for the first time in my life, I felt something real for a woman who wasn't my sister."

She licked her lips. "Is that it?"

"Christ, wasn't that enough? There isn't anything else. I swore to myself I'd take it to the grave. I didn't want you, or Linnea, or anyone to ever know…"

*…my darkest parts. The wrongness inside me.*

He waited and waited for Kelly to speak, but she just sat there. Her hand, limp in his, she didn't utter a word.

"Say something."

She swiped at her eyes, and after a moment that seemed to go on forever, she spoke, "Back in college, there was this professor. Good looking for an older man—forty was old to me then. Dark hair, graying at the temples. Glasses. Your typical academic type. He was imposing and authoritative like Brendan, flirty like Dillon— thought he was God's gift to women too." Biting her lip, she looked down at her lap. "I sort of had a crush on him. Anyway, I was at a bar over in Wrigleyville—Cubby Bear, you ever been there?"

"No, but I know the place."

College kids. Baseball fans. Plenty of booze. Acid churning in his gut, Kodiak had a feeling he knew where this was going.

"I don't know how he found me there, but he did. This 80s hair band was playing that night." With a toss of her head, blonde hair curtained her face. Kelly wouldn't look at him. "I was already wasted, but he bought me a drink. Next thing I know, we're in a cab. I don't remember anything after that. When I woke up, I was alone, naked in my bed. Torn clothes lying on the floor. His…his semen, crusted between my thighs. It was noon on a Sunday. I went to his office and confronted him on Monday. You know what he did?"

His throat went dry. And with his airway constricting, Kodiak couldn't answer.

"He laughed and said no one would ever believe me. I had no proof, and besides, I wanted it anyway."

*I'll kill the motherfucker. Feed him his own dick.*

He knew right then it was over.

After what happened to her, how could she love him knowing what he'd done? It all made sense now. Kelly became the ice queen to protect herself. And Stacy, that fucking bitch, she knew. She took advantage of a broken, vulnerable girl, and when things didn't go how she wanted them to, she left her.

If anything, Kodiak was glad he at least removed that vile woman from her life.

Surprising him, Kelly cupped his cheek in her hand. He held it there, tracing his fingers on her warm, soft skin, memorizing how wonderful it felt, while he still could.

"Yes, what you did was horrible and wrong. I know first-hand how those missing moments in time must be haunting her. But oddly enough, I understand why you did the things you did. You wanted her to see you, didn't you?"

As her husband, the man who'd always loved her.

"Your father was cruel—and sick. He put you in that position. Not. You." Digging her fingers into his biceps, she shook him. "I never thought I could ever be with a man again, but then came you. You are *not* the terrible things you've done. I see your heart, Seth Black. I see it and it's beautiful."

Not what he was expecting to hear, saline burned in his eyes.

"How do you learn to unlove someone? You don't. You can't. It's impossible. And I know that because there's nothing in this world that could ever make me stop loving you."

This woman.

His queen.

God knows, he didn't deserve her.

"I love you."

Her arms wound tightly about his neck. "Good, because you're stuck with me."

*Gladly.*

And with fireworks going off all around them, he kissed her.

# Twenty-One

The sky outside his bedroom window looked heavy and dank, brief flashes of lightning breaking into the darkness somewhere off in the distance. Nestled against his chest, Kelly lay asleep, her warm breath fanning his skin. He still couldn't believe it. This amazing, wonderful, and beautiful woman was his. And he was hers. For always.

Running his fingers through her hair, Kodiak glanced at the clock on the nightstand. Three o'clock in the morning. She'd be waking soon. Her typical day began early, but now that she and Leo had a full staff, Kelly could start taking more time for herself.

Maybe he'd get her the puppy she'd always wanted. A hypoallergenic one, like a doodle. Kodiak made a mental note to look into it.

And to start looking for a house.

They'd already discussed combining households. Kelly stayed at his place most of the time, but he couldn't live in his sister's old row house forever. Well, technically, he could, but he'd rather not. The loft, though convenient, was too small, the walls too thin, especially with Kevin around. Something close to First Avenue and Coventry Park would be ideal. A townhouse with room to grow and a little backyard. But properties like that didn't come along often, and when they did, they were snatched up before a 'For Sale' sign could make it to the front lawn.

Smiling to himself, Kodiak kissed her brow. It would come. They had all the time in the world, after all.

Warm and wet, her tongue peeked out, circling his nipple. He tipped her chin up, and bringing her lips to his, Kodiak took possession of her mouth. A fuck first thing in the morning was his favorite fuck of the day. He was up for it any time, all the time, but there was something about the realness and rawness of it then. Mind clear. Rested. His dick already hard.

Kelly slid down his chest. Kissing his abs, her nails teased his balls, and with a hungry-sounding moan, she took the tip into her mouth.

The sensation intense, he hissed at the contact. "Yeah, baby, suck me."

He could feel her wicked smile against his flesh. She paused briefly, her fingertips tracing the veins on his shaft, before greedily taking him down her throat. Gagging and sputtering, Kelly choked on his length, but nothing could deter her from reaching her goal.

Enthusiasm. It makes all the difference.

Fisting her hair, Kodiak tugged. "Let me see."

Pink-tipped breasts grazing his thigh, sultry blues flashed up at him. Hollowed out cheeks. Lips stretched thin, saliva dribbling from the corners. She looked beautiful.

"Fuck."

Fire ramping up his spine, he pulled her off his dick to kiss her. Kodiak didn't want to come yet, and when he did, it wasn't going to be inside her perfect, little mouth.

"I love how you suck me." Nibbling along her jaw, he penetrated her with his fingers. "Like you'll die if you don't taste my cum."

"I might. Why do I want you so bad?"

"Because you love me." Removing his fingers, he lined up his cock with her entrance. "And I love you."

In one delicious movement, Kodiak buried himself deep inside her.

Kelly made that high-pitched squeaky sound he loved like she was surprised how well he filled her. They just fit. There was no denying it.

His hand at her throat, he fucked her. A man on a mission, he thrust up, hitting that spot inside her over and over again. Kodiak knew her body as well as his own, learned all her tells. Straddling him, Kelly pushed out her breasts and arched her back, her wet walls clenching down on his dick.

"I'm going to put a baby in you," he rasped, as the pain of approaching relief sliced through him. "Fill this pussy up with my cum."

Then with a loud roar, he came like a freight train inside her.

They lay together after. Watching lightning flicker out the window, his fingers lazily strummed through her cunt, pushing his cum back inside. Not that it mattered. There'd be no baby. Kelly took her pill religiously every morning. Still, the thought that a part of him remained with her pleased him, made him feel more connected to her somehow.

The sky hadn't even begun to lighten when Kelly left for work. Too early to coax Linnea out of the house for a run, he put the kettle on for tea. His sister and Dillon were going through a rough patch. Grieving. Trying to start a new life together. All the conflicting emotions that come with it. Heavy stuff.

Settling himself on the sofa with his tea, he'd just opened his Mac when he heard a knock at the door. Kodiak didn't get visitors often, especially at this hour of the morning, and thinking Kelly must've returned for something and had forgotten her key, jumped up to answer it.

A sad, dejected-looking Dillon stood there on his porch.

"Sorry to show up here like this, but I figured you'd be up," he said, making his way inside.

Closer now, lightning illuminated a heavy sky. This couldn't be good.

"Is everything okay?"

"No." Plowing his fingers through the mop on his head, Dillon heaved a sigh. "Nothing is okay."

"Can I do anything?" Kodiak asked, even though he knew he probably couldn't. His sister and Dillon had to find their own way through this. "Just name it."

"Linn…I need you to look out for her and Charlotte for me." He rubbed his bloodshot eyes. The poor guy looked like he hadn't slept in a week, and knowing him, Kodiak would bet that he hadn't. "I'm going to Dublin for a while. Got a flight out this afternoon. That's why I came by here so early."

"I don't understand…"

But he did.

"When will you be back?"

"I don't know." With a shake of his head, Dillon took a ragged breath.

Kodiak placed a reassuring hand on his shoulder. "It's all going to work out."

And he wasn't just saying that. Linnea loved Dillon, of that he was sure, but she'd loved his brother too. That had to be fucking with her head. She just needed time to sort through all those feelings.

"Sure doesn't feel like it."

"Trust me, it will." And he hugged him. "Have a little faith, brother."

Dillon promised to check in from time to time while he was away. Kodiak promised he would look after his sister and the baby. Not that Linnea needed him to. She was the strongest person he'd ever known. But as her brother, he'd always be there in any way she wanted him to be.

Sipping on his now lukewarm tea, he skimmed through his inbox. "Jesus, fucking enough already."

Another email. They'd been arriving more frequently in the past few months. When was this going to stop? What in the hell could

Jarrid possibly want? Curiosity getting the better of him, his finger hovered. Then he came to his senses and hit delete.

Friday night, and he and Kelly were doing what they loved to do most. Absolutely nothing. Chilling with a beer on the patio, Kodiak had some ribs cooking on the grill, Cubs game playing on the TV. More than anything else, they enjoyed a relaxing evening at home together.

Opening the foil to check on the ribs, he glanced over his shoulder. Knees bent, Kelly held a Kindle on her lap, engrossed in whatever it was she was reading. *One of them dirty books with a naked dude on the cover, no doubt.* He smirked to himself. "Read me the first line of that book you got there, Snicks."

"I'm going to fuck you."

*Oh, yeah. Keep reading, baby.*

He chuckled. "Ribs should be ready in about thirty minutes."

"Cole slaw's in the fridge, beans are on the stove," she replied without looking up. "I'll get the corn as soon as I'm done with this chapter."

"I got it." Kodiak bent over to kiss her. "Read your book."

Husking corn is a bitch. Damn silks. No matter how he unzipped the leaves from the cob, some of them always remained. He was still trying to get them off when Kelly came in, looking guilty as all get out, with his phone.

"I'm sorry, but the caller ID said Decatur Memorial Hospital." She bit her lip. "I figured it was important, so I answered it."

"Thanks, babe. It's okay." Kodiak took the phone from her palm. "Hello."

She squeezed his forearm and took the corn out to the patio.

Ten minutes later, he cracked open another beer and joined her.

Sitting down beside her, elbows on his knees, he brought the bottle to his lips. The summer ale, bitter and sweet, seemed to stick in his gullet. Taking another pull, he forced himself to swallow.

Kelly rubbed his thigh. "You okay?"

"Yeah." Though he wasn't quite sure that was true. "My father is dying. Cancer. They want to transfer him to a hospice."

Her lips parted like she wasn't sure what she was supposed to say. Sorry? Good riddance?

"I'm his next of kin," he scoffed. "And his health care surrogate. They need me to sign some papers. I'm going to have to go down there."

"No," she said, emphatically shaking her head. "Fax. Scan. DocuSign. There's no good reason for you to go there."

"There is," he countered. Raising her hand to his lips, Kodiak kissed it. "I've got to clean out the house before the church folk get in there. Make sure final arrangements have been made."

"Why?"

*Because I'm afraid of what they might find if I don't.*

"I'm his son."

"He's done nothing but hurt you, baby." Kelly caressed his face, concern evident in her pretty blue eyes. And he loved her for it.

"He's dying, Snicks. He can't hurt me anymore." Was he trying to convince her of that or himself? "I feel, I dunno, guilty? He's been emailing me for months and I trashed them all."

"You don't owe him anything."

"You're right. I don't." Kelly didn't understand, but then how could she? Holding her close to him, Kodiak tried to convey why he needed to do this. "I don't want him to be a ghost that haunts my soul. He haunted me in life. I won't let him haunt me in death."

Resignedly, she nodded. "Are you looking for some kind of resolution?"

*"Close the circle."*

"Maybe."

She rubbed her finger back and forth across her lips, and after a long pause, Kelly spoke, "What about your sister?"

"What about her?"

"She's his daughter."

"I think you're forgetting something." He polished off the rest of his beer and snickered. "In his twisted mind, Linnea is my wife."

"Jesus, don't go," Kelly pleaded.

"He's still my father. I have to."

"I have a really bad feeling about this."

He kissed her forehead.

*Me too, Snicks. Me too.*

# Twenty-Two

He debated whether to tell Linnea at all. As far as she was concerned, Jarrid was already dead. But in the same vein that Kodiak couldn't move forward with Kelly keeping secrets from her, he couldn't keep them from his sister either. Besides, his heart harbored far too many. There wasn't room for another.

Glancing over at him from the passenger seat of their rented Chevy Tahoe, Linnea reached across the console and took hold of his hand.

Lacing their fingers together, Kodiak squeezed. He knew this was difficult for her. Returning to Crossfield was the last thing he wanted to do. Nothing there except bad memories for both of them. Linnea came along to support him anyhow, and just as any other siblings would, they'd see to their father's final journey.

But then he and his sister weren't like other siblings, now, were they?

"There's a rest area coming up if you need to stop and feed the baby or anything."

"That's okay. She's good for a while." Linnea peeked over at Charlotte, asleep in the car seat behind her. "I'd just as soon get there."

"And get it over with?"

Because that's what Kodiak wanted too. Once they attended to all this unpleasantness, they'd be free.

"Every mile that passes, the pit in my stomach gets bigger. What the hell do I even say to him?" Her laugh bitter, she muttered, "I know what I'd like to say."

"You don't have to see him, Linnea."

"This is going to sound strange, but I want to." With a token shrug, her gaze turned in his direction. "I want Jarrid to have to face me, knowing that I know what he did, and it didn't break us."

Maybe Linnea needed to close the circle too.

"Bo and Ava are getting married right about now." Glancing at the time, his sister changed the subject. A smile gracing her beautiful face, she added, softly, "You and Kelly are next."

"Think so, do you?" The corner of his mouth sneaking up, Kodiak chanced a look her way.

She nodded. "I know so."

"What about you?"

"What about me?"

"You and Dillon."

"We talked about it…" Her smile fell, and turning toward the window, Linnea sighed. "…I haven't heard from him since he got there. Have you?"

*Almost every day.* Devoted to his sister, he checked in often. Dillon made him promise not to tell her, though.

"He said to me once, there's no avoiding your destiny." Reassuring her, Kodiak squeezed her hand. "And you're his."

The stretch of highway familiar, fields of grain moved past the window. Silos. Billboards touting everything from clean restrooms and cheap gas to 'Jesus Saves.'

"We're almost there."

"I figured we should go to the hospital first." The road to

Crossfield was at the next exit. "We can grab some lunch and head over to the house after."

"Yeah, okay," she agreed. "Maybe we'll get lucky, and no one will notice we're there."

"Doubt that." He snickered. "You know how they are. The church folk will come calling the second they see us pull up in the driveway."

"Can't wait."

"I'll handle them."

They were considered defectors. Kodiak had his reservations regarding how he and Linnea would be received by their father's brainwashed worshippers—not to mention Crossfield's townsfolk. Whether welcomed or vilified, and he presumed it would be the latter, he was prepared to take on the brunt of it.

His arm around Linnea's waist, they were ushered into a little room by the nurse's station. The smell of rubbing alcohol and scorched coffee turning his stomach, he pulled out a chair for his sister, and then took a seat for himself.

The doctor, a nondescript man dressed in surgical scrubs of green, sat down across from them. "As I told you on the phone, your father's cancer is quite advanced—stage four. That means what started in his lungs has metastasized to other parts of his body—brain, bones, liver. If he'd have presented sooner, we might have been able to buy him some time, but…"

"I understand." Reaching for Linnea's hand, Kodiak wet his chapped lips.

"At this point, hospice is really the only option." His glasses perched on the end of his nose, he looked at them from over the frame. "He'll be kept comfortable."

"How is he?" Kodiak inquired, knowing it would seem strange if he didn't.

"Sometimes he's with us and other times not. He's easily agitated, confused, and that's to be expected. Your father is declining rapidly, which is why I contacted you. As soon as you sign the consent, I can initiate the transfer to hospice. We'll get him a bed there as soon as possible."

"All right," he said, nodding. "Thank you."

"I'll send the nurse in with the necessary paperwork." Shaking his hand, the doctor stood. "I'm very sorry."

"What a beautiful baby."

Smiling at Charlotte while Kodiak signed the stack of forms she brought in, the young nurse seemed uncomfortable. Acknowledgment by health care proxy. Do not resuscitate order. Consent to withhold treatment. No wonder she wouldn't look at him.

"Would you like to see your dad now? He's been asking for you."

Turning to Linnea, he nodded. Her hand clasped in his, holding the baby to his chest with the other, they followed the nurse down the hall. Thinner than the last time he saw him, cheeks sunken, his skin sallow, Jarrid lay semi-reclined on the bed. Oxygen tubing up his nostrils, intravenous fluids dripping into his veins, he wasn't nearly as formidable as Kodiak remembered him being either.

"Pastor Black, your son is here." Gently rubbing his shoulder, the nurse attempted to rouse him. "Jarrid."

Opening his eyes, he squinted at the fluorescent lights. He turned his head on the pillow and looking past him, a tear slipped from the corner of his glassy, green eyes. He fixed his gaze on Linnea and smiled.

"Grace."

She was quiet in the car. Staring out the window, Linnea hadn't spoken a word since they left the hospital.

Exiting off the highway, Kodiak turned onto the road that led into Crossfield. The silence deafening, he couldn't take it anymore. "Say something."

"He thinks I'm my mother."

"Today." *Tomorrow he could think you're the Queen of England.*

"You heard the nurse. They're giving him a ton of meds, and his clarity comes and goes. He's not in his right mind, Linnea."

"Was he ever?"

Blowing out a breath, he shrugged. *Debatable.*

"I'm sorry, Seth, but the way he was staring creeped me out." Adjusting the seatbelt, Linnea turned toward him. "They say people who are dying can see things we don't—the spirits of those who died before them, coming to help them cross over."

Glancing at his sister, Kodiak snickered. "Who's they? John Edwards? Tyler Henry? *The Long Island Medium?*"

*You shouldn't be watching that shit, little one. It's fucking with your head.*

"No, smart-ass," she said, smacking him on the thigh. "It's a well-known phenomenon. There's documentaries about it. Dying people pointing to something no one else can see, talking to folks long since gone. Anyway, I got chills. Because what if my mother was right there behind me?"

*As long as Catherine doesn't stop by, we're good.*

Raising his brow, he shot her a look.

"Do I resemble her all that much?"

It hurt his heart to think Linnea didn't know what her own mother looked like. He remembered her as ethereal. An angel here on Earth. A beautiful life wasted, rotting beneath the ground for twenty-five years now. Just another sin of their father's.

"Grace's hair was the palest blonde." Linnea's the color of rich buttered toffee. "But otherwise, yeah, you do."

Three wooden crosses, twenty feet high, appeared along the side of the two-lane road. Staring straight ahead, his sister reached for his hand. "God, I loathe this place."

*Welcome back to Hell.*

Old clapboard houses sporadically came into view. The rusted gates of the cemetery where Jonathan and her mother lay.

"God doesn't live here, little sister."

"It's more depressing now than it was seven years ago."

Midwestern Gothic at its finest, she slowly shook her head. "I didn't think that was even possible."

In all that time, Linnea had never been back. But then he hadn't either. The last time he was here, he took the portrait of Grace off his father's wall.

Stopped at the lone red light in the center of town, it all looked the same to him. Crumbling brick. Paint, peeling, cracked, and faded. "Lunch?"

"Yeah, I'm hungry."

He parked along the curb, in front of the sad-looking, little diner. "I'll order some groceries when we get to the house."

"This isn't Chicago, you know." Getting Charlotte out of her car seat, Linnea handed her to him. "Doubt that Kirby's delivers."

"There's a Kroger's in Decatur. I'm sure they do." Wrapping his arm around her waist, Kodiak sniggered. "C'mon."

The diner sure hadn't changed. Same checkered tile on the floor. Booths covered in red vinyl. An old-fashioned soda fountain. It'd probably looked like this since the 1950s.

Only one table was occupied. An older couple, dining on French fries and club sandwiches, sat by a window in the corner. Fortunately, he didn't recognize them.

She came out from the back. Grabbing a coffee pot, Hazel refilled the old lady's cup. She hadn't changed much either. Turning around to head over to their booth, her eyes went wide.

Kodiak chuckled. "She looks like she's seen a ghost."

"Who?" Facing the door, Linnea hadn't seen her yet. She turned around to look behind her.

The woman's jaw about fell to the floor. "Tommy."

A sandy-haired young man poked his head through the opening to the kitchen. The last time Kodiak saw the kid he was a gangly, pimply-faced teenager. He was a grown man now. His gaze flicked between him and his sister, then he burst through the swinging doors. Glancing to his mother, he walked over, Hazel following right behind him.

"Oh, good Lord." The woman he'd known all his life angled her head, peering closely at his face. "Seth Thomas Black, is that you?"

"It's me."

"With all that hair and the beard, I wasn't sure at first." With a quiet laugh she waved her hand in front of him. "You look like Jesus."

His sister hid a giggle behind her hand.

The stunned young man found his voice then, "Linnea?"

"Hi, Tommy."

"And who do we have here?" Hazel asked, patting the baby's curls.

"This is Charlotte."

"Bless her little heart, she's just precious." Holding her hand to her buxom chest, she smiled. "How old?"

"Seven months."

"Tommy's got himself a wife now and two boys," Hazel informed his sister as if she had some interest in her son. Then she took a step back, and casting her steely gaze on him, she glared. "Don't tell me she's yours."

"Yeah, Charlotte's mine." With a roll of his eyes, Kodiak sniggered. "Jesus, Hazel, she's my niece. That's all."

"I'm sorry, it's just that…" Flustered, the poor woman looked up at the ceiling. "…we'll talk some in a minute. Let's get some food in your bellies first."

They ordered their lunch, and while they were eating, he and Linnea caught Hazel up on the past four years—her marriage to Kyan, and his tragic passing.

"I'm so sorry, dear." Hazel squeezed his sister's hand. "He seemed like such a wonderful young man."

"He was." Linnea sniffled, dabbing at her eyes with a napkin.

The old couple got up to leave. Hazel stopped talking to wave to them as they passed.

"Lock the door, Tommy, and put the closed sign up." Looking between the two of them, she sighed, her expression turning deadly serious. "You shoulda stayed gone. What in tarnation did you come back here for?"

"We're not staying long," Kodiak explained. "Jarrid's at Decatur Memorial. We're getting him transferred to hospice. Cancer. So, we're just here to, you know, take care of things."

"I don't think they know." Staring absently through the glass, she pursed her lips.

*Huh?*

"What do you mean?"

"The folks at the crazy church." Tapping her nail on the Formica, Hazel emphasized every word. "I don't think they know he's taken ill. Saw him myself a couple of weeks ago and he seemed all right. Skinnier, I reckon, but…"

"That makes no sense, Hazel." Leaning forward, Kodiak planted his elbows on the table across from her. "It's Sunday. Someone had to hold services, because it sure as hell wasn't him, so they must know something."

"I'm telling you, they don't," she insisted, wagging her finger. "Things have changed since you've been gone, and not for the better, let me tell you."

"How so?"

"After Linnea left, Jarrid pulled in the reins." Hazel turned to his sister. "I'm so sorry, girl, he put the blame on you for everything. The rules they must abide by are even more strict. All the children are taught at home now—public school is forbidden. Associating with non-members is forbidden. No one marries unless he says so…

*Course not.*

"Do you remember Jeremy Blythe? Ada's boy?"

"I remember Ada." One of the church ladies, she was a devout member of Jarrid's flock.

"He's a few years younger than us," Tommy said in an attempt to jog Linnea's memory.

"Yeah." She nodded. "Skinny kid. Dark hair and braces."

"Well, the braces are gone, and he sure ain't a kid no more."

"Your daddy has taken up quite an interest in that boy," Hazel said with a tip of her chin. "Been raisin' him to follow in his footsteps."

*Am I supposed to give a shit?*

"Better him than me." With a shrug, Kodiak took a sip of coffee.

"Be wary of that boy when he comes callin'," she warned, her finger wagging again. "All I'm sayin'."

"C'mon now, Hazel, why should I worry about some twenty-something-year-old punk kid?" After surviving Reverend John, Jarrid, the very thought was laughable.

"You and Linnea have committed apostasy in their eyes. The power he's been given by your daddy has already gone to his head." Reaching across the table, she took both his hands in hers. "If I were you, I'd make it abundantly clear y'all don't plan on stayin'. Oh, and they believe the two of you are married. You might wanna let 'em go on thinkin' that."

"Why?" Taken aback, Linnea cocked her head. "Seth is my brother, and they should know it. They should know all the horrible things Jarrid has done. How twisted he really is."

"Girl, what you're speakin' is heresy to them looney tunes." Kodiak knew their way of thinking. So did his sister. Hazel wasn't lying. "You know what the punishment is for that, don't you?"

In biblical times it was death.

"Trust me, withholding the truth could be the one thing that saves you."

# Twenty-Three

So far, so good.

They'd been at the house for an hour now, and no one had come sniffing around. Yet. It was just a matter of time, of that Kodiak was sure. There'd be a knock at the door sooner or later.

While he and his sister had taken Hazel's warning to heart, it seemed to them she was also being a little dramatic. Fallen from grace, they expected dirty looks, to be the objects of their scorn, but it's not like they were in danger of being burned at the stake for chrissakes. And now, there were other matters to attend to.

Linnea wasn't wasting any time. Balancing the baby on her hip, she surveyed the family room off the kitchen and sighed. "We'll tackle one room at a time, sort, pack, patch, and paint. Might as well start right here. You keeping any of this furniture?"

"No, we can leave it. If Jeremy Blythe wants it, he can have it."

The house belonged to the church. Once Jarrid passed, and his successor was named, the new pastor would move in.

"All right then." She settled Charlotte in her Pack and Play. "We're going to need moving boxes."

"Already ordered some." He bent to kiss her cheek. "And the groceries. Believe it or not, Kirby's delivers. Should be here in about thirty minutes."

Staring at the wall of black and white photographs, Linnea shook her head. The spot where the portrait of her and her mother once was, had been replaced with a yearbook photo of Grace. "I do look like her. It's almost spooky."

"Didn't I tell you?"

"There's so many pictures of us," she commented, taking them down from the wall. "Catherine didn't keep any."

*Before Grace died, she did.*

"Jarrid was obsessed, obviously." Kodiak chuckled. "You must get that from him."

"These aren't just pictures, Seth. They're moments." Looking over at him, Linnea spoke so earnestly, "And it's moments that make up your life."

"Are you trying to say our father's sentimental?" Because he sincerely doubted it.

"I don't know. Maybe." She shrugged. "But they must've meant something to him. Could be his memories were all he had."

"Yeah, I guess." He picked up a photo of himself in a football jersey. Kodiak still didn't think so, but if it made Linnea feel better, he wasn't about to disagree with her.

The ringing of the doorbell startling him for a second, he dropped the frame onto the couch. "Must be the groceries. I'll get it."

Only it wasn't.

Standing as tall as Kodiak did, the twenty-something-year-old kid himself stood on the other side of the door. Clean-shaven. Green eyes. Dark hair, the ends curling at the collar of his button-up shirt. Creases pressed into his khaki pants, his hands folded neatly in front of him.

*Ah, Jeremy, surprised it took you this long.*

"Who are you?"

"I could ask you the same question. It's been a while, but even with the way you look now, I'm sure I know who you are. Seems you don't remember me, Seth." Politely, he extended his hand. "Jeremy Blythe."

"It's been a *long* while. You were a little kid."

"Pastor said he'd get you back here." He smirked, trying to peer into the house. "Where is he?"

Either Jeremy was playing games or Hazel had been right. Kodiak didn't trust him, or anyone from the church for that matter, but he saw no reason not to tell him.

"In the hospital. My father's quite ill. You didn't know?"

"I did not. He only told me he had personal business to take care of and asked if I would minister for him in his absence." Jeremy paused for a moment, his lips pressed together, before lifting his gaze. "I must go to him."

*Nope. Can't let you do that.*

Kodiak couldn't say what his reasoning was—a feeling in his gut, maybe—but he was going to keep this guy at arm's length. It was best to have as little contact with him and the church folk as possible. Besides, the last thing anyone needed was to turn Jarrid's deathbed into a looney-tune prayer revival.

"I'm sorry, except for immediate family, he can't have visitors," he explained, feigning a sympathetic smile. "I'm sure you understand."

"I see." Jeremy nodded, but oddly, he was smirking. "Kindly tell him he'll be in our prayers and do let me know if there's anything you need."

"We'll be sure to do that and thank you." Hearing his sister coming down the hall, Kodiak went to close the door.

"Is your wife here with you?"

Charlotte in her arms, Linnea opened it back up. "Hello, Jeremy."

"Oh, there's a child." Ignoring her greeting, Jeremy's gaze flicked from the baby back to him.

A subtle nod was his only response.

"The gifts of God are great. For this child, too, we shall pray."

But his smile was leering. "I feel I must tell you, Seth, you and your wife won't be welcomed back here."

"Wasn't expecting to be." Curling his arm around his sister, he held her close to his side. "We're only here for my father."

"Well, goodnight then." Jeremy grinned, and it was chilling.

Kodiak closed and locked the door.

With a flip of her hair, Linnea snickered. "I think I liked him better when he had braces."

She didn't want to be here.

It wasn't a special occasion or anything, just a backyard barbecue at Katie's, but Kevin cajoled her into it. So, Kelly made a melon-berry salad with goat cheese and honey to bring along, and here she was. It's not like she had anything else to do anyway. Though, honestly, she'd much rather be home alone, stretched out on her sofa with a pint of chow mein, binging something on Netflix. Or better yet, at the row house on Oak Street with her man. But he wasn't there.

Still in Crossfield, a week had gone by since he left. And it had been the longest damn week of her life. Because Kelly missed him. He called her every day, of course, and usually more than once. Texted too. Kodiak and Linnea had moved their father into hospice and were packing up his house. He sounded okay and claimed that he was, but she couldn't help but worry. That town was nothing except a minefield of triggers for him.

And so, to pass the time and keep herself from going crazy, she was here on Katie's patio watching Kevin with his dick up Brendan's ass while he cooked steaks on the grill.

"What do those two have to talk about anyway?"

"I don't know." Declan squirming to get off her lap, Katie scrunched her shoulders. "Guy stuff, I guess."

"C'mon now, Brendan could be his father." She snickered, waving a hand in front of her face like she was shooing at a fly. "What guy stuff?"

"There you go again, Auntie." Tossing her blonde waves, her niece tapped a finger to her cheek. "Let's see…sports, cars, sex."

She harrumphed with a roll of her eyes.

"You asked." Katie giggled.

"You're so bad."

"And she's so good at it." Bending over the back of the sofa, Brendan kissed his wife. "Steaks are ready."

*I did not need to know that, thank you very much.*

They moved over to the table. Sitting beneath an umbrella, strung with twinkling lights, they piled food on their plates. At least with only the four of them and the baby, Kelly wouldn't have to talk much.

"Do you know when Kodiak and Linnea will be back?" His gaze on her, Brendan cut into his steak.

"They're working on the house. Settling things." She couldn't help but sigh. "So, they'll be there until…you know. I wish he'd hurry up."

Everyone put down their forks to look at her.

"That sounded bad, didn't it?" Covering her mouth with a napkin, Kelly finished chewing and took a breath. "I didn't mean it like that. Not really. Well, kind of. He wasn't a good person, right? Even so, wishing for someone's death is horrible of me."

"It's okay, Auntie." Katie patted her back.

"I never met the man, though some of us have." Brendan tried some melon and goat cheese salad. Shrugging a shoulder, he licked his lips. "Interesting."

"Bo."

"Yes, Bo. Dillon, Jesse, and Chloe did too." He picked up his beer. Grasping the bottle at the neck, it dangled in his fingertips. "I know what he did to Kodiak and Linnea, the damage it caused, the pain he put them through. I was there to see the aftermath of it. Jarrid Black is *not* a good man, but he fathered two of the most incredible human beings I know, so I'd like to think there's something good in him."

Brendan raised the bottle, tossing back half its contents.

"He might not deserve the comfort of having his children with him as he leaves this world, but they deserve to have that peace, you know?"

She nodded.

"You know, Kelly, you're among family here. You can always tell us what you're feeling. We won't judge you. No matter how it sounds."

"I just can't shake this awful feeling I have." And she couldn't explain why. "I want it over and I want him home."

"I know, sweetheart." Coming around the table, Brendan got down on his haunches to hug her. "Soon."

Kelly glanced over to see Katie wink at her.

Kevin just smiled.

Maybe she'd misjudged him. Brendan wasn't a lecherous predator. He was actually a good and decent man, who loved and cared for everyone in his family.

*Including me, and after I've been so shitty to him.*

"I owe you an apology."

"Whatever for?" he asked, pulling his head back.

"For being such a bitch to you," she mumbled.

Shaking his head like he wasn't sure he heard her right, Brendan raised his brow.

"Well, you guys don't call me the ice queen for nothing."

He smirked. "Does this mean I get to call you Auntie then?"

Katie and Kevin grinned.

"No." She smiled. "Kelly will do."

# Twenty-Four

On Monday, Kodiak and Linnea got Jarrid settled in at hospice. A beautiful building with lovely pastoral landscaping, surrounded by woodlands, it looked homey. Like it could be someone's house. That was the intention, he supposed.

There were eight comfortable bedroom suites, each one well-appointed, spacious, and private. Floor-to-ceiling windows with tranquil views of nature. Shelves filled with plants and books. A pull-out sofa so loved ones could remain at the bedside if they wanted to.

A community kitchen provided home-cooked meals around the clock. The staff informed them their father could eat whatever he wanted, whenever he wanted it, or not at all. His choice. Toward the end, they should expect that. They were also told a typical hospice stay is three to seven days. Was it terrible he was counting them?

Jarrid was out of it more often than not. Most of the time he didn't know they were there. And others, he didn't realize who they were.

When Kodiak ran an errand in town, most folks didn't recognize him there either. Funny, considering Crossfield was the size of a fucking postage stamp, and everyone in it had known him all his life.

"It's all that hair and the beard. Hides your handsome face," his sister explained. "I didn't recognize you at first either, remember?"

How could he forget? And to this day, that still bothered him.

Visits with Jarrid were usually brief. Because what was the point? Linnea would glance around the room, waiting for a sign from the spirit world. Kodiak just stared at his father's chest, waiting for the moment he stopped breathing.

On this particular morning, when they walked into Jarrid's room, he was sitting up in bed. Awake and alert, the good book rested in his hands.

Startled to find him so, Linnea gasped.

Looking back at her, he tossed the Bible onto the bed and smirked.

"What have you done to yourself, boy?" His father scanned him up and down. "You look like shit."

"Could say the same for you, old man."

"Not old. Just dying." A corner of his lip curled, and he tipped his chin. "Is that my granddaughter?"

Exchanging a glance with Linnea, Kodiak nodded. "She is."

"At least you managed to get something right," Jarrid quipped, waving his son over. "Bring her to me. I want to see her."

He went to the bedside. Charlotte reached up to pull on his beard, as she so often did. Smiling down at her, Kodiak kissed her soft, dark curls.

"What's her name?" With rheumy eyes, his smile slack-jawed, Jarrid studied the baby in his arms.

"Charlotte."

"Oh, precious little angel." He stretched his arms out. "Let me have her."

Glancing back at his sister, Linnea's eyes widened in alarm.

Their father must have caught her reaction too. With a snicker, he smirked. "Don't worry, dear. Death's not contagious."

A nurse came waltzing into the room right then. Grateful for the interruption, Kodiak took a step back. Her smile effervescent, she offered Jarrid a small plastic cup. For some reason, she reminded him of Chloe.

"Looking handsome as ever, Pastor Black," she flattered him, combing the hair from his face with her fingers.

"Call me Jarrid, dear."

"And this has to be your beautiful family."

"Indeed, they are. My son and his wife." Then his face lit up. "And this pretty, little blessing is my granddaughter."

This was fucked up.

*Linnea's my sister and you know it, you sick bastard.*

Kodiak wanted to say it out loud, but he held his tongue.

"How about I grab the camera and take a picture? We can pin it up right there." The nurse pointed to a corkboard on the wall by the bed. "That way you can always see it. Would you like that?"

"You're an angel, dear. Yes, I would love that."

The nurse returned with a Polaroid camera. She took the shot, Kodiak holding Charlotte on one side of the bed, Linnea on the other. Then Jarrid reached for the baby, and with no other choice, he placed her in her grandfather's arms.

*You should get to hold your granddaughter once. So you know what you missed.*

Linnea came over to stand at his side.

The nurse smiled at this facade of a normal family. If she only knew the truth, she'd be mortified. "I can take one for you if you'd like."

"Yeah, sure."

Kodiak handed her his phone. Then she took the photo and left.

"Once again, God has fulfilled his promise." His voice gravelly, Jarrid stroked the baby's hair and glanced at Linnea. "I wish I'd have known sooner. You shouldn't have run."

"She's here now," he said, curling his arm around his sister.

"It's too late."

"For what?"

His laughter cynical, Jarrid shifted his gaze. "Are you staying at the house?"

"Yeah."

"Take what you want and burn the rest," he adamantly instructed. "Leave nothing behind."

Jesus, what could be in there? They hadn't found anything noteworthy yet.

"By chance, did they give you my wallet?"

"I've got it right here." Pulling it out of his back pocket, Kodiak tried to pass it over to his father. He waved his hand away.

"Open it." Jarrid tipped his chin. "There's a key with a number on it."

Small and silver, 319 was etched into the metal. "This one?"

Rubbing circles on Charlotte's little back, he nodded. "That's to a safety deposit box. Citizens Bank of Decatur. The main branch on Water Street."

"I know it."

"Once I'm dead, on your way out of town, go get what's in it. And not until then, you hear me?"

"Yes," he answered with a nod.

Inhaling Charlotte's sweet baby smell, Jarrid held his lips to her brow. "And don't ever come back here."

*No worries. Wasn't planning to.*

Showing off her two bottom teeth, Charlotte patted her grandfather's face. In turn, he kissed her cheek. Linnea stepped in, taking her daughter back.

"Hate me that much, do you?"

"You're not the least bit sorry, are you?" Her emotions raw, she held the baby to her chest.

"Linnea, always the defiant one." Jarrid chuckled, tipping his head to look up at her. "Now what do I have to be sorry for?"

"What you did to Seth. To me. My mother." Linnea glared at him.

His eyes shimmering, he closed them and sighed. "All I ever did was love her."

"You don't know what it is to love anybody." Her pain-filled voice punched a hole in Kodiak's heart. "She's dead because of you."

"Nothing could be further from the truth." Jarrid held his hand out, but Linnea stepped away from his reach. "Is that what Catherine told you?"

"She didn't have to."

"I'm not sorry for anything, daughter. God fulfilled his promise." Beckoning her to come closer, she went to him. Gripping her wrist in his bony fingers, he chuckled softly and grinned. "Has not the one God made you? He created Eve from the rib of Adam. Flesh of his flesh. Bone of his bone. As I have given you to Seth, and he to you. Is there any greater gift?"

Releasing her from his grasp, Jarrid closed his eyes. With his lips turned up at the corners, he slept.

*He is mad.*

Visibly shaken during the drive back to Crossfield, Linnea's hands fidgeted in her lap. Kodiak reached across the console, taking her palm in his. She inhaled sharply through her nose, and lacing their fingers together, leaned against his shoulder.

"I'm sorry."

"It's not your fault." She squeezed his hand tight. "If we were looking for some kind of validation, I guess that was it."

He was surprised they got that much.

"How about we stop at the Dairy Queen on the way home? I'll get you a Dilly Bar, just like I did when you were little."

*That always made you feel better.*

"I'm not little anymore, but I won't say no."

Driving past the high school, the football field where Jonathan took his life, Kodiak diverted his gaze. He went to grab his pen from the console, but then he remembered Charlotte was with them.

"Gosh, high school seems like forever ago."

*Feels like yesterday.*

Linnea looked up from his shoulder. "Can we go by Catherine's old house?"

*Jesus, why?*

It didn't look how he remembered it. No longer weathered and dreary, whoever lived here had painted it a sunny yellow. Planted flowers. Children were playing on the front lawn.

"It looks happy here now." Turning to him, his sister smiled. "I'm glad."

Kodiak smiled too. "Dilly Bar?"

"Yeah."

They were still smiling, licking chocolate-coated ice cream from a stick, as he pulled the Tahoe into the driveway. Until they saw Jeremy on the porch, that is. He stood there, hands on his waist, surveying the place like he already owned it.

Kodiak got Charlotte out of her car seat. "Don't worry. I'll get rid of him."

"Seth." He acted as if Linnea wasn't standing right here beside him. "I've come to see about Pastor. The hospital won't tell me anything."

*They can't. And besides, he's not there anymore.*

Kodiak just smirked.

"It's, um, time for her nap." Throwing a look at Jeremy, his sister took the baby. "I'm going to lay her down."

"You do that, little one." Holding Linnea to his chest, he kissed the top of her head. "I'll only be a minute."

She nodded, and after a fleeting backward glance, went inside the house.

Folding his arms across his chest, Kodiak stared Jeremy down. *Time to put this punk in his place.* "What?"

"I'm sure you can understand my concern." Displaying no emotion, he spoke without inflection, "How is Pastor?"

"Seeing his granddaughter had him in good spirits this morning."

"I need to speak with him."

*Yeah, I bet you do.*

"He should be coming home in a few days."

*It wasn't a lie.*

The muscles in Jeremy's face didn't so much as twitch. Kodiak couldn't tell whether he was relieved or disappointed with the news. He listened to his gut, and something wasn't right here. Holding this kid off would give them more time to prepare for whatever was coming. He just wasn't sure what that was.

"Good." Resembling a creepy Howdy Doody doll, he smiled. Sort of. "Then I'll be going."

"One more thing."

Jeremy turned back around.

"I won't stand for you disrespecting Linnea, understood?"

"She doesn't exist to me." He lifted his chin. "Yet I pray for her soul. I can't abide a murderess."

He tried to hold it in, but he couldn't. He burst out laughing. *Pray for your mama, kid.*

Shaking his head all the way to the back porch, Kodiak took a seat on an old milk crate. He drew on his pen, feeling better as soon as the vapor touched his lungs. Ada and Catherine. Two psycho peas in a pod. It sure as hell explained a lot.

He woke up his phone. Glancing at the photo that remained on the screen, he took another hit and closed out the image. Then opening his messages, Kodiak sent one to Kelly.

*I love you, baby.*

"Linnea." Well past lunchtime, he took to the stairs to see what she wanted to eat.

The baby was asleep in the spare room.

He poked his head inside his, but she wasn't in there either.

Linnea sat on the floor in their father's room. Sheets of paper clutched in her hand, she was crying.

"You wrote me letters." Glancing up at him, tears rolled down her face.

Sitting on the floor beside her, Linnea put the letter in his hand. He'd written it on her eighteenth birthday. Their wedding day.

Held together by a rubber band, a stack of them sat on her lap. Addressed to Linnea. His handwriting on the envelope.

*What the hell?*

Private and personal, those letters were meant only for her.

When she was just a girl, Kodiak sent words of encouragement. How is school? Mind your grandmother. But once they were married, his letters were from a husband who wanted his wife. So, what the fuck was Jarrid doing with them?

Linnea dragged a box from the closet. "Look, there's hundreds of them."

"Five hundred and twenty, give or take."

One every week for the ten years he'd been away.

"I never got any of them."

"I still have every letter you ever sent." *Every picture you drew me. Every photo.* "Remember when I enlisted, and I came to say goodbye?"

"That was a wretched day."

"You wouldn't talk to me. Stomped up to your room and cried yourself to sleep." He let the sheets of paper fall to his lap. "Seems like all I've ever done since then is make you cry."

"You have not," she said, reaching for his hand.

"I hated leaving you here, but I had a plan to get you out of this miserable place." His eyes looking into hers, Kodiak tucked a lock of hair behind her ear. "And until I could, I needed to know you were okay, so I made Jarrid promise you'd write me every week."

"Every Sunday, he'd be at the church steps with his hand out." Softly chuckling at the memory, Linnea retrieved her letter from his lap. "I was so mad that you never wrote me back, I stopped writing them."

*What? But…*

"When did you stop?" His brow knitting in thought, he cocked his head.

"Oh, I don't know. I had to be around fourteen, I think."

*Son of a bitch.*

Kodiak huffed out a breath. "The last letter I got was after Catherine died."

"But how? I didn't write them."

"Jarrid or Catherine must have." He snickered at his own

stupidity. He'd been played. "You started typing them in high school to practice for class. Except it wasn't you, I guess."

"This makes no damn sense. They wanted us together, didn't they?" Rubbing her temple, Linnea momentarily frowned. "So why would my grandmother keep your letters from me? And why does Jarrid have them now?"

*I have a hunch.*

"I can't say for sure." Pausing, Kodiak turned his head. "But I think Catherine might be dead because of it."

"She had a heart attack on the kitchen floor. I'm the one who found her."

"Sure about that?" Because he wasn't.

"Well, no, but...what are you saying?"

"Hear me out." Grasping her hands in his, he squeezed. "What if Catherine had a change of heart? Maybe she just played along with Daddy's twisted plan. And maybe she did what she could to stop it."

"I don't think so," Linnea said, emphatically shaking her head. "She witnessed my signature on the marriage license."

"Someone did a pretty good job signing your name." *At the bottom of every letter, even dotted the 'i' with a heart.* "My guess is that someone signed her name too."

"Jarrid?"

"Who else?" Their father was the most logical choice. "He must've figured out she kept the letters from you. We were married and I was coming home. What was he going to do? The only choice he had was to get rid of her."

"This is just too much."

*Yeah, but hasn't it always been?*

# Twenty-Five

It was just after sunset, that moment of dusk when the last vestiges of pink slip from the darkening navy sky. While Linnea put the baby to bed, Kodiak returned to his seat on the milk crate. Glancing down at his feet, he made a mental note to sweep up his father's old cigarette butts from the porch.

Hymns of worship could be heard coming from the church across the street. What night was this? He'd lost track of the days here, but if they were singing and carrying on like that, it had to be Wednesday. Prayer meetings were on Wednesdays. At least they used to be.

The meetings were a spectacle, really. Worshippers speaking in tongues. Outbursts of praise in unintelligible words. Dancing and shouting *in the spirit*. Raising hands and arms in prayer.

Can't forget the miracles, the divine healings, the prophecies that served as evidence to his sheep. Jarrid was filled with the Holy Spirit. He was God's chosen one. And only he could save them from the growing demonic forces in the world.

*"Satan does not succeed in taking the Bible from us, he works hard at taking us from the Bible."*

Kodiak had to hand it to him. His father put on a good performance. Jarrid was a terrific showman, not the new messiah. There were no miracles. A heap of snake oil and nonsensical ramblings is all it ever was. Folks ate it up, though.

Snickering to himself, Kodiak tipped his head back against the clapboard siding. He took a long hit on his pen, thankful Kelly convinced him to bring extras, because all this shit was fucking with his head.

Linnea had been upstairs a long time. No doubt she got caught up reading more old letters. God, he wished she'd never found them. He'd poured out his heart and soul to her in those letters. Feelings. Dreams. Desires. And she had done the same in return, or so he thought back then. Jarrid must've had quite the laugh at their expense.

The sound of katydids calling mingled with voices in song. Kodiak closed his eyes, slowly releasing the vapor from his lungs. He didn't open them when Linnea sat down beside him, resting against his shoulder.

"That day in the park was supposed to be goodbye."

"What?"

"When I left for Cali, I wasn't going to come back," he admitted.

Glancing up at him, she lifted her head. "Why?"

It was time to let the secrets go. There wasn't a reason to hold onto them anymore.

"Because I still had feelings for you, Linnea. I couldn't quite think of you as my sister." His hand over his heart, Kodiak tapped on his chest. "My head knew it, but not in here. I'd loved you for so long. I didn't know how to stop. So, I got as far away from you as I could."

"Alaska?"

"Yeah, I always loved it there. Thought I could heal in the one place I felt peace." After a pregnant pause, he turned his head to look at her. "I had to protect myself…and you."

"Protect me from what?"

"From me." Ashamed, Kodiak lowered his gaze. "See, there was a lot of fucked-up shit going on in my head."

"Seth, you've got to know it wasn't your fault." Reaching for him, Linnea palmed his cheek.

"We can't blame it all on Daddy, little one." He turned away from her touch, staring into the void of the night sky. "I was angry with myself for not claiming you as soon as I found you. I regretted that I didn't demand they give me leave to be with you on your birthday, marry you in person, and fuck a baby into you right then. I was going to take you back to Alaska with me. Build us a house there. We would have never known then."

*I regretted the one night I had you, I didn't take what I believed to be mine.*

*But I remember the way you taste.*

*And, fuck, I'm your brother. I shouldn't know that.*

"But we do know."

"But my heart didn't care, Linnea. I struggled with it for a very long time." Shaking his head, Kodiak still couldn't look at her. "After what I did, how could you want me to remain in your life as your brother?"

"Because I love you," she simply said, turning his chin toward her.

"Can I ask you something?"

"Anything."

"If the DNA test had gone the other way, what would you have done?" Not that it mattered, but he'd always wondered.

Linnea wet her lips, then softly cleared her throat. "Your desire will be for your husband, and he will rule over you."

The answer didn't surprise him. It's what she'd been taught, after all.

"I wouldn't have wanted it that way."

"I know." She kissed his cheek. "I understand more than you think I do."

Maybe she did.

"I'm okay now, little sister." And he was. "It took a while, but eventually my heart caught up to my head."

"I know that, too, big brother." Twining her arms around his, she laid her head on his shoulder. "You found your person."

Kodiak smiled. That he did.

Voices carried on the gentle August breeze, Jeremy's rising above the rest.

*"If there is found in our midst, a man or a woman, who does what is evil in the sight of the Lord, our God…"*

"Have they always been this obnoxiously loud?"

With a snicker, Kodiak shrugged. "I think he means for us to hear."

*"…we must bring out that man or that woman who has transgressed, done this evil thing…"*

"Well, I'm not interested in hearing it." Grabbing his hand, Linnea stood. "Let's go back in."

*"…we must cast stones upon them, purge the evil from our midst."*

He followed her to the door.

*Crazy motherfucker.*

Then he locked it behind him.

Kodiak spent the morning cleaning up around the back porch. He tossed the old milk crate in the trash, along with the cigarette butts he'd collected. After sweeping ashes off the wooden planks and hosing down cobwebs from the walls, no one would be able to tell Jarrid had signed his own death warrant here.

Wiping the dirt from his shoes, he went inside the house. Linnea stood in the kitchen, holding Charlotte with one hand, and whisking eggs with the other. Focused on her task, she inquired, "Are we going to see him this morning?"

"Here, let me take her." Scooping up his niece, Kodiak kissed her little head. "I thought we'd finish up here first. What do we have left?"

"Just his closet."

"We can grab some dinner in Decatur. See how he's doing after, okay?" he suggested, smacking his lips to Linnea's cheek.

"Okay." She wrinkled her nose. "You're all sweaty, Seth. Put the baby in her swing and go take a shower. You stink."

"Guess I better do what Mommy says, huh?" He chuckled, buckling the baby in. "Sorry, Charlotte."

After breakfast, they got to tackling what remained in Jarrid's room. As a kid, he never came in here much. Unless his father summoned him, it was forbidden. Bed stripped, walls painted, drawers emptied, it shouldn't take them very long to be done with it.

Kodiak spied a sealed box by the door. Written in bold, feminine script, his sister's name was on it.

*Damn letters.*

"Burn those, Linnea."

"They're mine, aren't they?" She didn't wait for an answer, tossing clothes upon the bed. "Help me empty out the closet, will you? It'll be easier to sort through it all this way."

Doing as Linnea asked, he took everything off the shelves up high and set them on the floor. "Done."

"Which suit, you think?" She held up two. "The gray one or navy blue?"

"Does it matter?"

Her brow shot up.

*Guess so.*

"Navy blue."

She put Jarrid's suit to the side, along with a crisp, white dress shirt and matching tie. "Donate the rest?"

"Yeah."

Once they'd bagged up all the clothes, Kodiak hauled them downstairs. Glancing at the church across the street, he loaded them into the back of the Tahoe. They'd been dropping off donations at the collection box in Decatur every time they passed through.

When he returned, Linnea had brought everything he'd dumped on the floor up onto the bed. Sitting cross-legged on the bare mattress, she reached for the closest box and looked up at him. "After this, we're done."

Nodding, he sat down across from her. Old receipts. *Playboy* magazines. Most of it was garbage, really.

*"Take what you want and burn the rest. Leave nothing behind."*

*What were you afraid they'd find, old man? Cigarettes, booze, and naked women?*

Snickering under his breath, he kept on going.

Small and white, the box itself was innocuous. He lifted the lid. A diary. Nestled in a bed of tissue, it was covered in soft, red moleskin and embroidered with flowers. Kodiak didn't have to look inside to know it wasn't his father's.

*Grace.*

His gaze briefly flicking to his sister, he turned to the first entry. She was fifteen when she wrote it.

"There's a box of really old photos here."

"Yeah?" Kodiak responded, but he was leafing through the pages.

"This could be him, but I'm not sure."

He went to her final entry, scanning the words she must have written shortly before she died.

*"All I ever did was love her."*

Perhaps in his own perverse way, he did.

Grace was certainly in love with him.

"Did Jarrid have a sister?"

"Not that I know of. He always told me we didn't have any kin." Kodiak held out her mother's diary. "Linnea, there's something you…"

"Who's Brandy then?"

Putting the diary aside, his brows cinched together, and he gave his head a shake. "What did you say?"

"Brandy. That's what's written on here."

"Let me see."

Linnea handed him a photo.

A woman's handwriting on the back, Kodiak read it out loud, "Joe, Jarrid, Brandy, and me. 1983."

"That would make Jarrid fifteen here, right?"

He studied the photo in his hand. Even as a teenager, his father looked pretty much the same, albeit younger. Shirtless, a cigarette tucked behind his ear, he was down on his haunches next to the girl, her chestnut hair in braids. She appeared to be around ten. A man and woman stood right behind them.

"My mother's name is Brandy."

"Oh, shit." Linnea gasped, clapping her hand to her mouth. "Do you think that's her?"

*It must be.*

"Are there any more?"

"Pictures?" Her grin smug, she pushed a good-sized box his way. "Weren't you listening?"

Dumping the photos into a pile on the bed, Kodiak attempted to put them in some semblance of order. Some had names and dates on the back, but many did not. Who were these people?

"Joe must be Jarrid's father," Linnea reasoned, her finger tapping on the man's image. "Dark hair. Green eyes. See the resemblance?"

He saw it. "Maybe, or his uncle."

But who was Brandy to his father? Would Jarrid finally tell him? Because that's what he wanted to know.

"Your phone, Seth."

It vibrated on the mattress beside him.

The caller was straight to the point and brief. *Hurry.*

Kodiak looked at his sister.

"What is it?"

"We've got to go."

# Twenty-Six

Sunlight streamed in through the windows, but Jarrid didn't see it. He lay there, his eyes closed, skin ashen, barely breathing. The photo they'd taken only yesterday, rested in his palm. Picking it up, Kodiak's fingers brushed his hand. It was cold.

*I should feel something.*

But he didn't. Not really.

Her arm around his waist, Linnea stood at his side. "What are we supposed to do?"

A nurse spoke up behind them. Kodiak thought that's what she was anyway. He hadn't seen her here before. "You can talk to him. He can still hear you. Hearing is the last sense that leaves us."

She moved to the other side of the bed, fluffed his pillow, and lifting the sheet that covered him, made sure he hadn't soiled himself. Satisfied Jarrid was comfortable, the nurse addressed them once again, "I can bring your dinner here if you'd like. There are extra linens and pillows in the closet for the pull-out. Call me if you need anything. I'll be in to check on him from time to time, but otherwise, I'll be respecting your privacy."

"Thank you."

Smiling, the nurse gazed at the Polaroid Kodiak still held. "He wanted it close to him. Said the board on the wall was too far away."

Stifling a cry, Linnea turned around.

He gently placed the photo back in his father's palm.

"You okay?" Rubbing her shoulders, Kodiak stood behind her.

"Yeah." With a sniffle, she shrugged. "I don't even know why I'm crying."

"It's a lot."

"I've never watched someone die before."

"Can't say I have either," he said, wrapping his arms around her. "We'll see each other through it, right?"

"Yeah." Her head nodded against his chest. "Do you think he'll wake up again?"

"I don't know."

But he didn't think so.

It was too late. Now, Jarrid would never be able to tell him about Brandy, not that he would have anyway.

The second hand on the clock seemed to revolve painfully slow. Shadows of the trees outside the window were cast upon the wall. And Jarrid still lay there, the picture in his palm.

Hugging his waist, Linnea kissed his cheek. "Thanks for setting up Charlotte's bed. She's asleep."

Remaining silent, Kodiak slipped his arm around her and hugged her back.

"Are you hungry? I can ask them to heat up your dinner or fix you something else."

"No, I'm okay." Stepping away, he went over to the window.

"Did you call Kelly?"

"Yeah, when I went for a walk."

The room closing in on him, Kodiak took a stroll through the gardens. Discovering a trail into the woods behind the house, he followed it. Then leaning against a tree, he pulled out his phone and his pen. Hearing Kelly's voice soothed him more than canna-bis ever could.

"How is she?"

"Anxious for us to come home."

He wanted this to be over.

He needed her.

Glancing at his niece sleeping so sweetly, Kodiak turned from the glass. "You should lay down with the baby. I'll sit with him."

"You said we'd get each other through this. I'm sitting with you."

And she did.

The hours passed. Giving in to exhaustion, Linnea slept be-side him. Slow and shallow, Jarrid's breaths rattled in his chest. He knew what that meant. Leaning forward, he held his hand. Kodiak supposed he should say something, but he had no words of com-fort to offer.

"After everything you've done, I don't know if I have it in my heart to forgive you, but I'm going to try. Just know your children are cared for, happy, and loved. So long, Dad. Whatever comes next, I hope there's peace."

Kodiak must've dozed off, because the next thing he knew, the nurse was rubbing his shoulder. "He's gone."

Gazing upon his lifeless body, a tear rolled down Linnea's cheek, but he didn't have it in him to cry.

Dawn was breaking by the time they got to the Tahoe. He and Linnea were both quiet, Charlotte happily waving in her car seat. On the way through Decatur, he took a turn on Water Street.

"Seth, where are you going?"

"Citizens Bank."

"No, no, no, not now. He said to go on our way back home. He was very adamant about that, remember?" Placing her hand on his forearm, she gentled her voice, "Besides, it's only six in the morning. The bank isn't even open yet."

"I remember." Sitting at a stoplight, Kodiak scrubbed his face with his hands.

"Are you okay?"

"I'm all right," he assured her. "Just tired."

"We should stop at Hazel's for a quick breakfast, then you can get some sleep."

Already knowing that wasn't about to happen, Kodiak snickered. There were still arrangements to be made. A funeral to get through. Once they were home, maybe then he could sleep. For now, though, he could do with some food in his stomach.

He took her hand and kissed it. "Sounds good."

Breakfast at the diner on a Friday morning wasn't much busier than lunch on a Sunday afternoon. As soon as they walked in the door, Hazel rushed over, coffee pot in hand. "You two look like you haven't slept in a week. How's your father doing?"

"He passed this morning," Linnea informed her. "Couple of hours ago."

"I'm so sorry, dear." She patted his sister's hand. Then pouring their coffee, Hazel called out to Tommy, "Seth and Linnea are here. Get me two breakfast specials, eggs scrambled."

"Thanks, Hazel." She was probably the only person he would miss from this town.

"And how are you?"

"We're okay." Holding her hand between both of his, Kodiak gave her a squeeze.

"Have the church folk been bothering you?" Arching her painted-on eyebrow, she pursed her garish red lips. "I don't suppose they know yet."

"Jeremy's been by a few times." Sipping his coffee, he shrugged. "And no, they don't. I'm going to have to go see him. Make the arrangements."

And he wasn't looking forward to it.

"Do we have to?" Linnea wanted to know. "Can't we just bury him privately?"

*I wish.*

"Don't think you'd be able to get away with that, dear." Hazel clicked her tongue. "They've got eyes everywhere around here, you know."

"He gives me the creeps."

"The boy ain't right." Bending down, the waitress cautiously whispered, "Just look at his eyes."

"Oh, I have." His sister's pause was loaded. "They're green."

"Exactly." Returning upright, she winked. "I see you get my meaning."

"What are you intimating, Hazel?"

"Just rumors, but you've got to wonder why your Daddy took such an interest in that boy once you and Linnea were gone." Her finger started wagging. "I told you, be wary of him. Especially now. The sooner you leave here, the better."

"We aren't staying any longer than we have to. Don't worry."

"Oh, I'm worried, all right," she said with a single nod. "And you should be too."

Kodiak glanced behind him. Linnea stood on the front porch with Charlotte, watching him cross the street to the church. Hazel was right, as soon as Jarrid's body arrived at the mortuary, news of his death would be all over town.

Bypassing the twelve steps that led up to the red front doors, he walked around to the back where his father's office was. Well, it was Jeremy's office now, he supposed. Then with a fortifying breath, Kodiak knocked on the door.

"You may enter."

He rolled his eyes and went in.

The robotic Howdy Doody smile appearing on his face, Jeremy greeted him. "Seth, I do hope you've come to tell me Pastor is well and at home."

"I'm sorry, Jeremy, I can't tell you that." Kodiak took a seat in front of his desk. "My father passed away early this morning."

"No." His eyebrows narrowed. "He was fine."

"He had cancer."

"And you kept me from him."

*I sure did.*

"It was a family matter. Obviously, my father didn't want anyone to know he was ill. And except for Linnea and myself, he didn't want anybody there."

"But I'm not just anybody."

*Oh? Just who are you then, Jeremy Blythe?*

Not that he really gave a fuck.

"Didn't he ask for me?"

"He didn't."

*Truth.*

"I see." His lips pressing together, the kid exhaled out his nose. "Did he leave you the key?"

"You can have it after the funeral. We got the house ready. A fresh coat of paint and everything."

"Not the house key."

Kodiak raised his brow.

"Never mind."

He leaned inward. "I'm here to make arrangements for the service."

"It will have to be Monday."

"Fine." He sat back.

Folding his hands on his desk, Jeremy smirked. "Your wife isn't welcome."

*Fuck off, preacher boy.*

"Then there won't be a service here at all."

"We all know what she did to Miss Catherine, God rest her soul. I cannot permit it."

"I think you've been drinking way too much Kool-Aid, kid." Kodiak stood up to leave. "You can just let the flock know Pastor was buried privately by his children. I'll leave the key under the doormat."

"Wait," he called out just as Kodiak reached the door.

He didn't bother turning around.

"The blood of our Lord pays for all sin, including the sin of murder, does it not? Very well, your wife may accompany you."

He was closing the back of the Tahoe when Linnea came out of the house with Charlotte. Everything they were keeping was packed inside it, and it wasn't much. Personal papers, his high school letterman jacket, a painting his sister wanted, and all the photos, of course. Save the furniture, they burned everything else.

*Just as you requested, old man.*

They'd be leaving to go home directly from the cemetery. He didn't want to have to come back here again. "You sure that's everything, Linnea?"

"I did another walk-through on my way downstairs," she said, getting the baby into her car seat. "I'm sure."

Toffee-blonde hair pulled back at the crown, she wore a simple black dress. Kodiak watched her clicking the latch into place. "Why are your hands shaking? Are you okay?"

"I'm a little anxious, I guess." Looking past him, Linnea gazed at the church across the street. "It's been a long time, you know?"

"Just hold onto me." He kissed the top of her head. "I got you."

His arm around her shoulders, they went up the twelve steps and stepped inside. The smell of beeswax and Murphy's oil soap immediately assaulted his nose. In front of the altar, Jarrid lay in repose, wearing the navy blue suit his daughter had chosen for him.

Glancing down at his sister, she nodded. They proceeded down the center aisle to their father. No one else was here yet, and he was grateful to have this moment without the church folk gawking at them.

*That didn't take long.*

Coming out of the vestry in full clerical garb, Jeremy approached them. "Pastor looks at peace, doesn't he? I kept vigil over him all night."

Tipping his chin in response, Kodiak tightened his hold on Linnea. She remained silent.

"My mother and the ladies have arranged a luncheon in the church hall following the graveside service."

"That's very thoughtful of them, but Linnea and I will be leaving right from there. It's a long drive, and we have to get back home." He looked to his sister, kissing her brow for good measure. "Please give Ada and the ladies our thanks, though."

"I really must insist. They've gone to so much trouble. They're looking forward to catching up with your wife and meeting your precious baby girl. You don't have to stay long. What's another hour?" Jeremy turned toward Linnea, leering at her, when she didn't exist to him before. That disturbing smile popped up on his face. "Say you'll come."

A sense of foreboding tingled at the back of his neck.

*"Be wary of him."*

Linnea didn't answer.

And taking her by the elbow, Kodiak led her to their pew.

# Twenty-Seven

One more hour.

Tops.

They just had to get through the graveside service, then they would be home free.

Moving at a snail's pace, the Tahoe followed behind the hearse as the cortège made its way through town. Headlights on, a purple funeral flag affixed to their hoods, cars pulled onto the shoulder to let them pass.

Kodiak loosened his tie a little. Just enough so he could breathe. It was strangling him. Staring straight ahead, Linnea fidgeted with the bouquet of flowers on her lap. He laid his hand on hers, quelling her movement.

Diverting her gaze, she looked over at him. "I'd almost forgotten."

"What?"

"How undeniably strange those people are." Her green eyes grew big and round. "Having been away for all these years, I can see it so clearly now. It *is* a crazy cult. They're all a bunch of brainwashed zealots, and I have a feeling Jeremy is going to be ten times worse than our father ever was."

"We got out, and that's all that matters," he said, patting her hand.

Linnea tilted her head. "Did we?"

Perhaps not entirely unscathed, but somehow, they'd managed to survive it. Bringing her fingers to his lips, Kodiak kissed them. "We did."

"I could feel their eyes on me, burning holes into the back of my head."

"Ignore them." Looking at Jeremy in the passenger seat of the hearse in front of them, he glowered. "As soon as we're done at the cemetery, we'll be on the road heading home."

"What about the luncheon?"

"We won't be attending." With a smirk on his face, Kodiak glanced at his sister. "They can have their little repast without us."

"I wouldn't put it past Ada to poison the food," Linnea said in a joking way and snickered.

Kodiak couldn't say that very thought hadn't crossed his mind. "Not Jeremy himself?"

"Nah, he wouldn't dare get his own hands dirty."

Crossfield's only cemetery was very old. And very small. Everyone who'd lived and died in this town was buried here. Driving through the rusted iron gates, that sense of foreboding returned. His heartbeat quickening, the hairs on his neck prickled. Linnea must have felt it too. She grabbed his hand and squeezed it.

The lead sedan came to a rolling stop, the hearse pulling in behind it. One by one they all followed suit. Jeremy was the first to exit the vehicle. His Howdy Doody grin out of place, he directed the six teenage boys selected from the congregation to carry Jarrid's casket.

"Ugh, I can't."

"It's almost over." Kodiak fixed his tie and got out. Then he went around to the other side, assisting Linnea, and her bouquet of flowers, from the passenger seat. "I'll get Charlotte."

Lining up behind the casket, he held the baby, and his sister held onto him. That's when he noticed a patrol car parked some fifty feet away.

The solemn procession proceeded to the freshly dug grave. It was an archaic, morbid custom if you asked him. Kodiak saw no reason to witness the lowering of a coffin into the ground. He was just thankful there weren't any bagpipes or a boys' choir singing.

They took their seats in the first row of wooden folding chairs. Nobody else sat with them. Folks were standing at the back, while the seats beside them stayed empty.

Jeremy started the service, and softy, Linnea began to cry. Pale-pink roses trembling in her hands, Kodiak followed her gaze. The grave of the mother she never knew was right beside their father's. Curling his arm around her, she laid her head on his shoulder.

"We commend to Almighty God our brother, Jarrid, and we commit his body to the ground, earth to earth, ashes to ashes, dust to dust."

And then it was done.

As the mourners filed past, Ada and her son appeared before them. His mother latched onto Linnea's arm. Jeremy took hold of his. "Come with us now."

"I made macaroni and cheese, especially for you." Ada's smile was just as creepy as her son's. "Used your grandmother's recipe."

Off to the side, in the distance, Hazel and a policeman stepped out from behind a tree. Holding a finger to her lips, she shook her head.

"We'd like a few moments of privacy to say goodbye on own, if that's all right." Kodiak pried Jeremy's fingers from his forearm. "And Linnea wants to visit with her mother. She brought her flowers."

Ada's face turned sour. "Every Sunday after church, Pastor came here to put pink roses on Grace's grave. He was so besotted—"

"That's enough, mother." Jeremy linked his arm with hers. Turning to Kodiak, those green eyes blank, his lip curled into a smirk. "Very well then, but we'll be waiting for you."

They stepped up to the grave. Once he and his sister were gone, the gravedigger would come and fill it with dirt. Kodiak picked up a handful and tossed it in. Taking a rose from the bouquet, Linnea threw it on top of their father's casket, then placed the rest on her mother's stone.

Tears in her eyes, she looked up at him. "Can we go now?"

Nodding, his arm circled around her, and they turned away.

They'd only walked a few yards when he saw it. *Beloved Son, Brother, and Friend. Jonathan Reynolds. 1988-2004.*

"Wait," his voice a hoarse whisper, Kodiak dropped to his knees.

*God, I miss you. I'm sorry…I'm sorry…I'm so fucking sorry…*

Linnea's hand caressed his shoulder as the tears streamed down his face.

*I love you, brother. Always.*

Tracing his fingers over the letters, he kissed the stone.

*I never got to say goodbye.*

"Seth." Gently, Linnea ran her fingers through his hair. "They're watching."

Kodiak glanced behind him. Jeremy and his mother sat in their silver Buick, glaring at them.

"They're not going to let us get away so easily."

"Fuck them." Getting up off the ground, he grabbed her by the hand. "We're going."

Not bothering to look their way, Kodiak buckled Charlotte into her car seat while Linnea secured her seatbelt. Sprinting over to the driver's side, he got behind the wheel, started the engine, and swung the truck around. Jeremy followed, but he wasn't fast enough. Pulling away from the curb, the patrol car blocked his way.

He waved to Hazel just before clearing the gates, and instead of taking a right turn back into town, he went left toward the highway.

"What are you doing, Linnea?"

On her knees in the front seat, she was looking out the back window.

"I'm checking to make sure he's not following us."

Glancing in the rearview mirror, Kodiak smirked. He hadn't seen a silver car for at least ten miles. "We're good. Even if preacher boy tried, he'd never be able to catch up to us now."

"You sure?"

"I'm sure." Smacking her backside, he grinned. "Once we get on I-55, we can stop somewhere for lunch. I feel guilty, being you missed out on Catherine's macaroni and cheese."

"Don't know who Ada thought she was fooling." Linnea huffed out a breath, turning around in her seat. "My grandmother never even made it. Not once. Cheese got her constipated."

Slowly turning their heads toward each other, they busted out laughing.

Regaining his composure, Kodiak reached inside the console. He'd almost forgotten to give it to her. The red moleskin in his fingers, he handed Linnea her mother's diary. "It's Grace's. Found it the day we were going through Jarrid's closet."

Opening the cover, she glanced at the first page, then closed it.

"Aren't you going to read it?"

"I can't." Pursing her lips, she placed the book in her bag. "These are her own personal thoughts. I doubt she intended for anyone else to read them."

"Probably not, but I think you should."

*It's there, written in her own hand. She loved you.*

Her green eyes glassy, his sister smiled over at him. "Someday, maybe."

Smiling back, Kodiak nodded. He understood. Grace's words would be there for her, whenever she was ready to read them.

Finally making it to the interstate, he took the first exit to get some burgers at a fast food drive-thru. Charlotte was asleep, and they didn't want to wake her by going inside. They parked, eating their lunch in the Tahoe, as they watched the cars whizzing by. Then Linnea glanced down at the black drawstring bag at her feet. It held the contents of the safety deposit box.

"Aren't you going to open it?"

"I'm almost afraid to," he said, taking another bite of his burger.

"Whatever it is, Jarrid wanted you to have it."

*And whatever it is, Jeremy tried like hell to get it.*

Kodiak licked burger sauce from his fingers before wiping them on a napkin. Gesturing to Linnea, she placed the bag on his lap. He untied the drawstring, then loosening it, took out a notecard lying on top. In Jarrid's handwriting, it said:

*Any man who does not provide for his own, especially for those of his household, has denied the faith, and is worse than an unbeliever.*

*1 Timothy 5:8*

Passing it to Linnea, he emptied the contents of the bag. "Jesus."

"What is it?" Glancing at his lap, she did a double take and gasped. "Holy shit."

Cash. And lots of it.

"Where the hell did he get that kind of money?"

*Skimming off the collection plates, no doubt.*

His flock provided for him. How else?

Linnea nervously surveyed the parking lot. "God, put it away before someone sees it."

"I should send them a check," Kodiak murmured, as he tossed wads of hundred-dollar bills, rolled up in rubber bands, back inside the bag.

"You will do no such thing." Reminding him of Hazel, Linnea wagged her finger in his face. "Jarrid wanted you to have it."

"I don't need it."

"Donate it then."

*Now there's a thought.*

The Trevor Project came to mind, an organization that provides crisis support to LGBTQ youth. In that small way, Kodiak could honor Jonathan's memory.

"Yeah." Feeling better now for taking it, he smiled. "That's what I'm going to do."

Less than an hour from home, the city skyline finally came into view. They had a distance to go yet, but it was a welcome sight. Kelly, his heart, his soul, and his true salvation, was waiting for him there.

*"I know first-hand how those missing moments in time must be haunting her."*

His smile fell. One secret still remained. He had to let it go. Turning to the girl who was tattooed into all the best and worst moments of his life, Kodiak took her hand. "I need to tell you what happened between us that night in my apartment. You deserve to know and—"

"Shhh." Her green eyes gazed into his. "Seth, I know."

"But Bo told me you didn't remember."

He'd always taken comfort in that, at the same time fearing he'd lose her if she ever knew the truth.

"I didn't at first. Just bits and pieces. But thanks to Monica, with time, I was able to put them all together."

His eyes filling, Kodiak swiped at them so he could see the road.

"I told you, I understand more than you think I do. Maybe nobody else would, but then nobody else lived our life."

"How the fuck could you forgive me?"

Her hand landed on his thigh. "I don't blame *you*. I will never blame you. Our father was the one at fault. There's nothing to forgive."

Gripping the steering wheel, he inhaled and held his breath, his knuckles turning white.

"I love you, Seth."

And he exhaled.

"I love you, little one."

"Don't you see? You've been looking out for me my entire life. Even when you didn't know it, you were my big brother." Laying her head on his shoulder, Linnea peered up at him. "I always wanted one, you know."

"Yeah?"

"Yeah." His sister smiled. "And I got the best one I could've ever wished for."

Kodiak made a promise when he was ten. And he'd kept it. It was for Dillon to love and protect her now. But as her brother, he'd be there whenever she needed him.

Park Place was just as they'd left it. Music drifted on the breeze from Kit's open window, but no one seemed to be around on this late Monday afternoon. Linnea carried Charlotte into the house. Kodiak hauled everything else including that damn box of letters. He didn't understand why she wanted to hold onto them. Maybe it was a girl thing. Peeking through the French doors into her backyard, for a moment he thought they were in the wrong house. It didn't look like this when they left.

"A hot tub, Linnea? What the hell have you been up to while we were away?"

"Building a new life." She grinned.

*And that's what I intend to do with Kelly.*

"When Dillon comes back, if everything works out…"

"There's no *if* about it." Smiling, Kodiak tenderly smoothed her hair. "And you know it."

"Then how would you feel about living next door?"

"Kelly and Dillon, neighbors? Christ, can you imagine that?"

Actually, he could.

Linnea giggled. "Even better, if you marry Kelly and I marry Dillon, they'll be brother and sister-in-law."

Her laughter infectious, he couldn't help but laugh too.

"You're going to ask her to, aren't you?"

With a smile so wide he could feel it in his cheeks, Kodiak nodded. "Yeah, I am."

"Good, I was hoping you'd say that." And she hugged him tight. "Kelly's so lucky to be loved by you."

*It's me. I'm the lucky one.*

"Want me to make us some tea?"

"Thanks, but I'm going to have to take a raincheck." He kissed Charlotte's little head, then his sister on the cheek. "Kelly's at the house waiting for me."

And he smiled.

They might never have all the answers.

But at last, the circle was closed.

# Twenty-Eight

She was waiting for him on the porch.

His friend. His forever love. His queen.

He tore up the steps, and without a word, he kissed her, pushing her inside. Kodiak kissed Kelly like he'd been without her for a thousand years, and not just fifteen days. They'd been the longest days of his life.

"I love you." And he kissed her again.

And again.

And again.

It would never be enough.

"I love you too." Clinging to him, Kelly had her arms clamped around his neck. "God, I missed you."

Kodiak lifted her up by the back of her thighs, and she wrapped her legs around him. And just like the first time, his lips never leaving hers, he carried her up the stairs. Down the hall. When he let her feet touch the floor, he was still kissing her.

Her purse sat on a chair near the bed. Kodiak rifled through it, then handed her the pack of pills. "Throw these away."

Grinning, Kelly tossed them into the trash.

"I'm going to put a baby in you," he told her, breathing the scent of her skin. "For real this time."

His desire for this woman burning him alive, Kodiak stripped off all her clothes. Then finding her already slick with need, he laid her on the bed. Feathering kisses all over her beautiful face, he knew he would love her, cherish her, and protect her with everything in him, from now until infinity.

Suckling the nipple that would one day nourish his children, he caressed the place from which they'd be born. Then praying, he worshipped every sacred inch of her. Kelly, his only religion.

He fingered her pussy, rubbing her clit until she cried out his name.

He licked up her sweetness until she screamed, "Please, no more."

*I win.*

"You sure, baby?"

"I'm sure." Kelly panted, out of breath. "I need you inside me… right now. Please."

He always loved it when she begged.

And Kodiak would always give her what she needed.

Holding onto her nipples, he pressed his aching dick inside and groaned. There was no better feeling on this earth. "I love how you take all of me."

His hips in the cradle of her thighs, Kelly leached him of his seed. Pouring himself inside her, Kodiak watched as she absorbed him. She was truly his, and forever, he was hers.

Unable to be fully free until they found each other, they would have such an incredible life.

"Truth for a truth, Snicks." He could feel her smile on his skin.

"What?"

"I love you and I want to spend every day of my life with you. Will you marry me?"

Lifting her head from his chest, her fairytale eyes glazed, she smiled. "I love you. Yes, I will."

And she kissed him.

"Did I ever thank you for the cookies?"

Kelly thought about it for a moment. "You know, I don't think that you did."

"Thank you," he said, slipping the ring on her finger.

Her jaw dropping, she just stared at it.

"Oh, by the way, you should start packing because we're moving."

"We are?"

"We are." He grinned. "You're going to love living on Park Place. Especially since it's so close to Beanie's and Katie's right across the street…"

Her eyes went wide.

"…my sister will be right next door."

"And Dillon?"

"Is going to be your brother-in-law."

He kissed her.

*I love you, Kelly.*

Yeah, they were going to have the most wonderful, extraordinary, beautiful life.

And after everything, Kodiak figured they deserved it.

# *Epilogue*

*Fourth of July, three years later…*

He stood on the deck, the dog at his side, watching her long blonde hair billowing out behind her as she chased after their little boy. He'd been right. Their life together was extraordinarily wonderful, magical, and beautiful.

Barely a month after Kodiak proposed, surrounded by the people they loved most, he and Kelly were married where they first promised to be each other's friend. Under the tree, by the lake, they promised to love one another forever. He was her husband, and she was his wife. She took a pregnancy test the next day. It was positive.

Dillon was back from Ireland by then, and just as he told Linnea it would, everything worked out. A few months later, on a beach in Mexico, they got married too. And a couple of years after that, his sister gave birth to twins. Kodiak had another niece and a nephew. Born on the Fourth of July, today was their first birthday.

Kelly and Katie were pregnant at the same time, due on the

same day, in fact. It was like a competition between them, as to who would have their baby first. Kodiak chuckled at the memory. He still wasn't sure how he and Brendan survived it. As it turned out, Leah was born first.

Their son came kicking and screaming into the world five days later. A head of dark curls, and eyes the color of a stormy tropical sea, Jonathan Kade Black was the most precious, beautiful gift he'd ever been given. Apart from his wife, that is. God, he loved her so much. And more so every day.

Handing him a beer, Bo came to stand beside him. Together, they looked out onto the lake house lawn. Ava, seven months pregnant with her first child, waddled arm in arm with Chloe, who was five months along with her fourth. Emery, who was six now, happily tossed a football with the boys.

Chuckling, Bo tipped his chin toward the lawn. "They're giving her a run for the money, huh?"

Leah ran as fast as her little legs could carry her. His son chased after her, while his wife chased after him.

"Slow down, Kade. You're wearing Mommy out."

Yeah, even though Kelly agreed to name their son after the boy he'd loved, everyone called him by the middle name she insisted upon. It was a K name, after all.

"Sure looks like it."

"How did we get so lucky?"

Some would say the universe, or God himself, ordained it. Maybe that was true, but he didn't think so. Sipping on his beer, Kodiak dropped his arm to circle Bo's waist, and he smiled. This man. This selfless, beautiful soul. He'd saved his life more than once and he loved him. He always would.

"Luck had nothing to do with it, brother." He squeezed him to his side. "But love is everything. Even at my lowest low, you showed me that. We earn the love we have, and we earn it by loving."

"Yeah, I suppose we do." Bo smiled at him. "I love you, man."

"I love you too." Kodiak smiled back. "I think I need to rescue my wife from our two-year-old." He patted his thigh. "C'mon, Bernie."

"And I'm coming with you." Bo chuckled. "I need to steal my wife back from Red."

Grabbing another beer on the way, they walked arm in arm toward the lake house lawn. And their wives. The Bernedoodle faithfully followed along. Bo went left to his Avie, while Kodiak went right to his Snicks.

"Gotcha." Scooping up his son, he hoisted him high in the air.

Kicking his little legs, Kade let out a belly laugh.

He lived for those.

"Thanks." Kelly seemed out of breath.

Kodiak set his son down between them, each one taking his hand. "You all right?"

"Yeah, just a bit winded." She elbowed him. "I'm not a runner, you know. He gets that from you."

"I know." He grinned.

Smiling at him, Kelly bit her lip. "I think we should have another baby."

"We can barely keep up with this one, Snicks. I'm thirty-eight—"

"And I'm late."

*Ohh.*

"You are?"

She nodded.

"How late?"

"A couple of weeks, give or take."

*We're going to have a girl. And I hope she's just like you.*

Lifting his son, Kodiak spun around with him in his arms. Bernie barking his head off, he kissed his wife. "I love you."

"You're happy?"

*Hell, yes.*

"So happy." He kissed her again. "You're going to be a big brother, Kade."

"We don't know for sure yet."

*I know.*

His love. His life. His queen.

Once there'd been nothing but darkness. And now, the future shined bright.

All because he took a chance and made a friend.

Then he took another, and another, and another…

Isn't it funny how life changes then?

# Epilogue

*Sloan Michaels*

Eyes glued to the screen, his fingers furiously worked the buttons on the controller. He'd been awake going on forty-eight hours now. Exhausted, Sloan wasn't sure how he kept them open. But he couldn't sleep.

Stress.

That was the issue.

His shrink thought so anyway.

Sloan knew different.

"Play a video game. Do something you enjoy," he said. "It can boost your mood and relieve some of the pressure."

Course, the dude meant a few hours a week, not umpteen hours a day.

Admittedly, he was addicted to them. But they took his mind off shit. And what else did he have anyway?

Nothing and no one.

*Right.*

His phone rang. As usual, he ignored it.

"Fuck off."

But it rang and rang and rang. Only to put an end to the incessant ringing, he picked it up.

"What?"

He listened, the voice on the other end cold.

*Dead…overdose…so sorry.*

"I see. Thank you for letting me know."

He always knew he'd hear the news someday. Maybe now that it had come, and he didn't have to think about her anymore, he could finally get some sleep.

Who was he kidding?

She was dead, and he was to blame.

No, stress had never been his issue.

It was her.

The End

…until *Rhythm Man*

# Acknowledgments

Holyyy Smokes!!!

I can't believe I just typed '*The End*'. You've probably seen me say Kodiak's story has been so difficult to write and believe me, it was. He's such a compelling, complicated character and his story is so complex. If everything that man endured in his life made it onto the page, he could've had two books, and this one about did me in, but no character I've written deserves a HEA more than he does. I'll admit, there were times I thought I'd never get this book finished—two rounds of COVID, my day job, a new addition to the household…you know. Life.

As I mentioned in my author's note, some elements in this book are disturbing. Sadly, it isn't fiction. Not only does conversion therapy exist, but it's also legal in most of the United States and many countries around the world. For more information, or to help provide crisis support to LGBTQ youth, you can visit thetrevorproject.org.

Many of the Chicago locations included in this series are actual places. *The Signature Room at the 95th*, the iconic restaurant in the John Hancock building (yes, I still call it that, and I always will) is one of them. Unfortunately, it fell victim to the post-COVID economy and was permanently closed while I was writing this book. Lucky for Kodiak and his Snicks, they went there for dinner when they did. So long, Signature Room. This Chicago girl is going to miss you.

The Pinterest board and the playlist for *Son of a Preacher Man* on Spotify and YouTube are open. Matt's story, *Rhythm Man*, book 7, is next in the *Red Door Series*. I hope you all were able to get your hands on *Whiteout* when it was published in *Billionaires & Babes*, the BABE 2023 charity anthology. The anthology is no longer available, but anyway, those nine chapters were just the beginning of this twisty story—you can find out what happens next very, very soon! As always, I've included sneak peeks following these acknowledgments. And did I happen to mention we're going back to Brookside? Well, giddy on up, *The Hardest Part*, Emily, Jake, & Billy's story, is next in that series.

I say it every time, and yes, I'm going to say it again—this is so surreal. Book 6. From the beginning, I planned a total of nine books for the *Red Door Series*. Matt, Kit, and Sloan are the only stories left to be written. That's not to say another side character won't start screaming at me, and we have plenty of them, but those three are who remain from the OG crew.

As always, I've got some people to thank. My family. My tribe. My heart. I wouldn't be here without them. I say this every time too— I'll try not to be so wordy. And as usual, I will more than likely fail.

Thank you to my babies. **Michael** & **Raj, Charlie, Christian, Josie Lynn** & **Josh, Zach** & **Sam, Jaide, Julian, Olivia, Jocelyn,** and our newest addition, born just a few weeks ago, baby **Jalina Isabel.** You're the most precious, beautiful gifts I've ever been given—I love you!!!

**Michelle Morgan.** Thank you for always being there. I love you, beautiful, and I'm always going to need you!!! xoxo

**Linda Russell** and the amazing team at **Foreword PR.** I would not be here without my Linda. Sorry for the gray hairs I gave you with this one—we did it, though, didn't we? I love you lots!!! Forever a Foreword girl!!! xoxo

**Michelle Lancaster,** my beautiful, talented friend, my Cover

Queen of Hearts—could those images be any more perfect? She's in my head, I swear!!! I told her I needed 'Hippie Biker Jesus' and good Lord, she found him for me! Took a year to convince **Reeff Kuhn** we *really* wanted him for this cover, but then we couldn't imagine another model for Seth "Kodiak" Black. My thanks to you both—I love you to infinity!!! xoxo

**Lori Jackson** did it again! Cover magic, I tell you. I love how her designs showcase Michelle's art. I love how easily we work together. I just love *her*. And there's more magic coming!!! xoxo

**Ashlee O'Brien**, my girly, alpha reader, book daughter, and the design goddess that is *Ashes & Vellichor*. Creative and original, she pulls all the quotes, and makes all the pretties, to tantalize and tease you along the way—she's damn good at it too. I'd be lost without her. I love you more than the mostest!!! xoxo

**Stacey Blake**, of *Champagne Book Design*, for making the pages so pretty every time. And for being so patient. Love you bunches!!! xoxo

My beta team—**Charbee Balderson, Jennifer Bishop, Heather Hahn, Kim Lannan, Marjorie Lord, Lee Ann Mathis, Anastasia Meimeteas, Melinda Parker, Sabrena Simpson, Rebecca Vazquez**, and **Staci Way**, together with my **ARC team**—sorry for any consumption of alcohol that may have been required while reading this book. Thank you for being so patient, and for taking the time out of your busy lives to read Kodiak's story, but most of all for being my ride or dies. I love y'all—who has more fun than us, my girlies? xoxo

**Bloggers, Bookstagrammers,** and **Booktokkers.** I can never say it enough—thank you, thank you, thank you!!! For supporting me and the books I write. Sharing posts. Creating so many wonderful edits, reels, and TikToks. Selflessly giving your time and talent to the book community. You make it a better place. I appreciate everything you do so much. xoxo

My beautiful **Redlings**—these humans are some of the most incredible beings on the planet!!! Love you all the mostest!!! They, and I, would love to welcome you *Behind the Red Door* on Facebook. xoxo

And as always, my lovely **readers**. Thank you for being here and loving the *Red Door* world. Your messages and emails make my day—I appreciate every one of them. Thank you for wanting more Kyan, Dillon and Linnea, Chloe, Jesse, and Taylor, Brendan and Katie, Bo and Ava, Kodiak and Kelly, Matt, Kit, and Sloan. We're not done yet.

Until *Rhythm Man…*

Much love,
Dyan xoxo

The doorbell rang.

"About time."

After a late night at the club, he was fucking starving.

Wearing only a pair of grungy old sweats, Matt opened the door. A girl stood on the other side of it. Long dark hair in a ponytail, her eyes a mix of sable and green, she cocked her hip, his pizza in her hand.

He licked his lips. "You're not Luca."

"Nope." Shifting her eyes, she scanned his bare torso and made a face.

"Who are you?"

"The pizza girl." She smirked, shoving the box into his hand. "It's gonna get cold."

Then, turning around, she skipped down the porch steps.

He was tempted to chase after her, but he didn't.

"Hey, you got a name, pizza girl?"

"Doesn't everyone?"

*What the hell?*

Her ponytail swinging, she glanced back at him from over her shoulder. Shaking his head, Matt took a step back inside the house.

"Gina."

*She'll be back.*

And closing the door behind him, he grinned.

Sneak Peek of

# Whiteout

# Chapter One

Five hours.

That's how long she'd been driving already, and Breanna hadn't even reached the California state line. Maybe she should've stayed on I-5, instead of cutting over to Route 39, but that's the way her GPS sent her, so she took it. Passing Klamath Falls, she cranked up the tunes and grinned. "Seventeen more miles."

Spotify playlist blasting, she excitedly waved goodbye to Oregon, as the 'Welcome to California' sign appeared. The state of her birth, though she wasn't going to be anywhere close to her family in LA. She hadn't even told her mom she was making the trip. She'd only worry. Besides, just hearing the name, Dalton, made Sarah Benjamin sad. Breanna was surprised she got to keep her dad's name.

Bad blood between her mother and her late father's family. Namely, her grandmother, Valerie Dalton, whom Breanna had never even met. She'd never met Shane Dalton either—not that she could remember anyway. He died when she was just a baby.

So when she received an official-looking letter from St. John, Maynard & St. John, Attorneys at Law, requesting her presence at Dalton House, on her grandmother's behalf, Breanna's curiosity was piqued. What did Valerie Dalton want? She doubted it was a desire to meet her son's only child after twenty-one years. But it could be, right? The woman had to be in her seventies now. Maybe she'd had a sudden change of heart in her old age.

*Yeah, and maybe shit doesn't stink.*

The correspondence, signed by one Derek St. John, didn't say much. No clue as to why she was being summoned. He only stated he was following the wishes of his client and advised Breanna to make arrangements to get there prior to the Thanksgiving holiday—and before the arrival of winter weather in the Sierra Nevada. Mountain roads can be treacherous when the snow comes.

Did he think she was an idiot?

Just because she was a California girl didn't mean she'd never driven in snow before.

After marinating on it for a week, she left word with the lawyer's secretary, letting him know when to expect her. The week of Thanksgiving break would have to do, and too bad if Derek St. John or her grandmother didn't like it. Breanna had friends to see, parties and classes to go to. Okay, she was on the flexible undergrad track for her BA in English. She could log in on her laptop, comfy in her pajamas, from the sofa in her apartment for most of her classes—or from anywhere for that matter, but the old lady didn't need to know that.

Her gaze flicked over to the snowcapped range of peaks to the east. Overcast, the midday sky looked dreary, but the clouds weren't ominous. *Yet.* She'd be fine. But Breanna still had five hundred miles, some seven hours of driving left before she reached her destination, and her ass was already numb.

A hundred and forty miles later, her bottom screaming at her to get up and stretch, gas gauge down to a quarter tank, she got off the highway. Refuel. Restroom. Coffee. There was no time to waste if she wanted to reach Dalton House before dark. Estimating she'd only need to make one more stop after this one, Breanna stood in line, Styrofoam cup in hand, rubbing circulation into her aching backside with the other. As long as the weather held, and barring any unforeseen hazards on the road, she should be good.

Her ass protesting once more, she sat back down behind the

wheel, burning her tongue on the steaming hot battery acid that passed for gas station coffee. *Yuck.* Breanna grimaced into the cup, her phone vibrating on the center console.

"Hey, Kay," she answered.

"Just checking on you. You there yet?"

Kayleigh, her closest friend at college, and her roommate, was a worrywart. An old mother hen in a twenty-year-old body. She was the girl who forbade the consumption of jungle juice at parties—especially those held on Greek Row—cockblocked the fuckboys, and forced her to eat something besides cheap ramen noodles for dinner. And Breanna loved her for it. God only knows just how many bad decisions she'd saved her from.

"Hell, no." She expelled some air, tipping her head back against the seat. "Just made it to 395."

"You're not being safe." Breanna could just picture Kayleigh shaking her head. "You should stop. Get a room and rest for the night."

"No, I'll be fine," she assured her. "It's only a few more hours."

"Stubborn." Kayleigh could be heard sighing through the phone. "Have you even bothered checking the weather, Bree? They're predicting—"

"Snow. I know." Swallowing a sip of the putrid battery acid, she glanced up at the sky. "I'll be there long before it gets here, so don't worry, okay?"

"Yeah, I bet that's what the Donner Party said too, and look what happened to them."

"So dramatic," Breanna said, chuckling. "I think it's pretty safe to assume no one's going to be eating me—dead or alive."

Kayleigh giggled. "Well, should that lawyer guy or Grandmama serve fava beans and a nice chianti at dinner. Run. Fast."

"Will do." And she started her car. "I'll text you when I get there."

The cloud cover grew more dense the farther she drove. No longer merely overcast, the sky appeared heavy, saturated in a deepening gray. Breanna wasn't too concerned, though. According to the GPS, Dalton House was less than an hour away.

Like a good, obedient girl, she exited off the highway when the robotic British male voice instructed her to. She preferred him to the Siri-sounding woman. A checkpoint was set up on the road in front of a mom-and-pop store. Coming to a stop, Breanna lowered the window.

"Evening, miss."

She tipped her chin. "Hello."

"You're gonna need to get chains on those tires before I can let you through. We're expecting a doozy of a storm. Can't have you getting stuck out there on the pass."

"But—" *It's not even snowing yet.*

"Sorry, miss." He pointed toward the little store. "Hank's got 'em if you're needing some. Seventy-five bucks and he'll put 'em on for you too. Have you back on the road in a jiffy."

"Okay, thanks," Breanna assented, raising the window. "This is some bullshit. Hank must be raking it in."

Figuring she might as well top off her tank before heading inside the store, Breanna pulled up to the gas pump. A cold gust slapped her face as she exited the car, causing her to clench the unzipped jacket tightly around her middle. Trees danced on either side of the road, their naked branches bending to the will of the wind in the thickening darkness. Gazing heavenward, the slate-gray altostratus ominously churned.

Triggered by a familiar tickle in her nose, she sniffed the air. The scent of an approaching storm mingled with sweet benzene. Breanna zipped her worn, black leather bomber, and winding a scarf around her neck, made her way across the small parking lot. Bells attached to the door clanked into the glass as she wrestled with it, a sudden squall pushing her inside.

It was as if time had forgotten this place. To her left was a small diner with a checkered floor, red vinyl seats, and an old-fash-ioned soda fountain. To her right, a counter with rows of penny candy—cost twenty times that now—and a cash register. In front of her were several aisles of grocery essentials and sundries.

A balding head popped up from behind the counter. "Need something, miss?"

"Yes. Yes, I do. Chains." Behind her, the door burst open again. Breanna shivered, tingles creeping down her spine. "The officer at the checkpoint told me to see Hank."

"That's me." Pointing a thumb backward at his chest, he cracked a crooked grin, revealing a crooked front tooth. "I'm Hank."

"Can you put them on for me?"

"Be happy to." His head bobbed. "Where's your car?"

"Right outside," she said, handing him her keys. "The white Miata."

Breanna heard a snicker at her back. A voice, rich and deep, muttered low, "Figures. Damn girly car."

She whirled around to find six feet of rugged man standing behind her. Bearded. Suede coat lined with sheepskin. A black Stetson on his head. Dark hair brushed his shoulders. Eyes the color of whiskey. "Yeah, well, I *am* a girl."

"I can see that." Smirking, he dropped his head to the side and winked.

*Probably drives one of those big-ass pickup trucks to compensate for having a puny dick.*

Flustered by the stranger's boldness, Breanna turned back to Hank. "How long will it take?"

"Not too long," he assured her. The crooked grin fixed to his face, he bobbed his head to the left. "Why don't you get yourself a cup of coffee while you wait? Have a piece of banana cream pie. My wife makes it. Best damn pie in the world, trust me."

"Can't pass that up, now can I?" She smiled at Hank, side-eyeing the tall, dark, imposing stranger. Brushing past him, Breanna took a seat on a vinyl-covered stool at the end of the counter.

Sweet on her tongue, she licked thick, whipped cream from

her lips. Hank did not exaggerate. The pie was chef's kiss, the coffee sublime, especially after the gas station sludge she'd been existing off of.

Rubbing his hands together, cheeks reddened, Hank came behind the counter as she washed down the last of her pie with a sip of coffee. "You're all set, miss."

"Great, thanks." Breanna handed him her credit card.

He just held it in his hand, staring at it. "Dalton, huh. You any relation to Valerie?"

"Yeah, she's my grandmother, why? You know her?"

Tucking his tongue into the corner of his lip, Hank nodded. "Well, I'll be goddamned. I had no idea. You have to be Shane's girl then."

"That's right."

Brows cinching together, his eyes flicked to the windows behind her. "It's startin'. Best get you on your way."

The bold one sat in a booth. Hat on the table, a mug of coffee poised at his mouth, he shook his head. "Suicide. Chains or no chains, she's gonna slide right off the mountain in that thing."

Standing from the stool, Breanna sniggered. "It's just a few snowflakes."

Slowly, he swiped his tongue across his lip and grinned.

"And every storm starts with just one."

Books by

# DYAN LAYNE

**Red Door Series**
*Serenity*
*Affinity*
*Maelstrom*
*The Other Brother*
*Drummer Boy*
*Son of a Preacher Man*
*Rhythm Man (coming soon)*

**Brookside Series**
*The Third Son*
*The Hardest Part (coming soon)*

**Standalones**
*Don't Speak*
*Whiteout (coming soon)*

# About the Author

Dyan Layne is a nurse boss by day and the writer of twisty sensual tales by night—and on weekends. She's never without her Kindle and can usually be found tapping away at her keyboard with a hot latte and a cold Dasani Lime—and sometimes champagne. She can't sing a note, but often answers in song because isn't there a song for just about everything? Born and raised a Chicago girl, she currently lives in Tampa, Florida, and is the mother of four handsome sons and a beautiful daughter, who are all grown up now, but can still make her crazy—and she loves it that way! Because normal is just so boring.

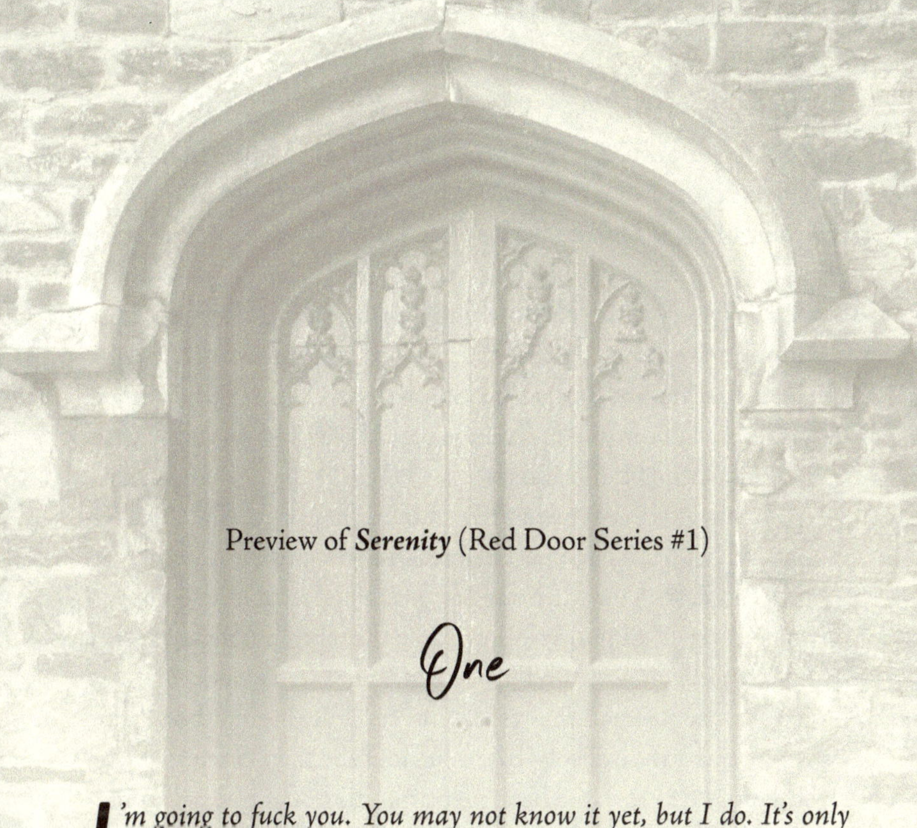



*'m going to fuck you. You may not know it yet, but I do. It's only a matter of time. I've been watching you. I swear that you've been watching me too, but maybe it's all in my head. No matter. Because I've seen you, I've talked to you and I've come to a conclusion: You are fucking beautiful. And I will make you lust me.*

The words danced on crisp white paper. Her fingers trembled and her feet became unsteady, so she leaned against the wall of exposed brick to right herself, clutching the typewritten note in her hand. She read it again. A powerful longing surged through her body and her thighs clenched.

Who could have written it? She couldn't fathom a single soul who might be inspired to write such things to her. Maybe those words weren't meant for her? Maybe whoever had written the note slid it beneath the wrong doormat in his haste to deliver it undetected?

Linnea Martin, beautiful? Someone had to be pulling a prank. *Yeah. That's more likely.*

She sighed as she turned and closed the solid wood front door. She glanced up at the mirror that hung in the entry hall and eyes the color of moss blinked back at her. Long straight hair, the color of which she had never been able to put into a category—a dirty-blonde maybe—hung past her shoulders, resting close to where her nipples protruded against the fitted cotton shirt she wore. Her skin was fair, but not overly pale. She supposed some people might describe her as pretty, in an average sort of way, but not beautiful.

Not anything but ordinary.

Linnea slowly crumpled up the note in her hand. She clenched it tight and held it to her breast before tossing it into the wastebasket.

Deflated, she threw her tote bag on the coffee table and plopped down on the pale-turquoise-colored sofa that she'd purchased at that quaint secondhand store on First Avenue. She often stopped in there on her way home from the restaurant, carefully eyeing the eclectic array of items artfully displayed throughout the shop. Sometimes, on a good day when tips had been plentiful, she bought herself something nice. Something pretty. Like the pale-turquoise sofa.

Linnea grabbed the current novel she was engrossed in from the coffee table and adjusted herself into a comfortable position, attempting to read. But after she read the same page three times she knew she couldn't concentrate, one sentence blurred into the next, so she set it back down. She clicked on the television and scrolled through the channels, but there was nothing on that could hold her interest. The words replayed in her head.

*I'm going to fuck you.*

Damn him! Damn that fucker to hell for being so cruel to leave that note at her door, for making her feel…things. The words had thrilled her for a fleeting moment, but then the excitement quickly faded, replaced by a loneliness deep in her chest. Love may never be in the cards for her, or lust for that matter, as much as she might want it to be.

Once upon a time she had believed in fairy tales and dreamt of knights on white stallions and handsome princes, of castle turrets shrouded in mist, of strong yet gentle hands weaving wildflowers in her long honeyed locks—just like the alpha heroes in the tattered paperbacks she had kept hidden under her bed as a teenager. She thought if she was patient long enough, her happily-ever-after would come. She thought that one day, when she was all grown up, that a brave knight, a handsome prince, would rescue her from her grandmother's prison and make all her dreams come true.

*Stupid girl.*

Her dreams turned into nightmares, and 'one day' never came. She doubted it ever would now. It was her own fault anyway. She closed her eyelids tight, trying to stop the tears that threatened to escape, to keep the memories from flooding back. Linnea had spent years pushing them into an unused corner, a vacant place where they could be hidden away and never be thought of again.

It was dark. She must have been sitting there for quite a while, transfixed in her thoughts. The small living room was void of illumination, except for the blue luminescence that radiated from the unwatched television. Linnea dragged herself over to it and clicked it off. She stood there for a moment waiting for her eyes to adjust to the absence of light and went upstairs.

Steaming water flowed in a torrent from the brushed-nickel faucet, filling the old clawfoot tub. She poured a splash of almond oil into the swirling liquid. As the fragrance released, she bent over the tub to breathe in the sweet vapor that rose from the water and wafted through the room. Slipping the sleeves from her shoulders, the silky robe gave way and fell to a puddle on the floor.

Timorously, she tested the water with her toes, and finding it comfortably hot, she eased her body all the way in. For a time serenity could be found in the soothing water that enveloped her.

*You may not know it yet, but I do. It's only a matter of time.*

At once her pulse quickened, and without conscious thought her slick fingertips skimmed across her rosy nipples. They hardened at her touch. And a yearning flourished between the folds of flesh down below. Linnea clenched her thighs together, trying to make it go away, but with her attempt to squelch the pulsing there, she only exacerbated her budding desire. And she ached.

Ever so slowly, her hands eased across her flat belly to rest at the junction between her quivering thighs. She wanted so badly to touch herself there and alleviate the agony she found herself in. But as badly as she wanted to, needed to, Linnea would not allow herself the pleasure of her own touch. She sat up instead, the now-tepid water sloshing forward with the sudden movement, and reaching out in front of her she turned the water back on.

She knew it was wicked. Lying there with her legs spread wide and her feet propped on the edge of the tub, she allowed the violent stream of water to pound upon her swollen bud. It throbbed under the assault and her muscles quaked. She'd be tempted to pull on her nipples if she wasn't forced to brace her hands against the porcelain walls of the clawfoot tub for leverage.

Any second now. She was so close.

*I'm going to fuck you.*

And he did. With just his words, he did.

Her head tipped back as the sensations jolted through her body. The sounds of her own keening cries were muffled by the downpour from the faucet. Spent, she let the water drain from the tub and rested her cheek upon the cold porcelain.

# Prologue

"**A**idan, baby."

His mother took him by the hand and pulled him along behind her as she hurried out of the kitchen. He'd only eaten half of his grilled cheese sandwich and some grapes when the banging started. It startled him and he knocked over his juice. By the time she went to the front door to see who it was, the banging noise was coming from the other side of the house.

"You can't keep me out, bitch."

It was a man. He was yelling. He sounded angry. Aidan didn't recognize his voice.

His mother seemed to, though. Her eyes got real big and she covered her mouth with her hand. It was shaking.

There was a hutch in the living room that the television sat on. It had doors on the bottom. He hid in there sometimes. His mother opened one of the doors, and tossing the toys that were inside it to the floor, she kissed him on his head and urged him to crawl inside.

"We're going to play a game of hide and seek from the loud man outside, okay, baby?" his mother whispered.

Aidan nodded.

The banging got louder.

"You have to be very, very quiet so he doesn't know you're here." It sounded like she was choking and tears leaked out of her eyes, but she smiled at him.

"Like at story time?"

Aidan's mother took him to story time at the library every Saturday, and afterwards if he'd been a good boy, she would let him get an ice cream.

"Yes, baby. Just like that." She nodded with tears running down her face. "Now stay very still and don't speak a word until I tell you to—no matter what, okay?"

He nodded again. "Okay, Mommy."

"I love you, Aidan."

"I love you, Mommy."

Everyone said the place was haunted. The kids at school. The people in town. It didn't look scary, but nobody ever went anywhere near the two-story white clapboard house that was set off by itself on the cove.

It was to be her home now.

Molly stood at the wrought-iron gate with her mother, holding onto her hand. She clutched her *Bear in the Big Blue House* backpack, that she'd had since she was four, with the other. A boy with sandy-blond hair sat on the porch steps. Aidan Fischer. He didn't pay them, or his father unloading their belongings from the U-Haul, any mind. He had a notebook in his lap and a pencil between his fingers. It looked like he was drawing.

The boy chewed on his lip as he moved the pencil over the paper. Even though he was in the fifth grade, and three years older than her, Molly knew who he was. Everybody did. He was the boy who didn't talk. And six days from today, when her mother married his father, that boy was going to be her brother.

# THE Third Son

Coming out of the bathroom, Arien stubbed her toe, close to taking a tumble over a stack of forgotten boxes in the hallway. "Ouch. Motherfu…"

She held onto her foot, hopping the rest of the way to her bedroom in the small townhouse apartment she shared with her mom. It was all packed up, cartons neatly labeled, identifying the contents inside. Bed stripped. Closet and drawers emptied.

It wasn't like she had a choice.

A moving van was parked outside.

Holding her towel closed, her back against the wall, Arien sat cross-legged on the bare mattress. She had exactly thirty minutes to put on some makeup and get dressed. It would only take her ten.

*This is so not fucking fair.*

She blew out a breath. A week ago, her room was pretty and her life wasn't packed away in cardboard boxes. That all changed when her mother and her boyfriend—if that's what you call a man in his forties—took her out with them to dinner.

And that alone should have told her something was up.

Jennifer Brogan had been dating Matthew Brooks for about six months now, but Arien didn't know him all that well. A real cowboy, her mother said. He had two sons and lived on some ranch up in Wyoming, an eight-hour drive from Denver. He'd come into town for business, and to see her mom, a few times a month.

He was the one to break the news to her. "Arien," he said with a smile, taking her mother's hand in his. "First off, I need you to know I love your mama very much. So much, I've asked her to marry me."

She about choked on her green-chili cheeseburger.

Her mom held up her left hand, waving the huge diamond glittering on her finger. "I said yes."

*Okay.*

Arien was seventeen, soon-to-be eighteen. She'd be going away to college at the end of summer anyway. Her mom deserved some happiness, right?

Swallowing down the cheeseburger, she put on a smile. "At least you won't have to change your monogram. When's the wedding?"

"Next week," her mother announced, biting her lip. "I'm pregnant."

"Three months already," Matthew said proudly, patting his new fiancée on the shoulder. "I'm coming back with the boys. We'll get married and have you all moved in before Thanksgiving."

*What? To Wyoming? Nope. Not happening.*

"Wait. You want me to move, to change schools during my senior year?"

"I'm sorry, sweetie."

"You're going to love Brookside." Her soon-to-be stepfather patted her on the hand. "We have a superior private school there. The ranch. The mountains. You can take lots of pictures."

"There's mountains right here."

Isn't thirty-six too old to have a baby anyway? Apparently not. And what happened to all those lectures her mother gave her about having sex, taking precautions, and all that stuff? She should've listened to her own advice. If she had, Arien wouldn't be going to a courthouse wedding to leave Denver, and the only life she'd ever known, behind.

*Only for a little while.*

True. She had her acceptance letter to UC. She'd be back.

"Sweetie, are you ready yet?" her mother asked from downstairs. "Matt and the boys are here."

*Dammit.*

"Almost," she answered, plucking through her makeup bag.

Clearly a lie. She hadn't even begun.

Holding a compact mirror in one hand, Arien applied mascara with the other, the towel slipping away from her.

She couldn't say for sure what made her look up. A feeling she was being watched, maybe.

Two boys—no, these weren't boys, they were hot-as-fuck men—stood smirking in her doorway.

"Who the hell are you?"

"I'm Tanner." The man smiled, and taking a step inside her room, he hitched a thumb behind him. "That's Kellan."

"And I'm naked." She snatched up the towel, covering herself.

Kellan snickered.

Tanner came closer. "Well now, that's a mighty fine hello, little sister."

# Cast of Characters

*In alphabetical order by first name*

Ada Blythe—Jeremy's mother

Aggie—owner of gift shop on Maple Street

Alicia "Allie" Robertson—older sister to Bo

Angelica—vamp (blood fetish) girl at masquerade ball (also appears in *Don't Speak*)

Anna—Kodiak's client

Ashton Michael Thomas Kerrigan Nolan—youngest child and son of Chloe, Jesse, and Taylor

Austin—boy at camp

Ava Liane Harris Robertson—wife to Bo, elementary school teacher

Axel—head of security for the Red Door

Barbara "Babs"—Kodiak's therapist in California

Bea—hospice social worker

Becky Brinderman—Taylor's date to senior prom

Bernie—Kodiak's Bernedoodle

Bethany—former high school sweetheart to Jesse

Elizabeth "Betsy" Bennett—mother to Michael, grandmother to Chloe

Billings—Kyan's friend from high school, now with the state attorney's office

Robert "Bo" Robertson Jr.—drummer of Venery, husband to Ava (also appears in *Don't Speak*)

Brandy Sullivan—Kodiak's mother

Brendan James Murray—eldest of the Byrne cousins, runs the Red Door/CPA, husband to Katie

Brigitta Thurner—wife/submissive to Hans, hostess at Red Door

Brittany McCall—high school classmate of Chloe, former fiancée to Danny

Cameron Mayhew—Katie's college classmate/former boyfriend

Casey—boy at camp

Catherine Lucille Martin (*deceased*)—grandmother to Linnea

Chandan William Arthur Kerrigan Nolan—eldest child and son of Chloe, Jesse, and Taylor

Charles Alexander "Xander" Byrne—son of Dillon and Linnea, twin to Madison, brother to Charlotte

Charles Dillon Byrne—brother to Kyan, cousin to Brendan and Jesse, second husband to Linnea

Charles Patrick Byrne (*deceased*)—father to Dillon and Kyan, uncle to Brendan and Jesse

Charlotte Kyann Byrne—daughter of Kyan (*deceased*) and Linnea, sister to Xander and Madison

Chester—Bo's Australian Shepherd

Chloe Elizabeth Bennett Kerrigan Nolan—wife to Jesse and Taylor

Colleen Byrne Nolan O'Malley—mother to Jesse, sister to Charley and Mo, aunt to Brendan, Dillon, and Kyan, second wife to Tadhg

Connie "Cici"—Shelley's next-door neighbor

Courtney—Kit's ex-wife

Curtis "CJ" James—Venery's manager

Cynthia Robertson—mother to Bo

Danielle Peters—photographer, wife to Monica

Danny Damiani—Chloe's high school classmate and former boyfriend

Declan Byrne (*deceased*)—father to Charley, Mo & Colleen, grandfather to Brendan, Dillon, Jesse, and Kyan

Declan James Murray—son of Brendan and Katie

Andrew "Drew" Copeland—Katie's dad

Ed—Bo's driver on tour

Elliott Peters—son of Danielle and Monica

Emery Sage Robertson—daughter of Shelley Tompkins (*deceased*) and Bo, sister to Kai

Eric Brantley (*deceased*)—son to Hugh Brantley

Gillian—bartender (former) at the Red Door

Gina Rossi—labor and delivery nurse, family owns Rossi's Pizza and Italian Bakery

Grace Martin (*deceased*)—mother to Linnea

Hailey—girl at warehouse accident

Hans Thurner—husband/Dominant to Brigitta, host/manager at Red Door

Hazel—Tommy's mother, waitress at diner in Crossfield

Hugh Brantley—real estate investor

Ireland Aislinn Kerrigan Nolan—2nd eldest child and daughter of Chloe, Jesse, and Taylor

James Murray (*deceased*)—father to Brendan, uncle to Dillon, Jesse, and Kyan

Pastor Jarrid Black (*deceased*)—father to Seth and Linnea

Jason—kitchen boy at Charley's

Jeffrey—boy at camp

Jenkins—construction/warehouse project manager

Jeremy Blythe—Ada's son, Jarrid's right hand in Crossfield

Jesse Thomas Nolan—cousin to Brendan, Dillon, and Kyan, husband to Chloe and Taylor

Jimmy Tascadero—friend of Bo's at age 14

Jonathan Reynolds (*deceased*)—childhood best friend to Seth

Jonathan "Kade" Black—son of Kodiak and Kelly

Kai Forrest Robertson—son of Bo and Ava, brother to Emery

Kara Matthews—third eldest sister to Kelly, aunt to Katie and Kevin

Katelyn "Katie" Copeland Murray—wife to Brendan, niece to Kelly, sister to Kevin, barista at Beanie's/college student

Kelly Matthews—aunt to Katie and Kevin, owner of Beanie's

Kelsey Miller—girlfriend (former) to Dillon

Kevin Copeland—younger brother to Katie

Kim Matthews—second eldest sister to Kelly, aunt to Katie and Kevin

Christopher "Kit" King—bassist of Venery

Seth "Kodiak" Black—son of Jarrid, half-brother to Linnea

Kristie Matthews Copeland—mother to Katie and Kevin, eldest sister to Kelly

Kyan Patrick Byrne (*deceased*)—brother to Dillon, first husband to Linnea, father to Charlotte, cousin to Brendan and Jesse

Kyle Donovan—Kelly's date to senior prom

Leah Brianne Murray—daughter of Brendan and Katie

Leena Patel Kerrigan—mother to Taylor

Leonardo "Leo" Hill—baker/Kelly's assistant at Beanie's

Linnea Grace Martin Byrne—half-sister to Kodiak, widow to Kyan, wife to Dillon

Logan—nephew to Bo

Lon—Venery's driver on tour

London Elizabeth Kerrigan Nolan—third child and daughter of Chloe, Jesse, and Taylor

Lucifer—friend of Brendan's, devil-masked member of the Red Door

Madison Margaret Grace Byrne—daughter of Dillon and Linnea, twin to Xander, sister to Charlotte

Marcus—manager at Charley's

Matthew "Matt" McCready—rhythm guitarist of Venery

Michael Bennett—father to Chloe

Milo Veronin—Angelica's partner (also appears in *Don't Speak*)

Mitch Rollins—State Senator, member of the Red Door

Monica Peters—clinical psychologist, wife to Danielle

Margaret "Peggy" Byrne (*deceased*)—mother to Dillon and Kyan, aunt to Brendan and Jesse

Maureen "Mo" Byrne Murray (*deceased*)—mother to Brendan, sister to Charley and Colleen, aunt to Dillon, Jesse, and Kyan

Meaghan O'Malley (*deceased*)—first wife to Tadhg O'Malley

Murphy—Brendan's childhood friend, detective with the police department

Nick Rossi—second eldest Rossi brother, same age as Jesse, family owns Rossi's Pizza and Italian Bakery

Paul—rigger on Venery's tour

Payton Brantley—son to Eric and grandson to Hugh Brantley

Perry Harris—older brother to Ava, Minor League baseball player

Phil Beecham—Brendan's attorney

Rachel—girl at camp

Reverend "Daddy" John—camp director

Robert Robertson Sr.—father to Bo

Roberta Torres—obstetrician

Roman—Jesse's Bernese Mountain dog

Rourke—alias of arrested priest and former Red Door member

Roy Francis Martin (*deceased*)—grandfather to Linnea

Ryan Sr.—husband to Allie, brother-in-law to Bo

Ryan Jr.—nephew to Bo

Salena Dara (*deceased*)—former hostess at the Red Door

Sean O'Malley—brother to Tadhg O'Malley, stepfather to Siona Dawson

Shelley Tompkins (*deceased*)—mother to Emery, groupie who instigated "baby mama drama"

Siona Dawson (pronounced *Show-na*)—receptionist at O'Malley Ink Emporium, step-niece to Tadhg O'Malley

Sloan Michaels—lead vocalist/lyricist of Venery

Stacy—former girlfriend to Kelly Matthews

Tadhg O'Malley (pronounced *Tige*)—Colleen's second husband

Tammy—hospice nurse

Taylor Chandan Kerrigan—husband to Chloe and Jesse, lead guitarist of Venery

Thomas Nolan (*deceased*)—father to Jesse

Timo—Chloe's Bernese Mountain dog (Roman's son)

Tommy—classmate of Linnea's, cook at diner in Crossfield

Anthony "Tony" Rossi—eldest Rossi Brother, same age as Brendan/Venery, family owns Rossi's Pizza and Italian Bakery

Vanessa Parisi—Journalist with *Revolver*

William Arthur Kerrigan—father to Taylor

www.ingramcontent.com/pod-product-compliance
Lightning Source LLC
Chambersburg PA
CBHW061757190726

48289CB00007B/1992